COLLAPSE - BOOK FOUR OF BEYOND THESE WALLS

A POST-APOCALYPTIC SURVIVAL THRILLER

MICHAEL ROBERTSON

Email: subscribers@michaelrobertson.co.uk

Edited by:

Terri King - http://terri-king.wix.com/editing
And
Pauline Nolet - http://www.paulinenolet.com

Cover Design by Dusty Crosley

Collapse - Book four of Beyond These Walls

Michael Robertson
© 2019 Michael Robertson

Collapse - Book four of Beyond These Walls is a work of fiction. The characters, incidents, situations, and all dialogue are entirely a product of the author's imagination, or are used fictitiously and are not in any way representative of real people, places or things.

Any resemblance to persons living or dead is entirely coincidental.

All rights reserved

No part of this publication may be reproduced, stored in a retrieval system or transmitted in any form or by any means electronic, mechanical, photocopying, recording or otherwise, without the prior written permission of the author except in the case of brief quotations embodied in critical articles and reviews.

READER GROUP

Join my reader group for all of my latest releases and special offers. You'll also receive these four FREE books. You can unsubscribe at any time.

Go to - www.michaelrobertson.co.uk

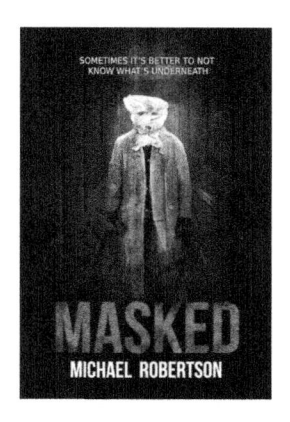

Michael Robertson

EDEN

A Short Story About The Zombie Apocalypse

RAT RUN

A POST-APOCALYPTIC TALE

Michael Robertson

CHAPTER 1

William jumped aside, avoiding Hugh, who charged at the creature. His mouth stretched wide, the veins visible on his neck, Hugh met the diseased's hiss with a shriek of his own. A wall of sound that would have startled many, but it appeared to energise the beast. His stick raised in a two-handed grip, Hugh expelled clouds of condensation in the damp morning air. He didn't miss a step when the diseased took off, coming at him, mirroring his zealous drive to destroy.

The loud *tonk* emitted a bass note of cracking bone that snapped through the walled-in area surrounding them. The creature's legs folded beneath it as it ran, its knees sinking into the soft ground and catapulting it face-first into the dewy grass.

While Hugh went to work on the creature, William watched his friend rather than the damage he inflicted. It didn't matter how many of them he had killed or seen killed, the bloody and pulped ruin in the aftermath always turned his stomach. As vile as the beasts were, they used to be human. He shared something with them. His skull would yield to the same concentrated violence.

William turned away a moment before the beast's skull broke with a *crack!*

When Matilda stepped towards Hugh as if to intervene, William reached across and laid a gentle hand on the top of her right arm. Despite her hard scowl, he shook his head, fighting against his need to flinch at Hugh continuing to kill the already dead monster. "He needs to do this." Although, even as he said it, he lost confidence in his words. Did he need to do it, or had he finally gone over the edge? Matilda raised an eyebrow as if she'd just read his thoughts.

Maybe she had a point, and it would be better coming from him than it would her. Hugh knew William well and would be more receptive to what he said. While approaching Hugh, one eye on the swinging stick, William waited for the right moment; enter Hugh's cycle of madness at the wrong time and he'd also get his skull cracked like an egg.

His teeth bared, Hugh delivered another full-bodied blow against the battered corpse. William darted forward and grabbed his friend's shoulder with his right hand. He reached his left arm out to prevent the next upswing of the bloody stick. Adrenaline surging through him, he battled his frantic pulse to keep his tone soft. "Hugh?"

If Hugh heard him, he didn't show it. The muscles in his jaw bulged, and tears ran down his cheeks, mixing with his glistening sweat, as he pushed against William's restraint.

William grabbed the stick and yanked it free, jumping backwards as Hugh turned on him.

But Hugh's tension left him and his words softened. "I thought they would have closed the gate in time. I wouldn't have done it otherwise. I didn't expect it to stay open. How could I have known?" While looking from side to side as if assaulted by things only he could see, Hugh clapped his hands to his face. His words quickened, one running into the next as they flooded from him. "Oh, what have I done? What have I done? It looked like it would be okay for me to leave. She looked so like Elizabeth, it stopped me thinking straight. It *was* Elizabeth; I could have sworn it was her."

The words came so fast William caught one in three, moving back a step as if Hugh's madness were catching. Matilda appeared at his side and shoved him back towards his friend.

Mechanical in his approach, William fought against his own reluctance and spread his arms wide before he wrapped Hugh's stocky frame in a tight hug.

About a minute passed while Hugh sobbed in William's arms. The power in the boy shuddered through them both. It felt like hugging a bull.

"Elizabeth," Hugh finally said. "She looked exactly like Elizabeth."

The dead diseased had once been a woman. To look at her now, on her back with her mouth stretched wide and the top half of her head folded in like an old wasps' nest, William struggled to see the resemblance. Maybe Hugh now saw Elizabeth in everyone.

They couldn't wait there all day. William pulled away from his friend, holding both his shoulders as he lowered his head to get into his line of sight. "Look, Hugh, whatever's happened, we need to put it behind us. What's in front of us now is what we have to deal with."

"But if I hadn't screwed up, what's in front of us would be very different."

"Where will thinking like that get us?"

At that moment, Matilda came closer and put her hand against Hugh's back. In her tense features, William saw her impatience to get to her brother, but she kept that to herself.

Because Hugh didn't know her like William did, he didn't pick up on it and visibly relaxed at her touch.

"Had you not told us about Artan," William said, throwing a glance at Matilda as if looking for her approval, "we wouldn't even be here. We'd be walking out into the ruined city thinking he'd been evicted. Your actions have given us hope."

"It might have given you and Matilda hope, but what have I done to the national service area?"

William looked at the large wooden gates, one of them slightly ajar. After a few seconds, he said, "I suppose we need to find out." As if adding to his reluctance, the wound on William's right foot throbbed with his steps towards the gates. Matilda and Hugh followed behind.

Closer to the reality of what awaited them, William could no longer ignore the groans and wails of discontent. Shrieks and cries. He knew what he'd see. Yet, when he poked his head through the gap to peer inside, every instinct told him to run.

CHAPTER 2

People everywhere.
　　Running wild.
Chaos.

No, not people.

Wherever William looked, he saw the crimson glare and open-mouthed fury of the diseased. In just a few short hours, the national service area had been lost.

"Shit," Matilda said as she looked in. "They must have all been sleeping when it hit."

"Caught with their pants down." When William stepped back, he bumped into Hugh. The boy moved aside, and all three of them stepped away from the gates.

William drew his sword. After Matilda had done the same, he said, "Whatever happens, we've got a fight ahead of us. So what do we do?"

Determination in her deep brown eyes, Matilda shook her head. "Nothing's changed."

"*Everything's* changed."

"What I mean is Artan's still in there."

"We think."

Matilda's breaths ran harder and she spoke through a clenched jaw. "And unless I see evidence he's not, nothing will change my mind."

A concessionary dip of his head, William waited for her to continue.

"So the plan's still the same," she said.

"Get to the political district?"

"Right."

While pointing at the large wooden barrier in front of them, William raised his eyebrows. "Through these gates?"

"Can you think of a better way? We could walk around the entire city searching for a part of the wall to climb and not find anywhere."

A warble broke Hugh's voice. "And they're not going to let the person responsible for the collapse of the national service area in through the eviction gates."

"I'm not sure they'll let anyone in through those gates," William said.

A streak of hair had fallen loose from Matilda's topknot, which she tucked behind her ear. The early morning sun glinted off the metal hummingbird. "We need to take this one step at a time. The first thing we need to do is get to the other side of the national service area. We find a way over those gates and we might be able to use this chaos to our advantage."

William frowned at her. "How so?"

"The political district will be caught up in what's going on. It might be the perfect time to find a way to get Artan out of there." When William and Hugh didn't reply, she added, "I dunno; I can't see exactly how this is going to play out, but Artan's our … Artan's *my* goal."

William reached down and held Matilda's hand. "*Our* goal."

Hugh nodded in agreement.

"Okay." Matilda's tone lifted. A renewed hope. "Artan's our goal. Let's make sure we take steps towards that, and always towards that. We'll deal with whatever's thrown at us on the way."

Hugh wrung his hands, holding them just in front of his stomach, his squat frame hunching around the action. He kept his head lowered as he said, "Are you sure you want someone like me with you? I don't want to make things harder than they already are."

A flash of anxiety spiked William's pulse when Matilda stepped towards Hugh. Her direct approach might not be the best right now. But he'd already given Hugh his backing, so what else could he say?

Matilda held both of Hugh's hands, her words soft. "William's right; we would have given up on Artan had you not told us about him. We're a team. We do this together and we stand by each other, no matter what."

When Hugh didn't reply, Matilda kept a hold of his hands and snapped them as if to break through his self-pity. "No matter what!"

Now nodding, Hugh inhaled, his chest rising. He fixed on the open gate with his watery gaze.

Fifteen minutes previously when they'd stepped through the hole into the newly walled space where the resting gates were due to be fitted, William had heard every shriek and cry in the national service area. He'd been able to ignore his ears, but now his eyes had confirmed what lay ahead, he couldn't deny it any longer. However he looked at it, they were about to enter chaos. But what else could they do? Artan needed them. "You both ready?"

Neither replied. Neither needed to. Before William led the way, Hugh raised his bloody stick like a batter preparing to swing, and strode ahead of them, marching towards the gates.

William pulled Matilda in close and kissed the top of her head. Did the trembling come from him or her? What did it matter? They both knew what lay ahead. They followed Hugh, the absence of their words palpable. Whatever they said, nothing would change the fact they were about to enter hell.

CHAPTER 3

Two hours earlier

OLGA SAT BOLT UPRIGHT IN BED, GASPING FOR BREATH. Her heart beat in her neck and sweat dampened her brow as she fought to calm herself. She pushed the covers away, the cool morning air biting into her damp skin. Although she had her curtains drawn, they didn't prevent the hazy light of the early morning from seeping into her room.

There might still be a few hours before she had to get up for work, but her chances of any more sleep today had been driven from her with her ragged respiration. She'd been here too many times before. Awake meant awake whether it suited her or not.

Olga got up and paced her small room. Ten feet by ten feet, most of it was taken up with her bed. She could have moved into her sisters' larger room. Or maybe she couldn't. Maybe her parents would have resisted if she'd asked. After all, since it had happened, they'd turned the room into a shrine to what they'd lost, everything remaining the same as if they expected the girls to suddenly reappear. And would she really want to sleep in there anyway? Like she needed any more reminders of their passing three years previously.

It had been six months since Olga had broken her left arm. It had healed enough for her to start work weeks ago. She dropped to the ground to begin her press-ups.

Forty-three reps later, the last ten lopsided from the weakness in her left arm, Olga fell flat, driving her heavy pants into the wooden floor. Her ulna had snapped like a twig on national service. She didn't need to push herself so it happened again; bones were fragile things. As she sat cross-legged on her cold bedroom floor, she recovered from the exercise and rubbed the area around where it had broken.

Olga's stillness opened the door on the real reason for her sleepless nights, the truth catching up to her. After Max had been taken away from the dorm they were resting in, Bleach told her about his fate. The labs for life. He'd spend the rest of his time in a luxury prison, but a prison nonetheless. Too dangerous to let a carrier of the virus loose in society, what else could they do but test on him? What if he provided them with the blood samples they needed to make an antidote? It sounded noble, right? But no matter which angle you looked at it from, the inescapable fact remained: Max now faced a lifetime of incarceration.

Birdsong dragged Olga's attention to her still-drawn curtains. A rare sound in Edin, you had to be up early to hear it. Very few birds came anywhere near the place. None appeared after about eight in the morning—too many projectiles from Edin's hungry residents after that time. Could Max hear birdsong from his cell? What freedoms, if any, had he been granted? Also, how bad was it compared to the life she had to live? After all, weren't most people in Edin prisoners in some capacity?

Olga stood up—using her right arm for support—and walked to her curtains. She'd sat still for long enough. Obsessively thinking about the same problem rarely led to a solution. Slowly, so as not to startle the birds, she let in the light of the day. The three wood pigeons directly outside took flight.

Blinking repeatedly, Olga tried to combat the glare of the early morning. Although, it was hard to tell if her eyes burned from the light or something else entirely. Her life had been enveloped in a haze since she'd returned from national service, and she'd held on to tears she couldn't cry. What right did she have to express her sadness? After all, everyone else had gone through it. She needed to get over herself.

From her bedroom window, Olga saw the top of the arena. Before national service, she'd had no desire to enter the world of the protectors. Then she found out how good she was at killing the rotten freaks. What she'd give to have another chance to make the trials. To have another six months with Max and team Minotaur. Too late now. A life in laundry lay ahead of her. Within two years she'd be broken by the monotony and, like every other adult in the city, would accept and live within Edin's arbitrary laws.

~

ROUGH BREAD AND RUNNY SCRAMBLED EGGS FOR BREAKFAST. Again. Olga's throat clamped in anticipation. But she had to eat it. Very few of Edin's residents could turn their nose up at protein, no matter how snotty.

The salty mess lay on Olga's tongue while she chewed the toast. A silent countdown in her head to psych herself up, she swallowed. She focused on the two plates opposite in an attempt to stifle her heave. Every mealtime, her mum set the table as if she expected the girls to return. The silence of their absence often dominated the conversation.

What must have been ten minutes passed before her father finally spoke. Quick on the draw this morning! A small rotund man with tight curly brown hair, a moustache, and a big nose. "So what are you doing today?"

Even though he watched his plate the entire time, Olga knew he intended the question for her. Eye contact left the house with her sisters. To look at one another caused too much pain. But Olga didn't reply like she normally would. Instead, she waited for the man to lift his attention. His wincing eyes pleaded with her to end the torture. "I dunno," she said. "Laundry would be my guess."

"Of course, of course." He returned to the safety of speaking to his gloopy eggs. "But scrubbing or rinsing? Which one you choose often affects how your day turns out."

And that was what it had come to. The days in Edin were a thing to be endured. The only variety in laundry was if you scrubbed or rinsed. You should carefully consider what you were: a scrubber or a rinser? Such mundanity while chaos roamed the wastelands outside the wall. No wonder Spike had made a run for it. But truth be told, it hadn't seemed so bad before she went on national service. It would be dull, sure, but she'd make good friends and find someone to love. With that, she could endure the tedium. And maybe she'd expected the mood in the house to lift when she returned from the experience. A reason for celebration after years of mourning. But everything changed in those six months. Everything changed for her, and nothing changed for her parents. She'd found out what she could do. She'd met people with life in them. Spirit. Hell, she even missed Ranger, the egotistical little prick. She'd met Max and now she owed him. By saving her, he got bitten.

She could do nothing for a diseased Max, but an incarcerated one …

Also, in the national service area, Olga didn't have the daily reminder of her sisters' passing. Her attention back on the two plates in front of her, she wrapped tight fists around her cutlery. Maybe her parents sensed something, because although they didn't look up, they both stopped eating.

"I didn't die, you know?" Olga said. "I returned from national service. *Alive!*"

Both Olga's mum and dad looked up. Her dad's eyes were ringed with dark bags from years of insomnia, her mum's lips tight. Avian, she had drawn features and a pointy nose. A slight wobble ran through her as if she held her grief on simmer. But neither of them challenged or questioned her. Since her sisters had died, her parents seemed to be awaiting the same fate. Days in Edin were to be endured. Life became a burden to carry until the weight of it grew too heavy and they were finally allowed the release of death. But Olga didn't want to simply endure.

While working through her mouthful of eggs and toast with quick chews, Olga's mum finally said, "I heard you waking again this morning. Did you have another nightmare? About national service?"

As much as Olga wanted to say no, to tell her the truth that the nightmares were never about national service but the life she now lived, she nodded.

"It'll get easier," her mum said.

That was what she wanted to believe. Although, what did it matter? The message was clear. Olga should get her head down and endure. If she did that—contrary to all the evidence in front of her—life would get easier.

∼

The rest of breakfast endured in silence, Olga still had some time before she had to leave for work. She'd returned to her room and now sat on her bed staring out of her window at the top of the arena. So close, but so far away. Guards stood between her and ever seeing it again. But did the protectors really have a much better life than those who worked in the districts? Were they slaves much like everyone else? Slaves to the people to put on a show. To impale heads on spikes and slay creatures as a way of reassuring them they were in safe hands? A way to remind them to keep working for Edin because Edin worked for you. She laughed and shook her head. "Yeah, right!"

But at least the protectors could go where they wanted. Be with whomever they wanted. If Max had won the trials, would he have come for her? They were close, but how close? Who was she kidding? What made her so special? What did she have to offer that every other girl in the city couldn't have given him? And what did it matter anyway? Neither of them had made it. But she couldn't forget about his current situation. Locked in a cell, not because he'd done anything wrong, but because he'd saved her life. But what could she do about it? She couldn't bust him out. How could she make it across the city over walls and rooftops when she couldn't even do fifty press-ups?

Olga lost her thoughts when her dad hammered against the other side of her door. "We're going to work in an hour. Make sure you're ready."

While letting out a hard sigh, Olga slumped and spoke to her toes. "Yay! Another day in laundry."

CHAPTER 4

As much as William wanted to call after Hugh to slow down, it wouldn't do any of them any favours. He pursed his lips to fight his urge as the stocky boy vanished through the open gate.

"What's he doing?" Matilda said. The day had warmed up, yet she continued to shake as they followed him.

The screams beyond the wooden barrier grew louder, one occasionally silenced by the *tonk* of stick hitting skull. "I know he's a bit rough around the edges," William said, "but he's a good fighter. Hugh's been a good pal. I won't turn my back on someone I care about. I need you to trust me, Matilda."

Her face slack, Matilda shrugged. "I'm not saying we should leave him. I trust you with my life. I always have. If you stand by Hugh, then I stand by him."

Fighting through the throbbing sting in his right foot, William quickened his pace, his sword raised as the steps of Matilda joined him.

The second he entered the national service area, William halted, Matilda crashing into his back. Hugh just a few feet in front of them, he gripped onto his thick stick with both hands as he swung for the diseased bearing down on him. The boy moved so fast, the stick turned into a blur. He hit their skulls with *cracks* and *tonks*, playing the beat of a skilled percussionist.

On his own, Hugh could defeat ten creatures—maybe even twenty—but there were many more diseased in the national service area who were yet to notice them. If he didn't wind his neck in, they'd be overwhelmed in seconds.

As several more diseased closed in on Hugh, William lunged for one with the tip of his sword. The best way to end the rotten bastards, he drove the point through its face. As it fell, pulling his blade with it, he withdrew, letting the creature crumple to the ground while keeping a hold of his weapon. A waft of rot and vinegar assaulted him as if the puncture wound had torn a gas leak in the beast.

Matilda doing the same on Hugh's other flank, William scanned the national service area again. A small pack charged their way, but the bulk of the creatures were too distracted to notice them, many of them running in the opposite direction over the brow of the hill and out of sight.

The veins on Hugh's neck were like thick twine, his skin glistening with sweat. Just as he set off to charge the next closest diseased, William caught the back of his collar and dragged him away from the fight.

Alive with berserker rage, Hugh turned, sending a chill through William. Would they really have to fight each other here? But then it softened, the darkness in his eyes lightening just a little. At first a frown crushed Hugh's features, fury giving way to confusion, and then remorse flooded in. Although he opened his mouth to talk, William dragged him towards the open gate, Matilda covering their backs.

Several feet clear of the gates, the screams of the pursuing pack on their tail, William turned Hugh back around. He stood on one side of him, Matilda on the other. The screams drawing closer, he tightened his grip on his sword and nudged his short and stocky friend. "Now we're ready to fight them."

Before Hugh had time to question it, the first diseased burst through the narrow gap in the gates. The small space created a bottleneck so they only had to face one or two at a time.

William stepped back a pace, Hugh and Matilda moving back with him and spreading out.

The first runner met the wide chopping arc of William's sword, the crunch of its yielding skull running through the weapon's grip. As the beast fell, Hugh and Matilda took out one each, and they all stepped back again.

They dropped the next three and stepped back. Then the next three, fighting in sync with one another, moving back with one another.

The flow of diseased ceased when they were about ten feet from the gates. A carpet of the fallen lay between them and re-entry to the national service area.

"We could call them all out," Hugh said, his face alive, his eyebrows lifting at the suggestion. "Use the gate to slow them down and destroy the lot of 'em."

Matilda's skin glistened, her cheeks red as she fought to get her words past her rasping breaths. "There's no chance of me doing that for any length of time. There has to be another way."

"I agree," William said. "I don't have it in me to fight that many. Let me lead the way. I reckon we can sneak past most of them if we're careful."

Although Hugh drew a breath as if to argue, William cut him off. "We go to war with that lot in there and we won't make it to the first dorm. Fighting is a *last* resort."

Hugh's frame sagged and he lowered his head.

Now he'd caught his breath, William glanced at the gates again. "Right, you ready for this?"

"Yep," Matilda said, her jaw set, her sword raised.

"Hugh?"

"Yep."

"Then follow my lead." A dry gulp, thirst pinching his throat, William walked through the slain diseased to the gap in the gates.

William poked his head in and looked across the national service area. Their immediate vicinity might have been clear, but there were plenty of diseased ready to notice them should they slip up. If they stayed close to the wall, it might help, but it would give them one less direction to run should they need an escape. It would also double the distance they had to travel. The dorms had to be a better option for cover: a more direct route through the national service area, and their roofs were too high for the diseased to reach. No time for consulting with the others, he led them up the small hill towards the first dorm.

Damn near deafened by his own hammering pulse, William's eyes burned from where he refused to blink. His two friends beside him, they seemed as equally focused on the diseased.

Several more packs ran away from them out of sight over the brow of the hill. What had they seen? His grip slick with sweat, William looked back at the gate. The nearest dorm was now closer than their escape out of the city.

When William reached the top of the hill, he stopped and waited for the other two to catch up. At least two hundred feet away, what looked to be seven or eight people stood on the roof of what had once been team Phoenix's dorm. Tens of diseased gathered around them, and more were joining the press of bodies all the time.

"What do we do?" Matilda said.

What could they do? It might have been harsh, but they

weren't here to save everyone. William held on to his reply. And then he saw him.

"Trent," Matilda said.

The unmistakable beanpole silhouette among the survivors on the roof.

"Who's Trent?"

"Someone from agriculture," William said.

"You know him well?" Hugh asked.

"Well enough. He was the kid we punched to get out of Edin last night."

"Shall we save him?"

Finally looking away from the boy from agriculture, William turned to Hugh and Matilda. When he saw no judgement in their eyes, he saw no reason to deviate from the plan. The words still didn't come easily. "We can't help everyone. If we die saving them, we have no chance with Artan and the others. Besides, they're distracting the diseased. I can't think of a better opportunity for us to sneak past."

William winced in anticipation of his friends' resistance, but Matilda nodded. "When we get to the other side, we can tell them there's survivors out here. Someone else can come and rescue them, some protectors maybe. They're safer up there than they are with us."

Maybe a twisted logic, but it would do. "Okay, so we're agreed? We keep going, yeah?"

Matilda nodded. Hugh took a second or two longer, his eyes glazing as if he lusted for a fight.

"Hugh?" William said.

"Huh? Yeah, let's go. We can't fight that many diseased."

"You sound sad about that." Although Matilda said it to Hugh, she looked at William.

Had he made the correct choice standing by his friend?

Would he prove to be too much of a liability? Too late to question it now. "Right," William said. "Let's keep going."

Just as he moved off, William froze.

"Spike!" Trent waved his long arms. "Over here. Help us, please."

The faces of what felt like hundreds of diseased turned William's way.

Matilda spat the word. "Shit."

His pulse fuelled by the diseased's cries, William gasped against his panic before taking off towards what had been team Chupacabra's dorm. The other two followed.

CHAPTER 5

Two hours earlier

"Half an hour until we leave for work," Olga's dad called, snapping Olga from her daze. No matter how many times she blinked, it did nothing to ease the sting in her eyes. She'd stared at the floor for so long, they'd damn near dried open. The prospect of another shitty day doing her same shitty job had ground her to inaction. Half an hour without moving. But she'd best accept this life now. Doing a job she hated and staying in a house where the ghosts had more to say than the people living there—that is, until she met someone appropriate enough to live with. And that was what it boiled down to: were they appropriate? Could she find someone she hated at least slightly less than her profession, so when she came home at the end of the day, it felt like a relief? Maybe she'd even look forward to it. But, no matter who she chose, it wouldn't be Max.

Despite lethargy turning her blood to syrup, Olga stood up,

bounced on her toes, and stretched to the ceiling. She couldn't live like this. Butterflies danced in her stomach. She needed to take responsibility for her life. She needed to be the change she wanted to see in this household.

Olga left her room, stepping into the suffocating silence of the rest of the house, and headed straight for the kitchen. Both her mum and her dad were sat at the table opposite one another. Each of them hugged steaming mugs of mint tea, their heads bowed. The places were still laid for her sisters.

"I've had enough," Olga said.

They both looked up.

Olga pointed at her mum first and then her dad. "Are you two going to say anything other than Dad giving the house a countdown until we go to work? Is this really the life you've chosen for yourselves?"

Still nothing.

"You must have *something* you want to say to one another? Something you want to say to me? How would Jacqueline and Nikki feel to see what you two have become? And how do you think *I* feel? I lost two sisters to national service, and maybe I need to accept I've lost my parents too."

When her dad drew a breath, Olga fixed on him, hope swelling in her chest. Then the light in his eyes died and he let go of a long sigh. She deflated with him.

"Come on, Dad, say *something*. *Anything*. Show me you haven't given up on life. Show me there's something worth living for, because at the moment, I'm wondering if coming back from national service was the booby prize."

A wince ran across her mum's face. And that was the hardest part. There was something there, but neither of them was prepared to share it.

A few more seconds of silence, Olga's dad fixed on her again. "Twenty-five minutes before we need to leave for work."

Olga clenched her fists, forcing her nails into her palms. The same apathetic glaze covered both her parents' eyes, and it took all she had not to turn their table over. But screw them. She'd tried. She'd given them their chance. After shaking her head, she left the kitchen.

∼

The bed took up most of Olga's room, so when she'd needed a desk for schoolwork, her dad had made her a lap tray she could work from. It had served a purpose. As she leaned over it now, the familiar pain at the base of her neck returned. Some days, she'd spent so many hours working she'd go to bed dizzy. A fresh sheet of paper on her portable desk, the second she touched the nib of her pen to it, the words flowed out of her. She'd drafted this letter a thousand times in her mind.

Dear Mum and Dad,

As much as I love you both, I don't love our life and what's become of our family since Nikki and Jaqueline have passed. It's hard enough to think about working in laundry until retirement. It's like you don't see me. Like you both died with them. I get it, but I need something more. I can't be a part of the sterile existence you two have accepted.

I met a boy on national service who was bitten and didn't turn. He's being kept in the labs as a prisoner. They're using him to run experiments on to see if they can find an antidote to the disease. I'm going to go to him and see if I can bust him out. He saved my life, which is how he got bitten, so I figure I owe it to him. It's going to be risky, but what have I got to lose? Besides, it's the right thing to do. I wouldn't be here now were it not for him. He gave me a life, the least I can do is live it.

I suppose if you see me again, then I've failed in what I've set out to do. If you don't, I want to say goodbye. Try to focus on the people who are still alive, because you can't have a relationship with the dead, or bring them back, as much as you might want to. There was a time when you both used to laugh and sing and dance. I'd like for you two to remember that. Not for my sake, but for your own. I'm going to be okay.

So please don't worry about me. There's nothing here for me anymore, and I want to have one last try at happiness. I want a different future.

I LOVE YOU NOW AND ALWAYS.

YOUR DAUGHTER,

OLGA
   xxx.

OLGA FOLDED THE LETTER, ADDRESSED IT TO HER PARENTS, AND left it on her bed. She packed a small rucksack with as many changes of clothes as she could stuff into it. Who knew how long it would take her to assess the labs to work out what she needed to do to get into them. Who knew what would happen after that if she succeeded in busting Max out. They'd have to find a way out of Edin. There were too many 'what ifs', but she didn't want the life in front of her. She had to act on that. Although, she had to be strong enough first. No use running away if her body couldn't cope with the task.

Olga dropped down into another round of press-ups.

"Fifteen minutes until we leave for work," Olga's dad called through the house as if nothing had happened.

"Forty-three …"

Olga shook on the way back up, her left forearm aching. "Forty-four …"

Sweat fell from her forehead to her bedroom floor, creating small circular patches slightly darker than the boards.

"Forty-five … forty-six … forty-seven …" The strength returned to her forearm. She had it in her.

"Forty-eight … forty-nine …" It had been fear holding her back.

"Fifty." Olga fell on her front, panting from the effort. She'd done it. As she sat up and looked first at her bag and then at the letter on her bed, she nodded to herself. Probably not the best time for her to make her move, but she couldn't wait any longer. If she didn't go now, she'd always find a reason to stay.

Olga stood up and slipped on her backpack. She opened her window, letting in the sounds of the laundry district waking up for the day. It stood in stark contrast to the graveyard silence of her house. While swallowing the lump in her throat, she climbed from her window and dropped to the ground outside, pushing her window shut behind her. Sad, sure, but not guilty. She had nothing to feel guilty for. She couldn't sink with her parents. She chose life.

Maybe the consequences would be grave, but they were worth it. And she'd deal with them if they happened. Anything had to be better than staying—even prison or eviction. But it wouldn't come to that. She'd reach Max and save him like he'd saved her. After one final look at her house, Olga turned her back on her family home for maybe the final time.

No more than twenty feet away, Olga froze. The call of a

diseased sent ice running down her spine, images from her time building the wall flashing through her mind. Blood ... snapping jaws ... bodies slamming into the living at full speed. She strained her ears and caught the wail of another one. Had they always been there? Did she only notice them now because of what she'd been through? After licking her finger and holding it up, she felt the coolness of the wind. It blew from a different direction to the shrieks, which came at her from the national service area. Maybe they were just extra loud today. What must the rookies be thinking as they headed out? Olga shrugged. Their problem, not hers. Fighting the diseased would probably be a hell of a lot easier than freeing Max.

CHAPTER 6

After two steps, William stopped. Matilda hadn't yet moved. His back to the diseased's stampede because he had to face her, he threw his arms up, shouting over the feral yell bearing down on them, "What are you doing?"

Matilda hooked her thumb over her shoulder. "Shouldn't we be going that way?"

"Chupacabra's dorm's much closer."

While bouncing on the spot—his right foot on fire from sweat running into the cut on his sole—William waited for Matilda to make her mind up. Just before he shouted at her again, she ran for the dorm.

Only then did William see Hugh had also waited. Were they both soft in the head? If they ran through the gates, the diseased would follow them. It took all of William's resolve to refrain from looking at the frenzied mob behind him and keep his focus on the dorm. And a good job too. If he'd done that, he might have missed the pack appearing from around the side of Chupacabra's hut. They fixed on William, Hugh, and Matilda with their crimson glares. Their jaws worked as if they could taste them in the air.

Without breaking stride, Hugh said, "What do you want to do?"

Another hellish call from behind, William fought against his heavy breaths. "What can we do? We need to get through them."

As Hugh raised his stick, William and Matilda did the same with their swords.

The small group in front charged. It didn't matter how many creatures William had already encountered, his legs threatened to buckle in the face of such a formidable foe. They attacked with no concern for their own safety. A hive mind of rage, they had just one objective: to eliminate humanity's consciousness.

Hugh ran ahead, reaching the diseased first. He took two down before William and Matilda caught up.

William drove his sword through the chest of one of the beasts, pulling it out so the falling creature didn't drag it from his grip. Matilda and Hugh went to work beside him in a flurry of hacking and slashing. William could hold his own, but even with just a stick, Hugh did more damage than he could hope to inflict on the beasts. The boy reminded him of Warrior as he played out a ballet of destruction, every swing done with purpose, each blow eliciting a deep crack or snap.

Beside Hugh, Matilda turned the air red with the spray of claret, executing the creatures with almost the same efficiency as the short and stocky boy. It didn't matter how well William fought, they fought better and they had it covered. Four diseased still on their feet from the group, all four of them were engaged with his friends.

There must have been a hundred or more diseased closing in on them. They ran downhill, the slope giving them a momentum that turned them into a foetid avalanche of chaos.

"I'll get the dorm open," William shouted and took off towards Chupacabra's hut no more than twenty feet away.

But the door didn't budge. Another shove, it moved, but only a little this time. While clenching his jaw, sweat running into his eyes and his heart hammering, he barged the door again. It rattled. It had been locked from the inside. He banged against it. "Let us in."

Matilda and Hugh dispatched the diseased with unerring synchronicity, dropping the last two at exactly the same time before running at William with the larger pack of diseased breathing down their necks.

Fighting the urge to kick the door from its hinges, William leaned his shoulder into it, opening a gap large enough to slide his sword through. He used the blade to knock the latch. As he fell into the dorm, Hugh and Matilda entered the place by leaping over him.

A strong grip wrapped around William's collar and pulled him back, choking him and punching stars through his vision. As Hugh dragged him away, Matilda stepped forward, fighting the diseased in the doorway. Hugh jumped over William and slammed the door shut, forcing the creatures out and trapping Matilda's blade. The weapon fell apart from the pinch.

His back against the door, Hugh shook from the vibrations hammered against it as the diseased on the other side tried to beat their way in.

William's head spun as he got to his feet and led Matilda into the girls' dorm.

Like every other room, it had two sets of bunk beds. William ran to the closest one and dragged it away from the wall. Although Matilda moved as if to help him, he shooed her away with a flick of his head. "Get that one. We need as many out there as possible."

Back in the hall, William toppled the bed over, the large wooden frame slamming against the floor. Hugh shifted away at the last moment, and together they used it to block the door. Matilda appeared with her bed a second later.

The hammering attack against the door shook through the bed frame while William pushed against it to prevent it from moving.

"William!"

Hugh and Matilda came at him with the other bunk bed. He jumped aside to let them throw it on top.

Hard to trust the barricade would hold, William watched it while Matilda and Hugh ran to the boys' dorm.

Although the bunk beds still shifted from the impacts on the other side of the door, they held. They were heavy, their wooden frames thick. When Hugh and Matilda returned with a third and lifted it on top of the other two, the barrier became more resolute.

Once they'd put the fourth and final bunk bed in place, they waited.

After a few minutes, Matilda said, "They're not getting through that."

William sighed. "Neither are we."

Hugh walked over to the swords on the wall and pulled one down. After tightening the bolts on it, he handed it to Matilda. "Sorry about your other one."

Despite already having a weapon, William abandoned his sword when Hugh handed him a new one, the metal clanging against the wooden floor. Like Matilda before him, he slipped it into the sheath on his back.

His breathing levelled, the sweat drying on his forehead, William gulped. "We need to find water soon. I can't keep going without having something to drink."

The attack continued against the door, forcing Hugh to shout so they could hear him. "We can't keep going unless we find a way out of here."

Matilda dragged in a deep breath and said, "Hopefully—"

Bang!

All three of them spun around. It didn't come from outside. "I've never seen one of those doors closed before," William said.

Hugh still had his sword in his grip and stepped closer to the team leader's room. "No—"

Bang! The door rattled in its frame.

The ring of steel as Matilda unsheathed her weapon. "It's definitely coming from in there, right?"

Chaos still hammering against the door behind them, the next *bang* went off like an explosion in comparison. Gulping did nothing for William's aching throat, but it helped him get his words out. "Yep, it's definitely coming from there." He too drew his sword and widened his stance. "I was wondering who locked the dorm. Now, who's going to open it?"

CHAPTER 7

Two hours earlier

GLAD TO LEAVE A LIFE IN LAUNDRY BEHIND HER, BUT something took the edge off Olga's sense of freedom. She'd made the correct choice, one hundred percent; whatever happened, she had to try to break Max out. She owed him. Maybe he would have done the same for her were the roles reversed. But what weighed on her as she walked away was just how easy she'd found it to leave. Had she belonged to a normal family—if such a thing existed—she might have been conflicted. But she only felt relief.

There were about fifteen minutes before the residents of the laundry district needed to start work, but many of them were already in the streets. Olga walked down the main road, a crisscross of washing lines above. Cleaning stations lined the middle of the wide thoroughfare. They were large stone basins with rough edges to run the garments against. Whenever a horse walked through laundry, they'd often try to drink the filthy water.

By midday, washing would be hanging from the sky, damn near blocking out the sun, the air heady with the reek of damp. Olga's hands would be puffy, wrinkled, and numb from the cold water. And they were entering the better half of the year for this kind of work, when the sun dried most of the washing. In the winter, every resident had a house filled with damp fabrics. On the plus side, they were given more wood than most districts on account of needing to keep their houses warm, but by the end of winter, nearly everyone had a hacking cough from living in such a damp atmosphere.

"Olga!"

The sound snapped Olga's shoulders to her neck, but she didn't turn around. She should have left earlier. Although she tried to ignore him, she heard the pat of his jogging steps as he ran to catch up before he jumped in front of her.

Mark Stuck, a letch of a human being. Only a few years older than Olga, half a foot taller, and dirty everywhere but his hands. Maybe the work had given him an aversion to cleaning anything else. Despite his youth, he had the demeanour of an aging pervert: roving eyes, a grin filled with yellowed teeth, and he always spoke through heavy breaths as if he couldn't control his lust. "Hey, I called your name."

"Did you?"

Even though Olga dropped her head and walked away, he kept pace with her, swiping his greasy hair from his face. "Are you going to work?"

"What do you think?"

"Can I walk you there?"

"Does it matter how I answer that?"

The two of them walked in silence for a few seconds. Mark grinned like a moron. "What's in the bag?"

"Did I ask you to follow me today?"

"Wow. I was only making conversation."

"And what if I don't want to talk? Have you thought about that? Maybe my right to walk to work in silence is as important as your right to have a conversation with someone."

"So what's in the bag?"

Olga clenched her jaw and breathed through her nose.

"Well?"

"*Lunch!*"

Mark laughed. "You planning on feeding everyone today?"

Before Olga could tell him where to go, the cry of a diseased in the distance stopped her dead.

For the first time since catching up to her, Mark's smile fell. "You hear that too?"

Were it anyone but Mark, she might have discussed it with them. Instead, Olga set off again.

But Mark caught up with her. "I just thought it was a hangover from being on national service. I wondered if the screams this morning were some form of PTSD. National service was hard."

For the second time since he'd joined her, Olga stopped. "We've all been on national service."

"I know."

"You're talking like you want sympathy from me. Like your experience was somehow harder than what everyone else has been through. Get over yourself, yeah? We've all done it, and while I don't doubt it was difficult for you, you need to talk to someone who cares."

Mark tilted his head to one side and continued grinning at her. "Do *you* want to talk about your experience?"

Another shriek called from beyond Edin's walls.

Mark tried again. "I'm here for you if you ever need me.

You're right; we have all been through it. Which is why we should talk about it."

When Mark reached across and held the back of Olga's arm, she fought to suppress her shudder and growled at him, "Remove your hand before I snap it off and shove it up your arse."

Before he could say anything else, Olga ducked down a nearby alley between the houses in the residential area. She didn't look back when he called after her, "You're going the wrong way to get to work."

After rounding the first bend, Olga stopped and balled her fists. She watched where she'd just come from. If he followed, he'd lose his front teeth. She waited for about thirty seconds. Maybe the boy had taken the hint for the first time in his life.

Each district had their own distinct look on the main streets, but when in amongst the houses in the tight alleyways, Olga could have been anywhere. A mess of wonky huts, some of them were pressed so close to one another she had to turn sideways to move between them. The place buzzed with domesticity: crying children, coughing adults, and general chatter; the banging and crashing of pots and pans.

Like many other residential areas in the districts, a line of houses in laundry backed up against the walls between them and their neighbours. About fifteen feet tall, the wall blocking her access to tailoring stood high enough to be a deterrent for most people. Hell, with punishments as they were in Edin, they could have made it lower and still seen very few attempts made from adults trying to get from one district to another. To move between districts without permission meant eviction, and the city made sure everyone knew who'd been punished for that crime. But she'd made her mind up; even eviction would be better than the alternative.

Olga walked with the tall wall on her right and the houses

on her left. A quiet part of the city, very few people walked this way because it led nowhere.

Up ahead, the alley pinched tighter where the back of one house ran close to the wall. The perfect spot. Olga quickened her pace. Then she saw the guard. "Dammit."

Olga's heart hammered as she looked at the tall man with the baton on his hip.

The guard stared back at her, his eyes tight slits in his angular face. His skin shock white, the sun reflected off his face like a mirror. His right hand went to his weapon, his brow wrinkling with his frown. Were his shoulders any wider, he would have had to turn sideways to move down the narrow walkway.

A million thoughts flashed through Olga's mind. If she had a genuine excuse for being there, it would have been much easier. Just a few feet between them and she still hadn't said anything.

"What are you doing here?" the guard said.

Olga's quickened pulse made her response breathy. "I'm looking for a guard."

"For what?"

"I'm worried there's going to be an attack."

Another shrill call from the diseased. They sounded closer than before. It even distracted the guard, who stared off in the sound's general direction. He finally looked back at her. "What kind of attack?"

"A boy I know, Mark Stuck, was talking all kinds of crazy."

"What do you mean?"

"I'm not sure, but he mentioned that he'd had enough. That he's going to take down some people to help them see the boring lives they're living. He kept rambling on about national service and how much it's screwed him up."

"It's screwed all of us up."

"He had a knife on him." The sound of footsteps came up

the alley from the other direction. Two women with babies. Olga raised her voice for their benefit. "He said he's going to take down whoever gets in his way. Women. Children ..."

The two women stopped and pulled their kids in close.

"I'm worried if someone doesn't catch him, there will be a massacre. He's a danger to himself and everyone else. I can't do anything about it, but *you* can."

The tall guard looked back at the women, who stared accusingly at him. His reply loud enough for them to hear, he said, "You'd best not be winding me up."

"I don't know what's going to happen. I know what he told me, and I consider it to be a very real threat."

"You saw the knife?"

Olga held her hands up and showed a gap of at least twelve inches between them.

Exhaling with such force his cheeks puffed, the guard shook his head before bursting into a jog, slamming into Olga as he passed.

In his absence, the two women watched Olga rub the shoulder he'd just slammed into. "I think it's going to kick off," she said. "If you value the safety of your children, you'd do well to get them inside before it's too late."

Without a word, the women left.

On her own in the alleyway, her legs shaking, sweat itching her collar, Olga fanned her shirt to cool down. She wouldn't get a better chance than this.

Olga jumped up and caught the edge of the house's roof. The jagged tiles bit into her hands, but she held on and found her footing on the jutting bricks in the house's wall.

The wind blew harder up on the roof, rocking her where she stood. Her legs weakened to look at the gap. Not only did it now appear wider and the top of the wall higher, but the rough finish would tear her hands to shreds when she reached up and tried to hold on. But if she waited any longer, she'd get caught. A two-step run-up, she leaped for the wall, fire in her palms from where she caught the top of the uneven barrier.

After she'd scrambled up onto the rough wall, she heard, "Oi! You!"

Her heart beat in her neck when she looked back at the wide guard charging down the alley. Baton in one hand, his whistle in the other, he blew a shrill *peep!* Did he seriously expect her to freeze?

Olga hung her legs down the other side and slid off into tailoring.

As she landed, the high-pitched call of the guard's whistle told the rest of the city's enforcers they needed to find her now —if they could catch her. She ran towards the heart of tailoring. Now she'd made her move, she needed to run with everything she had. Through tailoring first, and although she'd never been there before, straight through woodwork after.

CHAPTER 8

Bang!
He might have just asked who wanted to open the door, but as Hugh stepped forward, William grabbed him. "Hang on! That door's locked, and it's remained locked since we've been in here."

"What? So we leave the thing in there?" Hugh said.

"No, but as loud as it is, I'd argue it's not our priority. The door's locked. I say we run a quick sweep over this place before we come back. We can deal with this last."

Although neither of them replied, neither of them argued with him, so William pointed at the door. "Matilda, are you okay watching this room?"

A two-handed grip on her new sword, she nodded.

"If there's any problems, shout, okay?"

She nodded again.

"Hugh, come with me."

Bang!

Not unexpected, yet William still jumped away from the door. His cheeks grew hotter and he let out a nervous laugh.

"Whatever's in there, it sounds big." He hesitated for a moment. "Are you sure you'll be okay on your own?"

Matilda reached out and squeezed his hand before tightening her grip on her sword again. "It's not like you're going far."

Another three loud bangs hit the door in quick succession. It held, so William led Hugh to the girls' dorm.

Emptied of beds and with daylight flooding into the room, it took no more than a cursory glance to search it. The diseased beating against the doors, William moved to the window and slowly drew the curtains. "I don't think those things can see, but I don't want to risk it."

Back out in the hallway, William shared a look with Matilda. "Everything okay?"

"Have I told you otherwise?"

"I worry about you."

"Thank you, but you shouldn't; we both know I can handle myself."

Three remaining swords on the wall on his left, they rattled with the attack thrown against the locked front door. The foetid and cloying vinegar reek of disease damn near curdled the air.

The boys' room as empty as the girls', William went straight for the curtains. Just before he drew them, he felt the slightest breeze. The window had been left open. A small crack of no more than a few inches, but it would be enough to give the creatures the purchase to pull it from the frame.

The banging from the leader's room had increased in frequency and ferocity. His throat drier than ever when he stepped back into the hallway, William checked the bunk bed blockade. It held strong.

"So?" Matilda said.

"So?"

"You've checked everywhere else." She flicked her head in

the direction of the closed door to the leader's room. "What do we do about this? We can't put it off any longer."

"I'm not putting it off," William said, clearly not convincing himself or—judging by her raised eyebrow—Matilda. Hugh remained behind him, ready to go along with whatever they decided.

"Okay," William said. "I'll open the door and you take the thing down, yeah?"

In response, Matilda hunched into a more solid base, her feet wider apart, her knees slightly bent. Her knuckles whitened from gripping the sword's handle.

Hugh had deep bags beneath his glazed wide eyes. The slightest of twitches ran through him, but if they needed to fight, he'd be ready.

One hand holding his own sword, and one on the now shaking door handle, William trembled as he cleared his dry throat. "One …"

Matilda nodded, the tip of her tongue running over her pursed lips.

"Two …"

She raised her sword higher.

"Three." William pulled the door wide and stepped back into the girls' room. A shrill scream exploded from the small space, followed by the slam of clumsy steps beating against the floorboards.

Although Matilda stood ready, Hugh's eyes widened. He dropped his sword, and before Matilda could swing for the creature, Hugh charged at it.

The sound of bodies collided, and William jumped from the girls' room to see Hugh standing over the diseased. He kicked it as its teeth snapped, desperately trying to bite into his flesh.

The reaction suddenly made sense. "Sarge?"

Despite the man's age, his grey hair, and slight limp, he'd

always carried himself like he had the strength of an ox. Now he had the crimson glare of a diseased, he looked like he could tear the world in two. Even as he lay on his back.

"You let Elizabeth die, you fuck!" Hugh screamed, kicking the diseased Sarge in the face. "You did nothing about Ranger and Lance. You knew what they did to her, yet you gave *him* the apprenticeship."

Kick after kick to Sarge's face, the grizzled vet continued to snap his teeth, missing each time and being punished with another strike from Hugh's boot.

Every kick helped with the subduing of their old leader, William moving closer to Matilda as he remained focused on Hugh.

Having finally kicked the beast unconscious, Hugh stamped on his head.

William's stomach lurched as the skin sheared from Sarge's face.

Hugh repeated the action, his boot heel slipping every time he drove it down.

It must have taken fifteen squelching stamps before Sarge's skull finally yielded with a *crack!* Matilda looked like William felt, her skin pale, her wide eyes asking a question he couldn't answer. Had Hugh lost it?

Blood and brain matter leaked from Sarge's pulped head, his body limp. Hugh still shouted at him, tears and snot dripping from his chin. "You should have managed them better. You didn't need to be such an arsehole. We were kids. What does it matter if we couldn't fight? Most of us didn't want to."

When Hugh lifted one of Sarge's arms and raised his own leg, William turned away. The snap of bone drowned out the insanity at the front door.

"So many died because of you." Hugh raised Sarge's leg next. *Crack!*

Matilda spoke so only William heard her. "You have to stop him."

"I think he needs to do this."

"He's scaring you too, isn't he?"

How could he deny it? And who in their right mind would try to interrupt a madman in full flow?

Crack! Sarge's other leg. Or rather, what remained of Sarge. The man had been driven out by the disease. The disease had been driven out by Hugh's stamping boot. An inanimate and broken object, nothing more. And maybe Hugh did need to do this. Maybe this would exorcise his screaming demons.

After the crack of Sarge's other arm, William relaxed. The end—hopefully.

Marching past them as if they weren't there—his eyes swollen and bloodshot, his nose running—Hugh returned to his dropped sword, picked it up, and walked back over to Sarge's corpse. He used his blade to rip the man's stomach open, the reek of exposed bowels joining the vinegar rot.

His nose in a pinch, William stepped closer to Hugh. "That's enough!"

But Hugh still hadn't finished, stabbing Sarge again and again.

When Matilda shook her head at him, William said, "You have to trust me on this. Everything will be fine."

But she clearly didn't. And why should she? They had to depend on one another, and Hugh had clearly lost his mind. Then William saw something in Sarge's room. "Look."

It halted Hugh's attack, and although the boy fixed on him, his eyes were black as if the Hugh he knew had been pushed far down. After a few seconds, the boy's features softened.

"Sarge has water in his room," William said.

Hugh panted as he stood in the pool of blood spreading across the floorboards. He threw a brief glance into the leader's room. A flask sat on the shelf. Maybe he saw it, but his attention returned to Sarge and his mouth fell open. He pointed at the broken corpse. "Who did this?"

William shivered and he heard Matilda's unsuccessful attempts to stifle a gasp.

"Don't worry," William said, Hugh and Matilda both standing with their faces slack, "we've found some water. We need to drink. Whatever else happens, we're in this together as a team."

Neither replied, but when William walked into Sarge's room, shook the flask to find it half full, and then walked to the boys' room next door, they followed him. If he asked Matilda how she felt, she might have said something, but he didn't need to. He got it. They had to get through the national service area. They had to free Artan. Could they rely on Hugh in his current state? Maybe not, but what else could they do? Hugh had been a good friend, and friends didn't turn their backs on one another, especially when they needed them most. After he'd quenched his thirst with Sarge's water, he handed the flask to Matilda, holding onto it until she looked up at him. "What matters right now is getting some water into us and finding a way out of here. We need to look forward."

Matilda dipped the slightest nod before sipping the water. When she handed it to Hugh, she managed a half smile, her eyes kind. "Here's to looking forward."

Hugh visibly relaxed and toasted her with the flask. "To looking forward."

CHAPTER 9

Two hours earlier

Free for now, Olga had the advantage. She'd only get caught if she screwed up. Like with the laundry district, the people in tailoring were awake and ready to start their day. Tailors and their apprentices were on their way to work, many already inside their shops. She'd been here plenty of times when afforded the freedom of youth, which, now it had been taken away, seemed like an uncharacteristically generous gift from the powers that be in Edin. It made sense to use the main road. The cobblestones were uneven underfoot, but it didn't get any better in this city. The shrill call of whistles chased her. Two quick peeps. Although unsure of the exact meaning, she didn't need to be a genius to get the gist; they were onto her.

Every worker stared at Olga as she ran down the main road. As of yet, none of them had decided to be a hero.

Around the next bend, Olga slowed to a walk. The people stopped glancing at her. She transformed from criminal to customer and slipped into a nearby shop as if with the intention of buying something.

A bell above the door announced her entrance, Olga shrieking at the unexpected sound. The woman behind the counter looked up, her brow furrowed.

While ruffling her nose against the strong reek of dust, Olga took in the various fabrics stuffed into shelves and hanging from the rails. "What a wonderful selection you have here. I'm not sure I could even name all these colours."

"Can I *help* you?" the shop owner said.

A slight shuffle as if she could wriggle free of her own sweating body, Olga tugged on her collar. "I'm here to get some clothes."

"*Clothes?* Anything more specific than that, or shall I guess?"

"What's wrong, old lady, my custom not good enough for you?"

The whistles outside drew closer. She needed to wind her neck in. Too sassy for her own good, Olga looked out through the large shop window.

The tailor raised her voice. "You look *awfully* jumpy, my dear."

Olga laughed it off and for some reason mimicked the woman's accent as if to throw her own indignation back at her. "I'm very keen to get a blouse, and I'm in *quite* a rush."

"Clearly."

"I've been waiting for a long time to come here to get one. I must say, I was hoping for a more positive experience."

The woman walked from around the counter. Her back as stiff as the mannequin she held, she approached. The doll wore a light pink blouse, which the woman gripped with a pinch. She too glanced through the window, not even looking at Olga when she said, "Like this one?"

Why had Olga come in here?

The tailor had the moves of a neophyte magician, doing her best to distract Olga with the blouse while she used her free hand to grab a long and straight stick.

Olga stepped towards the door. "You know what? I've changed my mind."

Sharp with adrenaline, Olga saw the attack as if the woman worked in slow motion. The stick came her way at head height. She ducked as it thudded into the door, and swiped the woman's legs from beneath her.

The tailor hit the ground with a thump, yelling as she rolled onto her back while holding the base of her spine.

Olga jumped to her feet, threw the door wide with such force it sent several mannequins flying, and ran out into the street. She halted at exactly the same time as three guards on her right. "Oh shit."

As one, the guards—two men and a woman—put their whistles to their lips and drew their batons. They sounded three shrill peeps. They might have found her, but could they catch her?

Olga ran left up the main road. The chase had caused quite a stir, the street growing busier with spectators.

Dodging through the dense press of bodies, the gap between Olga and her pursuers grew. She had the beating of them in a straight race, and the crowd gave her even more of an advantage. The guards were built like enforcers, but she had the physique and stamina of an athlete. Let them try to keep up with her.

A sharp right, Olga came face-to-face with another guard. A wall of a woman, she had tanned skin, a shaved head, and a baton as long as her forearm. A jaw so thick she could chew through walls, she growled with a deep rumble.

Like with the tailor a minute ago, Olga read the swinging

blow and ducked. She balled her fist and slammed it into the guard's right kneecap. Fire ran through her knuckles like she'd punched a rock, but the guard roared. The woman dropped to the ground, holding her knee as Olga darted past.

As long as Olga stayed on the main road, she'd be in plain sight. She could lose them in the residential area. Unless they predicted her path and formed a blockade. After rounding the next bend, the whistles still behind her, Olga glanced back. She couldn't see them and they couldn't see her. She darted down the next alley.

Were it not for the residents shouting to the guards, Olga might have kidded herself into thinking she'd bought an advantage. Her legs burning, she turned left, right, left, left, pushing off the lopsided houses' walls to help with her sudden changes in direction.

The guards might have used a code Olga didn't understand, but maybe that didn't matter. As long as they blew their whistles, she knew where to avoid and she knew they hadn't given up the chase.

∼

OLGA'S LUNGS WERE TIGHT AND HER LEGS WEAK. THE GUARDS' whistles remained at two peeps—whatever that meant—but more sounded than before, springing from all around her. Surely it just had to be a matter of time before one of the city's enforcers caught her.

Although Olga made slow progress through the unfamiliar streets, she had the tall warehouses in the woodwork district as her target, and most decisions led her closer to them. Hopefully she'd reach the wall before the guards reached her. As a kid, she'd been warned away from woodwork. Something about the place and the levels of violence there. But she wasn't a kid anymore, and it was the quickest route to the labs.

Another right turn and the one-storey buildings on Olga's left changed into the tall wall separating tailoring from woodwork. A similar height to the one between laundry and tailoring, it stood about fifteen to twenty feet tall. The whistles far enough away, she slowed her pace and tried to calm her breaths. There had to be an easy way over. Although, none of the houses were close enough for her to leap from.

Several loud peeps behind her, Olga took off again, halting almost instantly when she saw him.

He leaned against the wall as if standing guard at the large hole leading through to woodwork. The boy had several scars she hadn't seen on him before and several fewer teeth. "What are *you* doing here?"

Before he responded, Lance tilted his ear to the sky to listen to the whistles. He smiled as he let a long knife slide from his sleeve, catching the handle when about twelve inches of blade had appeared. "I would say the same to you, but I think I've already worked that out."

Olga shook her head and ran past him, flinching when he twitched the blade at her. Despite the bright sun, what she saw of woodwork was shrouded in deep shadow.

"You want me to let you through?"

Olga stopped a few feet away. "If I want to go through, I don't need to ask for *your* permission."

Lance lifted his blade and winked. "Sure you don't. I wouldn't advise trying though."

"So let's say you let me through … what's the catch?"

"No catch, you just need to ask nicely. Talk to me like I'm a human being for once. I didn't even exist to you when we were on national service."

Olga stepped closer and shuddered as she peered into the

gloom of woodwork for a second time. She shook her head. "I'm doing all right on my own. I don't need your help."

More whistles, Lance let out a tittering laugh. "Clearly. Well, good luck."

Screw him. No way would she let him win. No way. Olga ran off. Besides, now she'd seen it, she didn't want to go into the woodwork district. A place shrouded in secrecy, maybe she didn't need to find out why. But then the shrill peeps of whistles in front of her ground her to a halt. The houses on her right were pressed so tightly against one another she had no alleyway to duck back into. The whistles grew louder, footsteps closing in.

"Dammit." Olga turned around and ran back towards Lance, his face alight with glee.

"Come back to ask me nicely?"

But she ignored him, glanced at his blade, then the shadowy entrance to woodwork, and continued back the way she'd come from.

Before Olga reached the alley she'd exited less than a minute ago, more whistles warned her against it. They were coming for her. Her pulse quick, her clothes sticking to her sweat-slick body, she turned to Lance again.

"Sounds to me like they have you surrounded."

Olga returned to the tall and dirty boy. "Is this a trap?"

"Would you trust me if I said no?"

The whistles closed in from either side.

"I wouldn't trust you if you said the sky was blue."

"And therein lies your dilemma."

Had she not witnessed it, she would have called it an impossibility, but Lance's already wide grin stretched wider. None of her breaths deep enough to sate her need for air, she lost another gasp when a diseased's shriek rang out. Closer than any of the others she'd heard that day. Even Lance's smile faltered.

The guards' whistles pulled Olga back into the moment. "Please let me through."

"Wasn't so hard, was it?"

Lance stood aside, and Olga darted into woodwork, taking off into the shadowy alleyways. Maybe she shouldn't fear the dark. After all, it would keep her hidden from the guards.

Although she rounded a bend and put Lance out of sight, she hadn't gone far enough to escape his words. "Tell them Lance sent ya."

Five or six silhouettes stepped out about thirty feet ahead of her, blocking her path. Olga stopped and turned around to find the same behind. She spoke to herself. "What the hell have you done, Lance? You twisted prick." The small amount of light in the alley bounced off their blades. Every one of them had a weapon. The walls were too high on either side to climb. The silhouettes closed in to the tittering cackle of Lance's laughter. "This one's from me. Enjoy. She's a feisty one."

CHAPTER 10

"This is the only food or water in the entire hut," William said as he reentered the boys' room after having searched the place. Hugh and Matilda sat together on the floor, more comfortable with one another since their unspoken reconciliation. Although, William knew Matilda. She'd agreed to move on. Whatever had happened in the hall between Hugh and Sarge stayed in the hall, but he saw her unease from a mile away. Hugh, on the other hand, seemed uncharacteristically oblivious to the unspoken tension.

The diseased outside beat against the door with less enthusiasm. Maybe they were getting tired, or maybe they'd forgotten what they were pursuing now they no longer had sight of them.

William sat down, the bunk beds rattling in the hallway. Some of the water remained in the flask. He lifted it up and shook it. "Probably too late to ask now, but I wonder if this is safe to drink."

"It is," Hugh said. "Whenever we did tests on rats and rabbits in the labs, we found the second they were bitten, they were one hundred percent consumed by the virus and then the need to spread it. We never saw any of them concerned with quenching their thirst after the change."

"But how do you know humans behave the same?" Matilda said.

William shifted in an attempt to find comfort on the hard wooden floor. He straightened his back, alert and ready to stop Matilda if her line of questioning grew too aggressive.

"As William said, it's a bit late to be worrying about it now. We've already drunk enough to turn."

"Hugh's right." William took another sip of water. "It is a bit too late."

While Matilda sipped from the flask and passed it on to Hugh, William removed his right boot. His foot throbbed harder than ever now he'd finally given it his full attention. First he rolled his sock down from the top, stopping just before the pain became unbearable. A silent countdown in his head, he clenched his jaw and ripped it off the rest of the way, dragging the bandage with it.

"My god!" Hugh pulled his head back. "That looks nasty."

For Hugh to give him such a strong reaction … William turned away. Did he really want to look now? But like his dad used to say, it was always better to know what you were dealing with than burying your head in the sand and hoping it would resolve itself. Very few problems were fixed without a well-considered plan.

William's blood-soaked sock had turned the skin on the bottom of his foot pink and wrinkly. The cut stood out as a blast of red in comparison; a deep glistening gash. Fluff and dirt had collected in the ravine of the wound. When Hugh handed William the flask, he double-checked his friend's intention. "But this is all the water there is."

"We'll find more," Hugh said. "You need to wash it out."

"Do you two mind?"

Both Matilda and Hugh shook their heads.

As he poured, William dragged air in through his clenched teeth, the cold water sinking a sharp bite into the wound. Most of the fluff gone and the blood flowing freely, he drizzled in a little bit more before passing the flask to Matilda.

Once the water had gone around again, Hugh handed it back to William. "I really don't need any more now."

"I'm good too," Matilda said.

Another cold splash, William clamped his teeth on his bottom lip and rode out the hot nauseating flush.

"I feel awful about leaving Trent on that roof out there," Matilda said.

"You shouldn't feel too bad." William emptied the rest of the flask over his cut. "He sent those things after us."

"But how will they get away?"

"I'm more concerned about how we'll get out of here."

"We'll get out of here," Hugh said. "And when we get into Edin, we can let them know there are people who need help."

The Hugh in front of him at that moment reminded William of the one he'd first met when they started national service. Kind and intelligent. He nodded. "Hugh's right, someone will come for them before it's too late. Besides, our priority is Artan. We can't risk our lives on a rescue mission when the city has an army of guards and protectors at their disposal. I say we let them take care of it." Now he'd washed his wound, he ground his teeth against the electric buzz of slipping on the bandage and then his sock. Once he'd tied his boot laces again, he looked up at Hugh. "Didn't Ranger try to get you with a nail?"

"Yeah, he got me pretty bad." Nowhere near the level of fuss William had made, Hugh undid the laces on his boot and removed it.

When Hugh finally pulled his sock off, William flinched

and looked away. "My god, Hugh. Why didn't you say something? We've used up all the water now."

His attention on his foot, white ooze seeping from it, the blood a brown soup from where it had mixed with so much dirt and sweat, Hugh said, "I dunno, you looked like you needed it more."

And maybe he did. No doubt Hugh had the worse wound between the pair of them, but he didn't seem bothered. The way he shrugged, dragged his sock back on as if he felt nothing, and retied his boot sent a cold wave through William. "How can you tolerate the pain?"

White bands beneath each eye from where his face hung slack, the new Hugh stepped forward again. "I'm numb to most things at the moment." Then he smiled. His dark eyes, however, didn't.

"Why are you smiling?" Matilda said.

The lethargic banging continued against the dorm's front door. "I was just thinking about James."

"Your brother?"

"Yeah. When I went back after national service, I promised him I'd introduce him to Elizabeth."

"But Elizabeth's—"

"Going to love him," William said. Although he addressed Hugh, he glared at Matilda. Her lips pursed and her face red, he'd seen this a thousand times before. Not one to hold her tongue, he waited for her to speak again so he could interrupt her a second time. After a few seconds, she hadn't said anything, so he turned back to Hugh. "Tell us about James."

"He's just a normal kid, you know? Inquisitive. Bored most of the time. Always up for doing something. I made him train with me a lot before I came to the trials. He's certainly fitter than he used to be." While picking at his nails, Hugh said, "I was worried about him. Tailoring's right next to the woodwork district and the gangs." He shook, his knuckles turning white as he formed tight fists. "But I made sure the gangs knew who I was and that Lance didn't feed him to them."

"What did you do?" Matilda said.

Hugh turned puce and lowered his head.

The facade of trust fell away, and Matilda said, "If you remember that, what do you remember of the last fifteen minutes?"

"We were chased in here, we barricaded the doors, and then someone had a fight with Sarge. Who was it?"

William beat Matilda to it. "It was me. He'd turned." What good would it do to grill Hugh about it now? How would it help them get out of there?

A hard frown spread wrinkles across Hugh's forehead. "But why so savage? Wasn't it enough just to kill him?"

"You'd *think!*" Matilda said.

Before the conversation could go any further, William cleared his throat. "Let's move on, yeah? We need to look forward."

"We need to save Artan," Matilda said. "I can't let anything stand in the way of that."

Despite Hugh's plodding demeanour when they'd first met him in the dining hall, he'd always had a sharpness to him. One of the smartest people William knew. But now he sat with his jaw slightly loose and his eyes vacant … had they lost their friend for good? He reached out and held Matilda's hand. "Nothing will stand in the way of us reaching him. We'll get to him as a team." He understood her anxiety. Hell, even he didn't know who Hugh was anymore. "You need to trust me."

"I do trust you."

"Good. Now hopefully the diseased will run over to Trent's cabin. If we give them a bit of time, they'll forget we're in here. They can see Trent and the others, so surely they'll go to them."

"And if they don't?" Hugh said.

"Hopefully, they will." If only William had something better than that. A loose plan and a loose cannon of a friend, he had to put faith in them both. "Besides," he said with a shrug, "a rest will do us good."

Matilda met his words with raised eyebrows. Her trust in Hugh hung by a frayed rope. William could almost hear the ping of snapping fibres.

CHAPTER 11

T*wo hours earlier*

ALTHOUGH LANCE REMAINED HIDDEN AROUND THE CORNER, HIS high-pitched laugh echoed off the high walls. Olga shouldn't have come here. They avoided the place for a reason; that should have been enough of a deterrent. What an idiot!

As the two groups of boys closed in, their own mirthful rumble drowned out Lance's manic mirth. Yet, even now, with a very tangible threat ahead of her, when Olga heard another diseased's cry, she shivered. What was going on out there?

One of the gang members—an older boy by the sound of his deep voice—pulled her back into the moment. "It's kind of Lance to send us a gift."

Her throat dry, her heart hammering, Olga gulped.

"We get a bit bored of the girls over here. Fresh meat's always welcome."

The collective sound of laughter swelled in the tight space, some of them female. Maybe she'd imagined the diseased's screams. Olga couldn't keep her words level when she said, "I don't know what the hell you're talking about."

"You don't need to," another one of the boys said.

"Whatever ideas you have in your thick heads, you need to forget them now."

Although different members of the gang replied, the shadows hid their identities, turning them into one multi-tonal mass. A girl this time. "Sounds like a threat."

"You'd better believe it is, sweetheart," Olga said.

"And why should we be intimidated by that?"

Another voice cut in. "We like it when they fight back. Gives us a better story afterwards."

"What makes you sound more heroic?" Olga shook, the tight walls throwing the gasps of her own panic back at her. "Just let me pass, you scumbags."

Both packs were no more than six feet away when those behind her spoke. "That works in your district, does it? Sounds to me like the men over there could do with keeping their women in check. Maybe, when we're done with you, you could bring some friends over. We could teach them a thing or two about knowing their place."

As Olga spun from one group to the other, she grew dizzy. No more than a few feet away, their faces remained hidden in shadow. It was as if their presence repelled the light. "Some heroes you are. You hide in darkness, and it takes ten of you to overpower one girl."

"It's not that it takes ten of us to bring you down. More that we all want our turn, even the girls."

Ragged breaths and her chest tight, Olga shook her head. "This won't end well for you."

Any closer and they'd reach out for her. She had to do something. Their faces were still invisible, but their blades glinted as if they had their own source of light.

It didn't matter how many of them there were, the narrow alley kept them three abreast. She could take on six of them. No, she couldn't, but better to go down fighting. Olga turned on the gang behind her, yelled so loud she made her own ears ring, and jumped, kicking off the wall on her right. Propelled towards one of the gang, her boot connected with his face with a loud *clop!* As she landed, the boy fell into the row behind. A small gap, but they were rattled. She charged, punching another one of them in the face. It stung her fist, but knocked the girl out of the way. The darkness now against them because they couldn't tell where they ended and she began, she barged through the pack and burst free.

One of the boys grabbed Olga's rucksack, yanking her back. She hit the hard ground before the boy dragged her towards him.

A quick twist and Olga slipped free of her bag's straps, jumped up, and ran again, the slam of footsteps chasing her.

Olga rounded the bend to meet Lance's leering grin. He'd left tailoring and stood in the darkened path, blocking her way. Realisation then swept across his features, his face dropping as he raised his knife.

She could turn tight and continue into woodwork with the boys on her back, or she could face Lance. Olga screamed and charged the lanky boy. His attack came from a mile away. She pulled up short, the blade sweeping across in front of her before crashing into the wall on her left. Two quick punches to Lance's chin and the lanky boy folded.

After prying Lance's blade from his tight grip, Olga ran into tailoring and instantly stopped. It now made sense why Lance had left. There were guards on both her left and right. They had their backs to her. The boys closed in from behind. If the guards caught her, she'd get evicted, especially with Lance's machete in her hand.

Before the guards saw her, Olga ducked back into woodwork. The boys to her right, she turned left and ran deeper into the shadowy district.

The alleys were tighter and darker than any she'd seen. The tall buildings on either side had large wooden screens jutting from their roofs to block out the sun. It gave her just a small bar of light overhead to guide her way.

Right, left, right, left, left, left—no matter how zigzagged her run, the thunder of steps continued behind her. Although she couldn't see them, the gang remained on her trail, many of them laughing at her futile attempt at escape.

The shadows weren't dark enough to hide the figures on the first floors of many of the buildings. They watched over Olga like sentries. Just before she took the next right, one of them jumped down and blocked her path. She continued straight. The same happened at the next left.

Several more jumped down and blocked her way, but none of them wanted to fight. A second later, Olga burst into an open space with a dead end. Surrounded by spectators, she spun on the spot while fighting for breath. The woodwork district's own arena and she was the diseased. At least twenty boys and girls followed her in, fanning out and cackling like they had all along.

One of the boys stepped forward while shaking his head. She still couldn't see his face. "Well, well, looks like you want to put on a show. It's a good job you've come here. There's a bit more space for us to queue up. More places for the others to watch from."

Olga's stomach tightened, and the skin at the base of her neck writhed with a caterpillar crawl. Sweat ran into her eyes as the silhouettes of the gang spread out like a dark mist. She swallowed back her instinct to beg. They were animals. They had less humanity than the diseased. They didn't deserve her pleas. It would probably spur them on.

"I'm the guv'nor," the lead boy said. "That means I go first."

Still several feet between them, she couldn't let them any closer. And they didn't deserve the same respect she'd give to a human. Lance's knife in her sweating grip, Olga screamed and threw it at the lead boy. It spun once before the deep blade stuck in his face.

The boy fell and Olga charged, getting to him as he hit the ground. She pulled the knife from his face and the one from his hand. Armed with both blades, she swung at the next closest person, catching her arm. The girl yelled and dropped her weapon.

While letting out a shrill cry to match any she'd heard from the diseased, Olga's pulse hammered as she attacked with everything she had. These kids weren't used to people fighting back. It drove panic through them.

The gang members scattered, opening up a path for her. Covered in the warm blood of her enemies, Olga made it back to the alley she'd entered through and took off again.

Although she'd left the gang in disarray, it didn't take long for one of them to deliver an authoritative, "Get her."

Her legs weak, Olga hated herself for crying as she willed her tired body forwards. On the edge of her balance, she could crash down at any moment. But the gang were farther back this time and chased her with less enthusiasm. Who would be brave enough to attack her again? A blade in each hand, they knew what would happen if they got too close.

Several turns later, the pack still on her tail, Olga burst out into the main street running through woodwork. Thank god! What appeared to be a family of a mum, dad, and three children stared at her. "Please help me."

Snot and tears ran down her face, the blood of her victims tightening her skin where it had already started to dry. She couldn't blame the mum and dad for pulling their kids away. "*Please*, a gang of boys are going to attack me. Please help."

Not just the family, but the other people on the street vanished. They already knew about the gangs. They were as scared as her. What must have been fifteen gang members ran out onto the main road. Olga shook her head, taking off again.

She might have had enough rage and front to defeat the gang, but as she stretched her mouth wide to drag in more air, and her muscles burned with fatigue, she wouldn't bet on it. She darted left, returning to the tight and dark alleys. While she still had a lead, she had to try to lose them. They'd outrun her on the main road.

Taking every turn, Olga ran left, right, right, left, left, left. Around the next bend, she found a house with its door open. An old woman beckoned her in. If she didn't trust the woman, they'd catch her. With no idea how to get out of woodwork, she needed sanctuary.

Olga darted into the house, the woman closing the door behind her. Gasping for breath, she tried to speak, but the woman placed a finger over her lips.

Footsteps thundered past the house. The gang had increased in number. She had a small army after her now.

∽

A GOOD FIVE MINUTES AFTER THE LAST BOY RAN PAST, THE OLD woman finally spoke. "You need to get out of here. This is a bad district. It's one of Edin's best-kept secrets, but this place is run by the gangs. They've been getting worse."

Her breathing had levelled out. Olga shrugged. "But how do I get away? This place is a maze."

The old woman pressed her ear against her front door before she opened it and stepped into the street. When she returned, she pointed to her left. "You get out of here and turn right. If you follow this alley for the next few minutes, you should come to a gap in the wall that'll lead you out to the labs."

"Thank god." A gulp against the dry pinch in her throat, Olga pressed her hands together as if in prayer. "Thank you."

The woman might have been old and frail, her face a mess of wrinkles, but she had the brightest blue eyes. "It's my pleasure." The azure glow faded. "I only wish someone could have rescued me when I was your age."

Before Olga could reply, the old woman hissed, "Now go. Get out of here while you still can."

∽

EXACTLY AS THE WOMAN HAD CALLED IT, OLGA RAN FOR ABOUT two minutes and found the gap in the wall. But before she got to it, she froze. Deep voices came from around the corner. Four boys then appeared, blocking her exit.

They stopped talking when they saw her. Too tired to run anymore, Olga stepped forward, her knives away from her sides and ready to swing. "I will cut whoever gets in my way."

The boys stepped back at her approach. Were she to guess, she'd put them at around fourteen. Not like the almost men and women she'd encountered when she'd first entered woodwork.

Too much time and she might lose her advantage. Olga charged at the boys. They ran.

Where the boys turned right, Olga burst through the hole in the wall and into the labs. She fell to her knees.

It took a few seconds for her to see the guard standing there. The short and squat man had a tight afro, dark skin, and biceps like boulders. He'd already drawn his baton. "Put the blades down."

"The second I put these down, you'll take me in."

It took the man a few seconds to find his words, and when he did, they stood in stark contrast to his resolute posture. In a febrile tone, he said, "I had a daughter who got dragged into the woodwork district. I've not seen her since. The city's officials won't do anything about it because woodwork have them over a barrel."

"What are you talking about?"

"Woodwork threaten the city with revolt if they don't leave them alone. They have wood quotas, which they hit, but other than that, they don't want Edin's interference. So if you think I care about what you've done in there, you're wrong. I want you to drop your weapons as proof that you mean *me* no harm."

Trust didn't get given freely in Edin. Especially when it relied on the whims of a guard, but what else could she do? The *ching* of her blades hit the ground and Olga shook her head. Hot tears streamed down her cheeks. "I'm tired of fighting."

As the guard approached her, he softened his tone. "You're safe now."

Olga tensed at the guard's proximity. When he wrapped her in a tight hug, she let the large man take her weight, her body releasing her grief in sobbing waves as if it had been the thing keeping her upright.

CHAPTER 12

For about ten minutes, William, Matilda, and Hugh sat resting on the floor in the boys' room. Although it felt like much longer, the day getting warmer, the diseased—although more muted than before—still reminded them of their presence at the front door. Every time William thought to say something, it died before he opened his mouth. What did he have to offer them? They were prisoners with no way out. Better than being turned, but they didn't need that scant consolation.

"I think they're forgetting about us," Matilda said.

William shrugged. "They do sound less enthusiastic."

Matilda winced. "But we need another plan. If Trent and the others are sensible, they've hidden so the diseased can't see them."

"So the diseased outside our hut have no reason to move?" William said.

Matilda nodded. "Right. So how long do we wait before we try something else?"

A murky glow hung in the room like fog from where William had drawn the curtain previously. "I've not said anything until now because it doesn't seem like a very good plan …"

Since they'd had the conversation about what had happened to Sarge, Hugh hadn't put more than a few sentences together, and his eyes remained distant as if he communed with his inner demons. Maybe he realised what he'd done. Maybe they were losing him. Either way, William looked to Matilda to help him decide.

"What are you talking about?" Matilda said.

"Sorry. The window."

"Huh?"

"I've stayed in two dorms now, and the windows were sealed shut in both of them."

"This is going somewhere, right?"

And he couldn't blame her for her impatience. Not only did Matilda need to keep herself alive, but if she managed that, she then needed to find a way to get to Artan. "When Hugh and I came in here, I had to close the window. It only opens a crack, which is why I didn't give it much thought, but I reckon we can force it wider and slip out the back." He walked over to the window, moving more easily because of his washed foot.

The thin curtains would have revealed the silhouettes of diseased were there any on the other side, but William still shook as he pinched the light fabric and drew them. The morning light burned his eyes. Matilda and Hugh also squinted. No diseased out the back; at least, none he could see. "If we can sneak out this way, we have a clear run to the gates."

"That's a big *if*," Matilda said.

"I'm trying my best."

After a pause, Matilda came to William's side and leaned against him. She rarely said the word *sorry*, but it would do. Hugh followed a second later. While looking out across the national service area, she chewed the inside of her mouth.

Dust motes danced in the sun's strong rays, distracting William for a second before he looked back out. Minotaur's dorm, the dining hall, and the gym stood between them and the gates separating the national service area and the rest of Edin. "We could use the buildings as cover to get from here to the gates. Unless anyone has any other ideas?"

Neither Hugh nor Matilda offered one.

"I think Matilda's right about Trent and the others. If they have any sense, they'll stay out of sight, so we could be waiting a long time if we don't make a move."

The sun bounced off Matilda's pale skin when she moved closer to the window for a better look. William turned to Hugh. "You down for this?"

If the boy had an opinion, he hid it well. A shrug, he then nodded.

"Tilly?" William said.

Matilda looked at him with a watering gaze.

"Are you okay?"

She used the back of her hand to dab her eyes. "The sun's bright."

"And the plan?"

"It's the best we've got."

"Yeah, I think so too." While holding his breath, William unlocked the window's catch, the small bracket creaking. The hinges ran along the top of the frame, a gap opening at the bottom as he eased it wider. At about three inches, it stopped. Even with such a small gap, the stench of the diseased came into the room as if it had been propelled by their moans and wails. There were a lot of them out there. "This is as far as it opens."

Matilda pushed against the window as if testing his assertion.

Before William could say anything else, she clenched her

jaw and shoved it even harder. The flimsy wooden frame popped at the weak hinges.

William lunged to catch the window but missed.

The frame hit the ground outside, the large pane shattering on impact with a loud *crash!*

CHAPTER 13

William and Matilda dropped at the same time, crouching beneath the now missing window.

When Hugh didn't move, William grabbed his belt and dragged him down with them.

All three of them sat with their backs to the wooden wall directly beneath the window, Matilda hugging her knees to her chest as she shook her head. "I'm so sorry. I didn't think it would give so easily."

William laid a gentle hand on Matilda's shoulder and pressed his finger to his lips. She knew what she'd done wrong; he didn't need to make her feel worse. He reached down and held her shaking hand.

A pack of diseased appeared around the back of the dorm. It sounded like half a dozen at the most, their snorting and rattling breaths drawing closer.

At least William didn't have to deal with Hugh. If his friend felt scared, he didn't show it, looking back across the boys' room with his now familiar distant glaze. Maybe their situation hadn't even registered with him. After all, he hadn't taken the initiative to hide.

The stench, as always, reached William before the diseased. Their presence curdled the air as their snuffling and snorting drew closer.

The curtain danced in the wind, flapping above them as if desperate to reveal their hiding spot. It goaded William, daring him to drag it down. Maybe they should make a break for it now. Only a small pack outside, they could fight them and run. Anything had to be better than waiting to be attacked.

A diseased then leaned in through the window above them, showing them the underside of its chin. It had a skeletal face as if it had turned months ago, its skin clinging to the bones like pallid leather. The glistening tracks of blood so common for the creatures had dried up on this one. How long did it have before it dropped dead? And where did the fresh supplies of people come from for there to always be so many of the freaks beyond the walls?

Matilda shook more than ever, so William squeezed her hand, his attention still on the beast above. The thing moved its head as if surveying the room, but it clearly couldn't see. As long as they kept the noise down, they'd be fine.

With Hugh as a model of calm beside him, William closed his eyes and tried to channel his friend's state. Deep and slow breaths, he filled his lungs with the creatures' foul stench and slowly let it out, breathing into his stomach while fighting his need to heave. In and out. In and out.

It took a nudge from Matilda for William to open his eyes. She pointed up. The creature had gone. The sound of shuffling had moved on too.

A few minutes later, William's heart went into overdrive as he got to his feet, drew his sword, and peered outside. Both ways were clear. "I'm not sure it's going to get any better than this." He stepped out through the low window frame, broken glass popping beneath his boots.

Once Hugh and Matilda had joined him outside, William pointed in the direction of the closest hut about one hundred feet away: Minotaur's old dorm. Matilda nodded. Hugh didn't. Hopefully, the boy would follow. William took off towards it at a crouched jog.

On his way to Minotaur's hut, William's view of the national service area opened up. It gave him a clear line of sight to Trent and his friends, all of them lying low so the diseased couldn't see them.

Before he reached Minotaur's cabin, William stopped and waited for Matilda and then Hugh to run past him into cover. The mob remained outside the hut they'd just left. Fifty, one hundred ... however many, they loitered without a cause.

As William moved from their line of sight, Matilda pulled back from where she'd peered around the other side of the dorm at their route to the dining hall. She gave him a thumbs up, which he returned before she led them to the next hiding spot.

William watched the rookies on the roof as he ran.

Matilda and Hugh nipped around the back of the dining hall unseen. Just before William joined them, he froze as if pinned to the spot. One of the kids had sat up and turned his way. They stared at one another. Neither moved.

William felt the attention of his friends on him, but he continued to watch the boy in Trent's gang. His sword still in one of his hands, he pressed them together as if praying. Even from the distance between them, he could see the boy deciding his fate, adrenaline flooding his system.

But the boy didn't shout or alert the others. Instead, he glanced around him and subtly returned the praying gesture, pressing his hands together in front of his chest. In that moment, they'd signed a deal. William would do what he could to make sure someone helped them. He bowed at the boy before joining his friends.

CHAPTER 14

The kid's grace still with him, William moved along the back of the dining hall towards Hugh and Matilda at the other end. The gym stood between them and the gates leading deeper into Edin. They'd still have to find a way to scale them, but at least they were close. And now he'd cleaned his foot, he'd beat most diseased over a short distance.

Before William reached his two friends, Hugh burst from cover and sprinted towards the gym.

Matilda leaned around the dining hall to watch him go before she turned back. "What the hell's he doing?"

"Huh?" William said. "How would I know? You didn't just tell him to go?"

"No, I can't see if it's clear. He's not right in the head, William."

"He hasn't been since Elizabeth died."

"Then—"

But before she could say it, William took off after his friend. "Come on, we can't leave him."

Several diseased's screams burst from behind the gym. A

small pack emerged a second later. So much for reaching the gates without being spotted. As Matilda caught up to him, William said, "Even if we were super cautious, we had no chance of seeing them."

Her reply came in the form of ringing steel from where she drew her sword and quickened her pace to catch up with Hugh.

Faster than William, Matilda sprang on the diseased while Hugh fought them, jamming her sword into the right ear of one, pulling it back out again with a wet squelch before she went to work on another.

Just one left for William by the time he caught up. He swung a hacking blow into its neck, knocking it to the ground before he stabbed the gasping creature through the face.

The three of them might have made quick work of the pack, but the diseased let the world know they were in a fight. A second or two of silence passed before the roar of the horde they'd left outside the hut flew at them from across the field. A leading pack of about ten had an army of at least one hundred spread out behind them.

William yelled, "*Run!*" and took off towards the gym. When he reached the wooden rungs leading up the back of the tall building, he stood aside for Matilda.

Before she got to him, her face red, her brow furrowed, she said, "What the *hell* are you doing?"

"*Climb!*"

Although Matilda followed William's instruction, she spat the word, "Prick," as she ascended the ladder.

William followed her up, dew from the grass turning the soles of his boots slick.

A few seconds later—the leading pack on his tail—Hugh reached the gym and climbed.

Matilda on the roof, William three-quarters of the way up,

and Hugh about six feet from the ground. The first of the lead diseased jumped and grabbed Hugh's feet.

William's stomach sank as Hugh got ripped from the rungs and dragged into the mob below.

CHAPTER 15

William gripped the wooden rung tighter as Hugh hit the ground, almost as if he could somehow hold on for his already fallen friend. Ten or so diseased, but Hugh knew how to fight. He'd be okay. He could take on that many. Not having had time to sheathe it before climbing, Hugh still had his sword in his hand as he jumped up swinging, temporarily driving them back. But they had him surrounded.

After dropping down several rungs, William mouthed an apology to Matilda, who'd already made it to the roof. She frowned, but before she replied, he answered her question by releasing his grip and kicking away from the wall.

William landed next to Hugh and then turned his back on his friend. Too concerned with his half of the pack to see what Hugh did, he went to work, his arms moving like pistons. Stabbing several times, he sank his blade into faces and chests, the creatures' stench spilling from them with their pints of rancid blood. Soaked in the beasts' warm spray, it took all he had to focus on them and not the pack ten times their number closing in from behind.

Four down, William spun around. A diseased closed in from

Hugh's right, its jaw stretched wide, its crimson eyes glazed. It took the end of William's sword to its temple, already dead when it crashed into Hugh.

The front runners down, William stood aside to give Hugh a clear path to the ladder. But Hugh charged at the larger pack instead.

Just before Hugh escaped his reach, William grabbed his collar and dragged him back. He then shoved him at the gym. "Get up on the roof, you fool."

For a second time, Hugh tried to break away. William caught him again and slammed him against the gym's back wall, driving a gasp from his stocky friend. "You're going to get us both killed!"

For the briefest moment, the Hugh William knew so well broke through the dark glaze in his brown-eyed stare. His face fell slack and the colour left his skin before he turned to the ladder and climbed.

Aware of Matilda peering down on them, William watched his friend, waiting for enough space to follow.

The chasing pack came at William like a landslide, but he sheathed his sword. It wouldn't be a fight if he remained on the ground. His body tensed. His lungs tightened. His pulse worked overtime.

Hugh finally climbed high enough for William to follow. His progress only as fast as his friend above, it took all he had to refrain from screaming at the boy.

William had climbed about six feet when the lead runner appeared, its arms windmilling as it slapped the heel of his left boot. It tore his feet from the rung, the lower half of his body swinging away from the building. But he'd learned from Hugh and held on, finding his footing again after several scrambling attempts.

Although others tried to grab him, William climbed out of their reach.

At the top of the ladder, William fell onto the roof, gasping as he rolled over onto his back and looked up at both Matilda and Hugh, who stood over him with the same furrowed expression.

"What was that about?" Matilda said.

Using everything he had to drag more air into his lungs, William only had the breath for, "Huh?"

"*That!*" Her finger pointed at where he'd just climbed up. "Letting me up the ladder first! You should know me better than to play that ladies-first bullshit. If we're going to survive this, you need to recognise me as a soldier. I'd kick your arse ten times over. You'd do well to remember that!"

Still too breathless to speak, William then faced Hugh's wrath. "And jumping down after me. I had it covered."

At least he could shake his head in response to his short and stocky friend.

Matilda's face had turned puce and she balled her fists. "That was suicide jumping off after Hugh."

William finally found the breath to reply. "Firstly, Matilda, it was nothing to do with ladies first. I let you up before me because you're the fastest climber and we needed the ladder clear." A pause to level himself out. "I knew you'd get up it the quickest."

Although her face contorted, Matilda held onto her response.

"And, Hugh, had I not jumped down, you'd be one of them by now. You're one of the best fighters I know, but you're not *that* good. And why the hell did you try to fight the larger pack?" But Hugh's eyes had glazed before William had even finished. Matilda's raised eyebrows weren't lost on him, and although he continued to focus on Hugh, the words were for her. "We're in this together. I'd go after you again, Hugh."

The run had aggravated the pain in William's right foot, and he shook as he stood up. Hugh remained locked in his trance while Matilda had more to say. But as she spoke, he lost track of her words and pointed in the direction of Edin. "Um, you two."

Matilda saw it first. "Shit! Those gates outside, waiting to be fitted on the latest extension of the wall …"

"Must have been taken from in here," William said, a large space where the gates between the national service area and the rest of Edin should be.

Hugh's thick shoulders slumped. "Could there have been a worse time for me to let the diseased in?"

From their current position, they saw most of Edin. Where the districts had been characterised by difference over the years —the coloured fabrics of textiles, the factories of woodwork, the vibrancy of ceramics, the fields of agriculture—they all now had one major thing in common: chaos. In every street of every district ran scores of diseased. The virus had brought their home to its knees.

CHAPTER 16

Two hours earlier

THE GUARD CONTINUED TO COMFORT OLGA, HIS THICK ARM around her while he led her from the labs. At first, she'd been so preoccupied with being caught and the fact that she'd killed at least one person in woodwork, she hadn't looked at the district. Now settled by the guard, she took the place in. It had more open space than anywhere else she'd seen in Edin. But not like agriculture, which had the open space of fields because they were being used for the greater good. Instead, the labs were set in a vast expanse of wasteland. Kids were being massacred on national service for extra room, and the labs had acres to spare.

Not only did the labs have more open land than Olga had ever seen, but the buildings were different too. Much like the structures in the national service area, the labs were constructed from wood. But the huts here were placed end to end in one sprawling complex. Compared to the squalor everyone else lived in, it looked positively luxurious.

As they approached the labs' exit, Olga said, "You mentioned the woodwork district revolting and wood quotas. What did you mean?"

"Didn't you ever wonder why woodwork was so locked down as a district?"

"I had theories, one of them being how close it was to the labs."

"The place is run by gangs," the guard said. "As you've just found out. They decide how to run the district, and Edin lets them as long as they meet their production quotas."

"Why?"

"They threaten to revolt if they're not left alone. It's the only district organised enough to be able to overthrow the government, so they have an agreement."

"But?" Olga said. "How—?"

"How have you not heard about it before?"

"Yeah."

"They keep to themselves. The gangs have a tight enough control to keep their citizens silent. The punishment for anyone who talks is severe. It's also why they don't give their children the same freedoms as everyone else."

"But they send them on national service?"

"Another requirement from the powers that be. No one gets out of national service."

"So you're from woodwork?"

"No."

"But ... your daughter?"

"They took her from tailoring. There was nothing we could do. No one wants to get involved. The life of one girl isn't worth inciting a revolution." He spoke through gritted teeth. "Unless it was the child of a politician—I'm sure they'd go to war for that. But as you know, all life isn't equal in Edin, and the outspoken get evicted. The only power I had was to get work in the labs ..."

Olga left the silence hanging to allow him to explain.

"The labs are even more locked down than woodwork. They always have diseased in here, so they need guards to keep out any unauthorised people. They give us the power to kill if we think the threat warrants it."

"So it allows you to deliver justice to the gangs from woodwork? It gives you the power to decide they're a big enough threat?"

A frame of pure muscle, even the guard's jaw had lumps when he tensed it. "Yep, and I always do."

The pair walked out onto the main street, the guards at the entrance to the labs watching Olga but letting them through. She cast one last glance back at the sprawling layout of the buildings. Where were they keeping Max? Whatever happened, she'd get him out of there.

The guard said, "Where are you from?"

"Laundry."

He led them back towards her home and shook his head. "Tough break."

"Is it?"

"I mean, none of the jobs in this city are dream jobs, but I can't imagine washing clothes all day is much fun."

Olga shrugged.

"So what brings you over here? Whenever we catch adults moving through the city, they always have a story."

"I've just come back from national service."

"It gets easier."

"Huh?"

"Reintegration into society. After years of having freedom

as a kid, then seeing half the people you care for torn apart by those things—"

As if on cue, the shrieks of several diseased pierced the morning air, and Olga said, "They sound louder today."

"They always do after national service. You'll get used to them again. Soon they'll be nothing but background noise. Anyway, as I was saying, reintegration's hard. The life in front of you is going to be dull and monotonous from here on out. And not just your life, the life most of us have to live. We'll work the same job until we retire, and the likelihood is we'll be as good as dead by then anyway. Living in this place is like serving a prison sentence on death row. The end will come as a relief."

"Should you be saying all this to me?"

"Everyone else lies to you, kid. I don't want to be a part of that. You're smart, and I'm sure I'm not telling you anything you don't know. Other than maybe how they run woodwork."

The farther they walked back into Edin, the busier the main street became, the people watching her and the guard as they passed. The press of her blood-damp clothes heightened Olga's paranoia. But if those who passed them had thoughts, they kept them to themselves, their faces impassive. They did what Edin's citizens always did in the main street: they moved with the purpose of whatever job they'd been sent to do, lest they get their privilege of being let out taken away. And if they were kids enjoying the freedom of youth, they were too caught up in their peers to notice a blood-soaked girl and a guard.

Woodwork now on their left, the wooden hatches of Edin's underground storage on either side of the street, the guard said, "You never said what you were doing."

"In woodwork?"

"Yeah."

"Heading for the labs. I wanted to find someone I was on

national service with. He saved my life and got bitten in the process. But he didn't turn."

The whites of the guard's eyes stood out against his dark skin. "So what have they done with him?"

"They've locked him away. He's their latest science experiment."

"And you want to *free* him?"

"Yeah." As the word left Olga's mouth, a chill crawled up her back. She'd said too much.

"Don't you worry that he's carrying the disease?"

"Maybe. I was going to take both of us out of the city and away from here. So even if he is a danger to Edin, it won't be a problem."

Olga's stomach sank when the guard shook his head. The air damn near crackled between them as the atmosphere changed, a deep scowl hooding his eyes. "I can't have that."

"What do you mean?"

The guard wrapped his hand around Olga's left bicep. A grip of iron, she had no chance of escape. "I can't have one of our citizens thinking it's okay to release an infected person into society."

Half-hearted, but she had to try, Olga tugged against the guard. She'd only get free when he decided. "What are you doing? I thought you understood."

"I didn't want you getting in danger in woodwork, but I don't understand why you'd want to risk the lives of an entire city."

Another shrill diseased's scream, closer this time.

"It's still my job to protect Edin and the people in it."

Olga slammed her right heel on the guard's left foot. She could have sworn she felt something crack. The brute screamed and dropped to the ground.

A moment to react, Olga snatched his baton before sprinting

back towards the labs, the peep of the guard's whistle calling after her. She had nothing to lose now. Once she got Max, they could both get out of there.

Another whistle joined the first as other guards responded. She could outrun them. She could run faster than most—especially guards dressed in their full uniform—but not on the main street. She had to lose them in a district.

Then Olga's escape plan abandoned her and she slowed down. The whistles behind drew closer. But she didn't turn to look. She couldn't. Instead, she watched what came towards her. A wall of them as wide as the open street. Screaming, hissing, snarling … They bit at the air, their limbs flailing. There had to be hundreds of them.

Olga turned from the stampeding diseased and ran back the way she'd come. Shrieks and cries on her tail, she passed several stunned guards. One or two of them still had whistles in their mouths. Whatever else had happened up until that moment, it all became irrelevant. Judging by the size of the mob swarming through the streets, Edin now belonged to the diseased.

CHAPTER 17

A city William didn't recognise stretched away from him as he swayed in the strong winds because of his elevated position on the gym's roof. The life he'd known had gone. A gap of no more than two feet had ushered in the destruction of an entire city. Edin had always had the order of an ant colony, everyone serving their monotonous purpose for the greater good. But now, with chaos tearing through the streets, it bore little resemblance to his home.

Matilda's dark eyes narrowed. "Artan's in a cell."

William didn't reply.

"That *has* to be one of the safest places in the city right now. If they're strong enough to keep the prisoners contained, they must be strong enough to prevent the diseased from getting in."

The words sank through William and he swayed where he stood. "You think we can get through Edin?"

Matilda shrugged. "That's not the question."

"Then what is?"

"Is Artan still alive?"

"What if someone's already let him out?"

"What if they haven't? And why would they? If you had to

run for your life, would you waste time freeing someone you believed to be a murderer? Someone due for eviction anyway. Also, don't you want to see if your mum and dad are okay?"

"Of course, but …" The wind blew too hard for William to shout over.

All the while, Hugh stared down at where the gates between Edin and the national service area had once been. His eyes were glazed and he stood perfectly still, impervious to the wind's effect. Were his cheeks not damp with his tears, William wouldn't have known he was crying. Whatever anyone else said to the boy to reassure him, this was his fault. Not that William blamed him, but there seemed little point in trying to convince him otherwise.

Matilda pulled William's attention back to her. "I'm going whether you come or not. I have to assume he's alive, and there's no way I'm going to let him rot in a cell."

Even as they spoke, the diseased spread out, finding every corner of the city. Several districts close to them were already alive with fury, and those farther back, like tailoring, had already fallen and were growing more populated by the second. William chose not to look at his home district. There seemed little point. What could he do about it from his current position? "Okay, I'll go with you. But I'd like to pass through agriculture on the way."

"Of course," Matilda said.

Before either of them could ask Hugh, the short and squat boy said, "I'm with you both, wherever that leads us. We're in this together, right? But if we're going in, I also need to go through tailoring."

Hopefully Hugh hadn't noticed Matilda's reaction. Although her features fell at the prospect of him joining them, she righted them a second later.

William spoke before she could. "We'll find James, just like we'll find my mum and dad and Artan." And it would do them good to have Hugh with them. The boy could take on armies of diseased by himself.

Hard not to focus on the creatures tearing through it, William followed the line of the main street all the way to the back wall. On foggy days, the city stretched so far into the distance he couldn't always see the other side. The clear morning gave him a view straight to the wooden scaffolding. "We need to plan to go out the back."

"Through the eviction gate?" Matilda said.

"Yeah. There seems little point in travelling all the way through the city to then turn around and do it again on the way back. Besides, the eviction gate died with Edin's collapse. It's just a gate now."

A wet sniff, Hugh turned to them again. "There's just two more things we need to think about before we go."

Both William and Matilda waited.

"First"—Hugh pointed at Trent's crew on the roof of the dorm—"what do we do about them?"

Although Matilda turned around, William didn't.

"If we go through the eviction gate," Hugh said, "how will we help them?"

Matilda said, "We have our own path to tread. I hate to say this, but getting to our loved ones *has* to be our priority. It's certainly mine."

The kid in Trent's crew had saved their lives no more than ten minutes earlier. They owed him, but what else could they do? William finally looked their way and then out into the wasteland and ruined city beyond. "And even if we do get them off the roof, where will we take them? Everywhere's a mess."

"Okay." Hugh nodded.

"And the second point?" Matilda said.

Hugh peered over the edge of the gym, the mob below screeching at the sight of the boy. They were surrounded on all sides, the ladder their only possible escape. "How do we get down?"

CHAPTER 18

Two hours earlier

THE GUARDS HAD FOCUSED ON OLGA AND WHAT SHE'D DONE TO one of their own, but now, as she tore back through them, several of them still biting down on their whistles, they had much greater things to worry about than her. More diseased on her tail than she'd ever seen in her life, she tore through the uniformed enforcers and Edin's citizens alike, running with everything she had.

The charging creatures at her back released a call that sounded like hell had been torn open. But it was the very human cries and screams of Edin's citizens falling to the swarm that took almost all the strength from her legs. As much as Olga hated many things about the city she'd grown up in, she didn't want to see it collapse. Not like this. So many innocent lives wiped out because … because of what? How did they get in?

Even with her broken arm, Olga had maintained her training. The second she could, she'd started running again, and a good job too; many of Edin's citizens would fall because they weren't fit enough. Although she'd left her mum and dad behind when she'd gone to find Max, she had to get back to them now and make sure they were okay. The route to laundry clear of diseased, if she kept this pace, she'd reach them ahead of the creatures.

A small lead on the swarm, Olga looked back. The diseased filled the street, the mob so dense they could block somewhere twice the width. Shoulder to shoulder, they flooded forwards. While some of the front-running diseased disappeared into ceramics on one side of the road, others ran into woodwork. Hopefully the gang she'd encountered would get hit first. But even with the numbers vanishing to each side, the pack didn't thin.

As Olga turned back around, a guard slammed into her, his shoulder sinking into her stomach and driving the air from her lungs. She landed on her back, the guard on top of her.

It was the guard whose foot she'd stamped on. Olga shoved him, but he wouldn't budge. "What are you doing?"

"If I'm going down, so are you." The guard sprayed spittle in her face. "You've broken my foot, you spiteful bitch!"

He was easily three times heavier than her; Olga wriggled and squirmed, but she couldn't get free.

The guard leaned so close, the whites of his eyes dazzled Olga. "And to think I saved you from woodwork."

"*Saved me?* You wanted to arrest me."

The guard raised a balled fist, and from the tight clench of his jaw, he clearly intended to punch her unconscious. But when he moved to ready his blow, he shifted his weight, giving her the chance to bring her knee up between his legs.

Olga's kneecap sank into his crotch, driving the guard's mouth wide in a gasp. As he leaned to the side, she used his momentum to throw him off, jump to her feet, and crack him across the face with his own baton. He moved as if to get up, so she cracked him again, knocking him out with the second blow and sending a spray of blood from his mouth.

The diseased no more than twenty feet away, Olga turned to run but stopped instantly. Ahead of her, a swarm of the creatures flooded from tailoring. As the neighbour of woodwork, they must have moved through the gaps in the walls. They'd cut off her route to laundry. "Shit!"

CHAPTER 19

The kids on the roof of Phoenix's old dorm had clearly seen William and the others, all eight of them facing their way. The lanky figure of Trent stood at least a foot taller than those around him. Obviously still pissed from when William sucker-punched him, he watched them with a hard scowl crushing his features. The kid who'd let them through without raising an alarm fixed William with a silent plea, a reminder of what he'd done for them.

But it would be hard enough going forwards without returning to save a group of rookies. They needed to find their own way. Every person for themselves. And when it came to a straight choice, it might have been harsh, but loved ones were more important than strangers.

Matilda and Hugh peered over the side of the gym at the diseased. Maybe they didn't feel the guilt, or maybe they simply chose not to engage with it. William joined them. "There must be one hundred of them down there."

"At least," Matilda said.

Hugh shook his head. "Too many to fight." He sounded disappointed.

Most of the diseased looked up and worked their jaws, showing their bloodstained teeth in their dark mouths.

William shuddered to be on the receiving end of such an intensified hatred, so he broke eye contact with the creatures and looked out over the fallen city. Their experience on national service had nothing on the chaos now running through the streets of their former home.

The squeak of cartwheels and clop of hooves below, a large piebald horse walked around the corner of the gym, dragging a carriage behind it. It moved at a slow pace, cutting a path through the diseased. Despite their close proximity to one another, the diseased and the horse existed as strangers. The diseased focused on anything human; the horse wandered aimlessly, suddenly deprived of the job it had done for years. Another one of Edin's displaced residents.

William pointed down at the creature. "Surely that's our way out of here."

"It looks like it'll pass through the diseased without any problems," Hugh said.

Matilda nodded. "And the carriage's roof will keep us high enough from the ground. But there's one thing I don't understand. When we were in training, a diseased attacked a sheep. Why are they ignoring the horse?"

"There are several animals they attack, and many they don't." Hugh said. "Regardless of all the testing we did in the labs, we never understood why they went for sheep and not horses. They also attack pigs for some reason, but not deer. So if we can get to the horse and carriage, we're safe, but how do we get to it?" Hugh said.

With the horse and carriage a good eight feet from the gym's walls, he had a point. They were too high up to jump from the roof, and it hadn't yet walked close enough to the ladder. Yet. "I think it'll come closer," William said.

"Through that lot?" Matilda pointed down. The closer the diseased were to the gym, the denser the crowd.

There seemed little point in discussing what could and couldn't happen until they tried something. William moved across to the ladder and climbed down it backwards.

About two feet from the reach of the tallest diseased, the heady and palpable reek of rot in the air, William held onto a rung with one hand and reached towards the horse with the other. While clicking his fingers, he made a kissing sound through his teeth.

The horse had one brown and one white ear. They swished in response to the sound.

William tried again, and the deep brown eyes of the languid creature turned his way. So intent on alerting the horse, he didn't care about the reaching arms from the sea of creatures below. He shut out their cries and shouts, kissing through his teeth again.

"That's it," William said when the horse took steps towards him. Despite the press of bodies, the creatures yielded to the horse's unstoppable progress.

While still clicking his fingers, he continued to kiss through his teeth. "Come on, boy."

"How do you know it's a boy?" Matilda said.

Although he remained fixed on the horse, William shouted up, "Do you really need to ask me that?"

Where there had been a gap of ten feet or more between William and the horse, his efforts coaxed the creature closer. Eight feet. Six feet. But then it stopped. Were it any nearer, he'd be able to step onto the roof of the carriage.

"Come on, boy. Here, here, come to William. Come on."

But the density of the crowd prevented it getting closer.

Matilda showed how well she knew William when she

called down, "The gap's too far to jump. Don't even think about it."

When he didn't respond, she added, "Remember the time when you tried to jump from a wall onto the roof of the factory in textiles?"

"That was *once*. In *all* the times we climbed up there, I missed once."

"You think you have a second chance if you screw up *this* jump?"

As William climbed a few rungs higher, his attention on his friends above, Matilda let it go. She meant well; he understood that. But the amount of times she'd reminded him of his fall when he'd tried to get on the roof of the factory in textiles ... Once! He'd only failed the jump once, yet she brought it up again and again as if it got funnier in the retelling.

Still several feet from the gym's roof, William turned back to the horse. It had watched him climb, remaining about six feet from the building.

"William! Don't!"

William jumped, kicking away from the wall to propel himself through the air towards the carriage. He flew over the heads of the diseased. Wide red eyes watched him, and he nearly watched them back, but he remained fixed on his intended target.

Falling slightly short, William hooked his hands over the far side of the carriage, his knees cracking against the near side. The sharp sting sent a hot wave of nausea through him. Despite his now sweating palms, he held on. A hard enough task on its own, the hands of several diseased then grabbed onto his hanging feet.

William kicked his legs, but the landing had robbed him of his strength to pull himself up onto the roof.

The wooden cart shook and wobbled as more diseased

crashed against it in their desperation to get to him. The horse whinnied, the carriage moving back and forth with its steps.

His grip still sure, his arms still too weak to pull him up, William held on as the creature bolted, tearing off across the national service area, dragging him away from the diseased.

Dragging him away from Hugh and Matilda.

CHAPTER 20

Two hours earlier

THE RESIDENTIAL PART OF AGRICULTURE BUTTED UP AGAINST the main street. The fields stretched out to Edin's external wall. With one side of the city falling quicker than the other because of the gaps between woodwork and its neighbouring districts, Olga had no choice but to dart right.

The diseased spilling from tailoring into the main street, Olga moved at a flat-out sprint when she jumped and kicked off the back wall of one of the many one-storey houses, catching the roof and pulling herself up as several crazed creatures slammed into the building a second too late.

Looking at the uneven spread of roofs stretching out ahead of her, she pressed her ribs. Tender from her collision with the guard, but probably not broken. The diseased hadn't yet entered agriculture. Maybe she could give the people a heads-up on her way to laundry. No more than a few feet ahead of the creatures, she stuffed the guard's baton into her belt and took off, her feet twisting and turning with the roofs' angles.

Olga jumped from house to house, clearing several narrow alleys as she aimed for agriculture's main street. Filled with people who appeared to be going to work, but many of them had stopped and looked at the sky as if it had answers as to why they heard so many diseased. "Get inside your houses now. Edin's fallen; the streets belong to the diseased!"

Maybe they didn't hear what she said, because despite her warnings, the citizens stared at her like she'd lost her mind. Not a single one of them moved.

"Go now, you fools. Hide before it's too—"

The shriek of the diseased cut her off. They'd entered the district. The ones at the front took down citizens in their path, but it didn't slow their forward momentum, those behind driving the pack on at the same frantic pace.

Still ahead of the beasts, Olga shouted with everything she had. "Edin's fallen. Get to safety before it's too late."

The same blank looks regarded her, now dividing their time between the crazy girl on the roofs and the chaos charging through the streets towards them. Yet the stupid bastards still did nothing. Olga said it more to herself than agriculture's fallen residents. Too late for them now. "What the hell do you hope to achieve staying down there?"

That part of agriculture now lost, Olga shook her head and continued towards laundry.

When she reached a busy but narrower street, a guard pointed up at her and blew her whistle. "You, girl, get down from there."

"Edin's fallen. Save yourself before it's too late."

If only the guard had drawn the baton to fight the diseased rather than as a threat to her.

Olga could do nothing more than watch as her angry glare

fell slack when she turned to face the onrushing madness. Seconds mattered, but none of them got it. Like the other people she'd tried to warn, she watched the disease roll right over the guard.

No way could she beat the diseased to laundry or help the people of agriculture. Why waste the energy? Soon she'd be a minority in the city, if not already. She needed to save her strength. Olga made her way back across the rooftops to the soundtrack of screams and cries that were now Edin's requiem. She jumped several small alleyways—all of them jam-packed with insanity—until she reached the city's main road. As packed with diseased as the rest of the place, she stared over the heads of the beasts in the direction of the laundry district. Her mum and dad had probably already fallen, but she had to check. Although, with at least twenty feet of road packed with the foul creatures, checking might not be so easy.

CHAPTER 21

So focused on holding on, it took William a few seconds to stop kicking his legs, the diseased now far behind him as the horse continued to gallop away from the hut.

The beat of the horse's hooves and the shaking of the rickety carriage sent William's body into a pendulous swing. It seemed as if every bump in the ground shot through the wooden vehicle, stinging his hands and challenging his grip. But at least they'd broken away from the diseased.

The gap between William and the diseased had opened wide enough for him to let go. He could get on the roof of a nearby dorm. But what good would that do? That would only leave him in the same shitty situation as Trent and his friends. And what if he fell when he landed? The rumble of the carriage's large wooden wheels spoke volumes for what they'd do to his brittle body.

The window frame in the carriage's door protruded by about an inch. The tendons in his fingers ready to snap, William clamped his teeth, grunted, and lifted his right foot onto the ledge.

One foot in place, he braced his swinging body, halting it

enough to get the second foot on the small lip. His fingers were still about to fail him, but it bought him a few more seconds.

The horse appeared to be running without direction, clearly spooked by the riled diseased. But they were now far enough away for the large stallion to slow to a canter.

William boosted off the window ledge and scrambled onto the roof, falling onto his back while opening and closing his hands. As his pain subsided, so did the ferocious cries of the charging diseased. From where he lay, he couldn't see them, so they obviously couldn't see him. They might have still been following, much like when they'd remained outside the dorm, but like outside the dorm, they sounded like they'd forgotten their reason for being there.

A moment to catch his breath, William massaged his knuckles. By the time the mob caught up to the now stationary horse and carriage, he'd relieved the fiery pain. From the shrieks and tormented cries, the diseased were clearly as disturbed as ever, but their calls lacked the focus of the hunt. All the while he'd assumed they were blind; how could they see through bleeding eyes? But there had been times when their behaviour challenged that assumption. Like how could they fix on their prey when they were surrounded by hundreds of baying spectators in the middle of a packed arena? They were probably very far from twenty-twenty, but they clearly saw something.

From where he lay, William saw Matilda and Hugh on the gym's roof, both of them at the edge, staring down at him. Trent and his friends had adopted a similar pose on the roof of Phoenix's dorm. Careful to remain out of the creatures' line of sight, he raised a thumb in Matilda's direction. She returned the gesture with a smile.

As long as he remained hidden, William had time. He took a minute to recover in the morning sun. The moans and groans of dissatisfaction continued around the carriage, but the creatures soon ran off, back towards the gym or to gather at the foot of Phoenix's dorm.

The horse's reins were attached to the driver's seat. If William sat on the bench, he'd be in plain sight. The horse might have been impervious to the disease, but their frenzied state had rattled it. If they were to get anywhere, he'd have to remain hidden, for the horse's sake if not his own.

Maybe the diseased would hear him, but he had to try something. William spoke to the horse. "Hey there, boy." The creature's large ears twitched. One brown, one white like the colouring on its body. "I need your help to get through this city. Can you do that for me?"

The sound of the few remaining diseased around them grew louder, but they didn't flip into the rage of the hunt. They might have heard something, but they couldn't locate him.

While rolling over onto his front, William reached out for the reins, stretching across the gap. A gentle tug, he kept his tone soft. "There, there, boy. We're going to go on a little walk. There's nothing to worry about. We just need to pick up a couple of friends, and then we can take a slow plod into the city." A tug on the left rein turned the horse left.

A big stallion of pure muscle, the horse followed William's lead, twitches and spasms firing across its velvety skin. This relationship went both ways. It could bolt whenever it liked. Show it respect, and hopefully it would do the same in return.

They moved at a slow plod, leaving many of the diseased behind as they walked back towards the gym. They took the most direct route, even though it meant passing Trent and his crew. As they got close, William and the boy from agriculture glared at one another. A tug on the left rein, William coaxed the horse to give the hut a slightly wider berth.

When they were close enough to Phoenix's dorm, Trent leaned towards them, the diseased around the foot of the hut responding with hammering blows against the wooden walls. The boy hissed one word. "Coward!"

William got it, he really did, and were the roles reversed, maybe he'd be as pissed, but Trent had already played his cards when he sent the diseased after them. The kid next to Trent, however—the one who stood about five and a half feet, the one with the kind face who'd not raised the alarm when William, Matilda, and Hugh were exposed—William had made a promise to him. As they passed one another, he repeated the promise, pointing at him and mouthing, *I'll be back for you.*

Although, silent words were easy; the hard thing would be fulfilling his pledge.

CHAPTER 22

Two hours earlier

OLGA MIGHT HAVE BEEN SAFE ON THE ROOFS IN AGRICULTURE, and now she'd moved to the edge of the district, she stood just twenty feet from laundry, but the relatively short distance might as well have been miles with the sea of diseased between her and her destination. Laundry had clearly fallen like everywhere else. Maybe she should give up on her mum and dad. Her parents weren't exactly survivors. They'd be the first to lie down and die; in fact, they'd welcome it with open arms. Still, she had to know their fate before she moved on.

Every diseased face in the street turned her way, but Olga kept her eyes on laundry. A view across the rooftops of the city showed her several other survivors. Several from ten thousand. Maybe, like her, they were on the search for loved ones. Even if she did get into laundry, how the hell would she get out again? "One step at a time," she muttered. But even that first step seemed an impossibility.

She then heard the slamming of fists beating against a door. Muffled voices cried for help, louder than the shrieks of the diseased. Olga stepped closer to the edge of the roof, the crimson eyes widening as if she'd give herself over to them. It took for several diseased to move before they uncovered the hatch in the ground. Two large wooden doors, they granted access to the storage tunnels. Agriculture had more hatches than most districts because they needed somewhere to keep the harvested food. Now at the end of winter, they'd be emptier than ever. Although, from the bangs and screams, they clearly weren't completely empty.

Even the diseased moved their focus from Olga to the hatch. The doors lifted again. An inch or two, no more, before slamming shut from the weight of the creatures standing on them. They must have been down there when the city turned. If they knew what waited for them, they'd remain where they were.

The hatch opened again, only a small way but enough to release a man's voice. "Help us! We're trapped. Please, someone help."

If Olga replied, she'd pull the attention of the diseased back on her. And if her run through agriculture had taught her anything, it was that people were hard to help in a crisis.

Although Olga hadn't been in the storage basements and interlinking tunnels, she'd heard about them. A fascination for many of Edin's residents, especially the kids. Large spaces off the main streets where they stored goods—mostly food for rationing during the winter—a maze of tunnels linked them all together as a distribution network. Some said they stretched under the entire city. Hundreds of caves, where access to one would lead to the others. She never knew what to believe though because she didn't know anyone who'd actually been down there.

The doors slammed again from the weight of the diseased.

Although this time, the creatures seemed to get it. Olga shook her head as they moved away, clearing the hatch. Before she could warn the people, the hatch flew open, the heavy wooden doors swinging wide and slamming against the road with a thunderclap. Five men dressed in tailored suits. Fat bureaucrats, they must have been planning how to manage the rations while they no doubt took more for themselves. Olga suddenly felt less guilty about not being able to warn them.

Five relieved faces fell slack as the first of the diseased crashed into them, driving them back into the darkness. Half an eye on the wretched creatures as they flooded into the pit like they'd flooded through the rest of Edin, Olga pulled the guard's baton from the back of her trousers and gripped it as she moved to the very edge of the roof.

Where before the creatures had watched Olga, they now fought to get into the pit. Those not descending were waiting to descend. For the time being, she'd become invisible.

Still far more than she could fight, but gaps were opening up in the mob. They continued to spill into the underground storage, alive with the excitement of the hunt.

Olga sidestepped along the roofs until she'd put a gap of about thirty feet between her and the open pit. The rumours of the space down there must have been true: the dark mouth swallowed the diseased with no sign of slowing.

A gap opened up on the main road. A direct route between Olga and laundry. Despite resistance locking her muscles, if she waited too long, it would close again. Another opportunity might come, but it might not.

Too long to think about it and she wouldn't go, Olga jumped down from the roof, the shock of landing on the hard ground snapping through her. Most of the diseased remained focused on the basement, but those closest turned their attention to her.

A diseased just a few feet away opened its mouth to scream. Olga slammed it shut again, driving her baton into it with a swift uppercut. The diseased fell back as she took off towards the other side of the road.

She couldn't fight them all, so Olga picked carefully, waiting for a diseased to get close enough before she swung for it, her baton cracking bones and driving back the imminent threats.

Most of the diseased twigged only after she'd passed them. Just a few feet between her and the buildings in laundry, Olga jumped like she had in agriculture and kicked off against the wall, grabbing the roof of the building. As she pulled herself up, a diseased hand clamped around her right ankle and yanked hard.

CHAPTER 23

William led the horse and carriage towards the gym. When they got to within about fifty feet, Matilda pointed at the ladder leading down the side of the building as if to ask if she should descend it. He replied with a raised thumb. It would rile the diseased, but what other option did they have?

Like when William had lain on the carriage's roof, Matilda and Hugh were invisible on the gym. The diseased had calmed almost as soon as they'd disappeared from sight. The second Matilda hung a foot down for the ladder, the creatures grew more animated and screamed louder. The pack had halved from where many of them had followed the carriage, but the sight of Matilda brought them all back and then some. They swarmed the base of the ladder, their arms outstretched as if reaching for her would somehow make her fall.

The horse then stopped, still at least forty feet from the gym.

"Come on, boy," William said.

Another twitch of its ears and nothing more. Apparently, they'd gone quite close enough.

William kissed through his teeth and flicked the leather

reins. "Come on, boy, keep going. We need to rescue Matilda and Hugh."

The same circular twitch of its brown and white ears, but the creature remained rooted to the spot.

"Come on, you don't need to be scared of those nasty things. They can't do *you* any harm, as you've already seen. There's a good boy. Come on." This time, William flicked the reins slightly harder, a gentle slap where the leather hit the creature's velvety hide.

The horse stepped back several paces. Maybe the stress of the situation made him imagine it, but William could have sworn the animal shook its head at him.

"Okay, I get it," William said before raising a halting hand at Matilda. He'd be there soon. She needed to trust him. While she waited on the ladder, inviting the wrath of the creatures below, Hugh paced on top of the gym's roof. The short and squat frame of his friend wound tight, his steps quick. He scanned the national service area as if he had plans of his own. Whatever they were, he couldn't be allowed to execute them. One of the deadliest fighters he knew, Hugh's once sound mind could no longer be relied upon for decision making.

When William moved from lying on his front to sitting up, Matilda's mouth fell wide. About twenty diseased remained around the carriage, but they hadn't yet noticed him. It wouldn't be long before they did.

William moved slowly so he could get into a good position before the insanity started. He shifted over the roof of the carriage and climbed onto the driver's seat.

His pulse quick, the diseased still shambling around the carriage, William nodded at Matilda before reaching forward and patting the horse's hide. "You ready, boy?" In a voice loud enough to attract the diseased, he then said, "Let's do this."

The diseased's shriek lit the horse's fuse and it charged towards the gym.

With only the reins to hang on to, William pushed against the footrest, planting the soles of his boots as he hopped and bounced on the hard wooden seat. The large wheels drowned out the sound of the chasing diseased, but did little to soften the journey.

With no control over the horse's speed, William gritted his teeth and tugged on the left rein. The horse moved where he guided it. A gentle tug on the right and he got a similar response. As long as he didn't get thrown from the carriage, he'd be fine. "I'm coming for you, Tilly. Just be ready, okay?"

If she acknowledged him, William couldn't tell. Too focused on not getting thrown to the ground, hopefully she'd heard him at the very least. About twenty feet from the gym, his vision blurred with the vibrations. He guided the horse around the left side of the building. Many of the diseased waiting around the base of the ladder watched him. Some of them gave chase.

As they passed around the gym, the thunder of the carriage echoed off the wall on their right. The vibrations ran up William's back, sending a sharp ache into the base of his skull. He tugged on the right rein, keeping the horse close to the building. The diseased stood no chance of catching them, but they were trying.

Around the next bend they came to the pack of diseased by the ladder. Already less than before but still four or five bodies deep. Too many to get close to his love. It hurt William's throat to shout over the insanity. "Wait there. I'll come back around."

Again, William had no way of knowing if she'd heard him or not, everything moving so quickly as he tugged on the right rein to take the horse and carriage on another lap around the gym.

When William passed Matilda for a second time, the crowd of diseased were only two deep. "Get ready to jump on the next pass."

Although, on the third lap, more diseased had gathered than before, forcing the horse wider than William would have liked. Thankfully, Matilda read the situation and remained on the ladder. She shouted, "It's not working."

Unsure what to expect when he rounded the corner again, William came back for a fourth time. The crowd had halved in number. While grinding his jaw as he tugged on the rein, William pressed against the footrest with his right boot and guided them close enough for Matilda to jump.

As his love flew through the air, William let go of the reins and reached out to her. Not that he needed to; Matilda landed as if she'd done it a thousand times before, and because he'd let go of the reins, the horse charged away from the gym, straight at team Phoenix's hut.

The touch of his love against his back, William bounced on his seat as he fought to retrieve the reins. The leather straps danced around like snakes on a drum.

When he finally caught them, William pulled back, a little too hard at first, the horse fighting him. He let up some of the pressure and the horse slowed. They'd opened a gap between them and the diseased. "Well done, boy." The horse's hide hot and clammy, the creature shivered at William's touch. "Well done. And thank you."

The same swishing of its ears, the horse's wide ribs swelled and deflated with its wild breaths. His hand still on its rump, William whispered, "I know that was hard, but I need you to do it again."

William winced as he pulled on the right rein, but the horse did as he asked, following his lead until they faced the gym again. "Good boy."

If Hugh saw what they were doing, he showed no sign of it. Instead, he looked over the side at the diseased below him. When he finally looked up, William pointed down to instruct him to descend the ladder.

"You think he'll be okay?" Matilda said.

"He just watched you. Hopefully he'll copy that."

"Hopefully."

"Only one way to find out."

The diseased who'd chased them from the gym were nearly on them. William patted the horse again and focused on keeping his pulse even as he gently flicked the reins. The animal quickened its pace and moved on.

As they rounded the gym for the first time, a similar mob behind them like when they'd rescued Matilda, William's stomach lurched. The glaze in Hugh's eyes told him everything he needed to know. No matter what he said—

Hugh leaped at the horse, a wall of diseased at least three deep beneath him. He hadn't even aimed for the carriage. He flew through the air, his arms outstretched so he could hook himself around the creature's neck.

The horse whinnied, reared, and kicked its front legs as Hugh slapped against it and held on like he wanted to wrestle it to the ground. The entire carriage tilted to the left. William caught the right side of the bench and held on. Matilda slid from the roof and vanished over the side.

CHAPTER 24

Two hours earlier

The diseased tugged on Olga's right foot, and several pops ran up her spine from the hard pull. Painless, but the sensation turned her weak and she nearly lost her grip. Before the creature tugged again, she kicked out, catching the beast in the face. It stumbled back, the opening she needed to pull herself onto the roof before it slammed into the wall as it lunged at her for a second time.

A moment to get herself together, the roof shook beneath her as several more diseased crashed into the hut.

Olga stood up and stretched. No niggles at that moment, but hopefully it would prevent her back from seizing later on. The route she'd taken across the road had now vanished, the street once more packed with diseased. The flow into the storage basement had slowed. The five bureaucrats must have fallen. Good riddance. Now she had to go and check on her parents.

Olga had stood on the roof of her house for the past ten minutes. The early morning sun warmed her skin, encouraging her tired frame into a state of dazed inaction. She stared down at the tiles and tried to block out the sounds of the diseased in the streets, with little success. Every once in a while, the splash of one of them falling into a washing station rose above the chorus of discontent. The only way into her house would be through the roof. At present, she stood over what had been her sisters' room.

No matter how long she waited, Olga would have to face it sooner or later. She raised the baton she'd stolen from the guard and slammed it down against the tile by her feet.

Like many things in Edin, the tile did a job—just. The blow she'd driven against it had enough force to shatter the thing. Olga moved on to the next one and cracked it. Then the next, smashing tile after tile until she'd cleared a space about four feet square.

After exposing the wooden ceiling beneath, Olga used the end of the baton to bash through the boards. On the second one, she gasped. Her mum and dad stared up at her through the crimson glaze of the disease. The tears they'd needed to cry before they'd turned now ran as trails of blood down their pallid cheeks. Even now, when taken over with the virus, they'd found their way to her sisters' room. Even now, with nothing other than the need to destroy running through them, they looked like they wouldn't leave even if the chance to infect someone arose. Despite being diseased, they still held their grief. Their snapping jaws—half-hearted in their efforts to get to her—seemed more like a warning than a threat. *Just leave us be. Go away.*

Olga only realised she was crying when she backed away from the hole. The creatures in the room below were as much her parents as they'd ever been. Diseased or not, she'd lost them years ago. At least she could finally mourn their passing.

As Olga looked out across the city she'd once called home, she dragged in a deep breath. Everything had changed and nothing had changed. She still had a debt to pay. She still had to get to Max. It wouldn't be easy and wouldn't be quick, but it wasn't like she had anything else to do. A tightened grip on her baton, she wiped her eyes, faced the direction of the labs, and said, "Just hold on in there; I'm coming for you."

CHAPTER 25

"Matilda?" William turned so hard it sent a sharp rod of electric pain into the base of his skull. He kept a hold of the seat as the carriage's right wheels slammed back down again, bracing against being catapulted over the other side. The carriage shook and wobbled from where the spooked horse galloped, Hugh still clinging onto his neck.

Even with the bumpy ride, William slid from the driver's seat to the roof of the carriage. "Matilda?" He saw her fingers gripping the side of the wooden vehicle, white with tension.

Pulling himself so he could peer over the edge, William saw her using the window ledge to stand on much like he had, her free foot driving back the snapping jaws of the diseased.

Nothing more than the weight of his body for leverage, William let his feet hang over the other side of the carriage, now lying horizontally across the wooden vehicle. He reached down and wrapped a strong grip around the back of Matilda's right wrist.

William held on tightly enough to prevent Matilda from pulling away. A natural reaction to his unexpected touch, she looked up. The briefest of glances, she returned to kicking the diseased with more ferocity than before, each blow landing with a loud *clop!*

"Three ..." It hurt William's throat to be heard over the thundering escape. "Two ..." On *one,* he pulled and she pushed off the window ledge, the diseased so desperate to get to her, many of them got dragged beneath the cart's large wheels.

On the roof of the carriage, both of them breathing heavily, Matilda jabbed a finger in Hugh's direction, her face nearly as crimson as a diseased's stare. "*He* nearly got me killed."

And were it not for the battle still raging between Hugh and the horse, the carriage still shaking and wobbling beneath them, William might have replied. Instead, he left Matilda to recover and shifted back towards the driver's seat.

William pulled on the reins, slowing them a little. "What the hell are you doing, Hugh?" Although, even as the sentence left his mouth, he let it go. With the horse still trying to throw the stocky boy from its neck, neither the animal nor his friend would benefit from his rage.

Like he'd done so many times already, William reached over and patted the horse's hide. The creature's muscles tightened at his touch. "There, there, boy. Calm down. He's just an idiot trying to get to safety."

The diseased had caught up to them again, but the height and strength of the stallion as it flung Hugh around like a rag doll kept the stocky boy from their reaching hands. Although, it would just be a matter of time before one of them caught him.

William stood up and thrust his arms out for balance.

"What are you doing?" Matilda said. "Don't put yourself in danger again. Not for him."

With Artan as her first and foremost worry, she couldn't see much beyond that. And William didn't blame her, but they owed Hugh. They wouldn't be here were it not for him. Besides, he'd calm down with time. They needed to stand by him until then. Were William in danger, Hugh would help him in a heartbeat.

Two wooden poles ran from the carriage to either side of the horse's wide body. They attached the vehicle to the creature's harness. They were lower down than the driver's seat. Were the diseased not so focused on Hugh, William might have thought twice. Just one of the vile creatures could drag him from the poles. But as the stallion shook its head, the flinging Hugh served as the perfect distraction for the foetid mob. The horse now moving at a slow walk, William jumped down, kicked off the left bar, and landed on the animal's back on his knees, tucking his feet beneath him.

For the second time, the horse reared up. The carriage lifted on one side, and Matilda shouted, "*William!*"

The large wheels slammed down with a *crunch* of breaking bodies, the weight of the vehicle making light work of the diseased.

Matilda had managed to hold on, so William reached out and stroked the horse's neck. "Calm down, boy. We'll get this lump off you, but you need to trust me."

Like when he'd talked to the horse from the carriage, the animal's ears twitched in response to his soft words, and the stallion settled.

While Hugh kicked out at the diseased grasping for him, William reached towards his friend. "Take my hand now."

Their grips locked, William dragged Hugh clear of the mob. Both of them on the stallion, the horse lifted its front feet as if it might rear again. William's stomach did a backflip; he had nothing to hold on to. But the horse resisted as if reassured by William's presence.

The clawing hands of the diseased reached after Hugh as William let him past on the horse's wide back.

"Thank you," Hugh said and stepped onto one of the poles

before jumping up to the carriage, his knees whacking the wooden side with a loud *crack!* The horse shifted at the sound, and William thrust his arms out for balance again.

The screams around them grew louder, the horse shaking as if about to explode. If William waited any longer, he'd be a goner. Too many diseased around the poles, he took a two-step run across the horse's back and leaped for the carriage.

William landed on the footrest of the driver's seat and spun around, sitting down on the bench, trembling from the adrenaline flooding into his system. A gentle flick of the reins sent the horse away.

When they'd broken into a canter, Hugh laughed. "That was a ride!"

Matilda responded through clenched teeth. "Just lie down, Hugh, before I knock you out and shove you off this carriage."

CHAPTER 26

Matilda on his left, Hugh on his right, William now lay on his front on the carriage's roof. He reached out to hold the stallion's reins and guided them towards Trent and his friends on Phoenix's dorm. The diseased might not have known why they followed the carriage, but they still had a group around them. Too many if they wanted to make good progress through the city.

As they drew closer, Trent stood up. "Finally, you're coming to help us."

Matilda spoke from the side of her mouth. Not that she needed to keep quiet; the sight of the tall boy riled the diseased around the hut, drowning out anything they might say. "How will we fit them all on here?"

"We could lock them inside," Hugh suggested.

A few steps closer to Phoenix's old dorm, the rest of the diseased around the carriage rushed over to the hut.

William had an awareness of Trent in his peripheral vision. The boy glared at him, awaiting an answer. But he didn't look back, tugging on the horse's right rein to guide them away from the small wooden building.

It didn't take long for Trent to see his plan. "You're a snake, Spike Johnson. You'll get yours."

The boy's words had nothing on the corrosive guilt inside William. Matilda had already said it; they didn't have room for all of them on the roof of the carriage, so they couldn't take any. But they needed to shake off the diseased. As much as he didn't want to, he looked at the boy who'd let them live when they were vulnerable. They owed him their lives. Unlike Trent, he didn't glare rage at them. He stared betrayal. Confusion. Could they really leave them there? Who made them God, giving them the power to decide who lived and who died? The promise seemed like an empty one, regardless of William's intention, so he didn't make it again. But they would be back for them. They'd make sure they helped them off that roof. But first, they needed to get to their loved ones.

∽

As they walked through the gap where the gates had once separated the national service area from the rest of Edin, Hugh shook his head. "If only they'd left them up for another day."

"If only you'd closed the gate behind you when you came to find us," Matilda said.

The air damn near crackled, and before Hugh replied, William reached out and patted the stallion's rump. "Goliath."

It dragged the focus of his two friends away from their volatile conversation. "That's his name."

"How do you know?" Hugh said.

"Because I've just given it to him. A name befitting his stature."

"And we're lucky he has such a calm temperament," Matilda said. "Otherwise, we'd all be dead."

Before she could go any further, William said, "That's enough. We're clear of the national service area now. We're where we need to be, so let's move on, yeah? We can't change the past."

The metronomic clop of Goliath's feet beat against the cobblestones as they passed the diseased, invisible to them on the roof. While lying on his front, the morning sun beating down on them, the muscles in William's body relaxed, but his heart quickened as a warning. Whatever happened, if they lowered their guard, they were dead. They might have had a clear path to follow, but things could change in an instant.

The edge gone from her tone, Matilda said, "I don't think those kids on Phoenix's dorm will have wanted to come this way anyway. They'll do much better getting the hell out of Edin. I can't even imagine what we've got ahead of us."

William shuddered at the sight of the shambling monsters on the main street. As much as he intended to return to the national service area, they'd have to survive this first.

CHAPTER 27

Goliath's rhythm sent William into a trance, his hooves clopping against the cobblestones, his thick body moving with a hypnotic sway. The leather reins still in his grip, William stretched his eyes wide for what felt like the twentieth time in the past five minutes. The warmth from the spring day did little to dispel his fatigue.

Before William could talk to the others—anything to keep a conversation going so he didn't drift off—Hugh tapped his side and pointed over to their left. "That's the labs."

The most private district in Edin, the labs were hidden behind a two-storey-high wooden wall that ran around the perimeter. A narrow corridor provided the only access to the place. Before Edin fell, the district had been manned by twice as many guards as any other. Very few citizens had the authority to enter, and those trying to gain unauthorised access risked their lives. Woodwork and the science labs: two places not even the kids in Edin bothered with. "I've never seen any more of the labs than this," William said.

"They have to lock the place down. We were always testing on the virus and had so many live samples we couldn't risk any mistakes. If just one of them escaped ..." Hugh left his words hanging, the shambling chaos on Edin's streets the obvious end to his sentence.

"*Live* samples?" Matilda said.

While nodding, Hugh continued to stare at his old district. "Yeah, there were always several diseased in captivity. It was the only way to test the virus."

As they passed the labs, it gave them a clearer sight down the narrow road leading into the district. Diseased shambled around the tighter space like everywhere else—at least, everywhere else they'd seen so far. With canted stances, they stumbled on the edge of their balance.

"I suppose at least now we don't have to worry about the disease getting out of there," Matilda said.

William gripped the reins with his right hand and touched Matilda's side with his left. She'd made her point; Hugh knew what he'd done. She needed to lay off him now.

If Hugh picked up on her jibe, he let it slide. "I think you're missing my point."

Before Matilda replied, William said, "Which is?"

"Max is in there."

"We know," Matilda said.

It killed the conversation. As if on cue, a crow cawed as it flew over the now dead city; even the scavengers knew Edin had been lost.

Hugh said, "Uh ... we can't leave him behind."

Matilda said, "We can, and we will."

"Tilly," William said, "Hugh has a point."

"What about Artan? What about your mum and dad? What about James?"

"We'll still go to them."

"So why risk our lives now?"

"We owe Max, like we owe Hugh."

"You don't owe me anything," Hugh said.

Matilda's eyes widened as if to tell William she agreed. Fortunately, she kept it to herself.

"Had Max not told us about Artan," William said, "and then helped Hugh break out so he could get to us, we wouldn't even be here. Just like we can't leave Artan to rot in a cell—which is exactly what would have happened had Hugh not found us—we can't leave Max."

Matilda shifted across so his hand fell from her. "Sounds like you've already made up your mind."

"There's three of us here, Tilly, and two think it's the right thing to do."

For most of their conversation, William had watched Goliath's swaying form. When Matilda didn't come back at him, he turned to see tears in her eyes. The watery surface shook with her rage. "If this diversion puts Artan in greater danger, I will *never* forgive you."

"We go back a long way, Tilly—"

"Yet you're still prepared to do this to me. To Artan!"

"I hope I can trust you at some point like I want you to trust me now. This is the right thing to do."

"It sounds to me like this conversation's over."

Even Hugh knew to keep his mouth shut at that point.

A gentle tug on Goliath's left rein, William led them towards the entrance to the labs. He fought to keep his focus on what lay ahead. He could think about Artan, his parents, and James when they got closer to the political district. For now, they'd made the right decision.

Despite William's certainty, his stomach still turned backflips. Had he just risked his future relationship with Matilda by delaying their route to Artan? Would entering the labs be a challenge they couldn't overcome?

CHAPTER 28

Goliath's steps and the squeak of the cartwheels bounced back from the close walls on either side of them. The steady rhythm served as both a signal of their intention and a desperately tense countdown to whatever lay ahead. Had William really thought this one through? What if the delay meant the difference between life and death for Artan? No use in questioning himself now; the decision had been the right one with all the information they had available.

The diseased who didn't move were shoved aside by Goliath's slow and unrelenting progress. Several were dragged beneath the cart's large wheels like cockroaches beneath the sole of a boot. Tempted to look over the side, William remained flat against the roof with Matilda and Hugh flanking him. No sense in revealing himself to sate his morbid curiosity.

As they walked free of the tight entrance, the space opened up, Matilda gasping in response. "Wow," she said.

Unlike anything they'd seen anywhere else in Edin, the complex stretched out like it belonged to a different city. A one-storey wooden building, it had many rooms with corridors linking them together. It took up a space that would have accommodated over two hundred houses in one of Edin's residential areas. The district also had acres of wasteland to spare. What agriculture would have given for all that extra space. Like the dining room in the national service area, the complex had large windows running along its sides. Not only did they let light in, but they also revealed the building's interior.

Morning had given way to afternoon, the bright sun bouncing off the panes of glass. "It looks empty," William said, squinting to see in.

Hugh pointed in the direction of a pack of diseased. "That's the main entrance they're gathered around. It looks like they haven't made it in."

Matilda lifted her head. "So where are all the people from this district?"

"She has a point," William said. "Why can't we see anyone?"

"We can't see all of it. That down there"—Hugh pointed at the end of the large sprawling building to show a windowless section—"is where they keep all the test subjects. It's also the safest place to hide out."

"So you think Max is there? With the people from the labs?" William said.

"That would be my guess."

William saw a skylight on top of the building and guided Goliath towards it. "Is that the only skylight in the place?"

"Yeah," Hugh said. "Not much need for them with so many windows."

"Do you think it's our best way in?"

Hugh nodded.

When they got close to the roof, the top of the carriage level with it, William tugged on Goliath's reins to halt him and stood up. The diseased responded to him with cries and shouts as they rushed towards them, slamming into the side of the wooden vehicle, rocking it from their impact.

Goliath added to the movement beneath William's feet, small steps back and forth, the diseased clearly bothering him. "There, there," William said as he jumped from the carriage onto the roof. A metal chimney close by, he hooked Goliath's reins around it while the other two hopped over. They moved out of sight from the diseased while William walked along the edge of the building, leading the creatures away from his horse.

About ten feet away, William said, "Now don't worry, Goliath, we'll be back."

The same twitching of Goliath's white and brown ears met William's soothing words.

"Take care, boy. Thank you and we'll see you soon."

If horses could talk, Goliath would impart an encyclopaedia of wisdom. His deep brown eyes spoke of an understanding William could only dream of attaining. But what he could read in his horse's kind gaze was that he would be there for them when they came back.

As William walked away, the splash of shattering glass pulled his shoulders into his neck and he froze. Hugh stood over the skylight he'd just smashed, using the heel of his right boot to kick more of the glass out. It excited the diseased around the large building, but revealed none of them inside. It might have been a clumsy entrance, but at least it served a purpose. They now knew the labs were clear.

Hugh already had one leg hanging into the building when Matilda said, "I'm not going in until we have a way out."

After leaning his head inside, Hugh pulled himself back up and pointed. "There are some ladders in there. See?"

And good job they could see them because Matilda needed proof. When she saw the wooden A-frame ladders leaning against a wall, she nodded. "Okay. Let's set them up before we go exploring."

The smile on Hugh's face should have triggered a warning for William. A sane mind would be approaching this with dread. The boy then dropped into the room below, Matilda and William following after.

The large windows muted the diseased's hammering against the glass. Many of them pressed their faces to it, leaving the tick of enamel from where they tried to bite through the transparent barrier. While Hugh set up the ladder, William stood frozen, his skin alive with revulsion to take in so many bleeding eyes, yellow teeth, and trails of crimson smeared on the other side. Even with the glass between them, he could smell the things, their scent embedded in his sinuses like it would never leave.

William jumped when Matilda appeared beside him. "You think the glass will hold?"

As he took in the decaying panorama, many angry fists desperate to get at them, he shrugged. "Maybe?"

"It will," Hugh said. "It's extra thick, designed to contain the diseased in case of an outbreak. Although it was meant to keep the infected in, it'll work both ways."

The diseased, William had seen a thousand times before. As he spun on the spot to take in the sparse interior of the building, he shook his head. "I've never seen anything like this."

"It has to be clean and empty to make it a viable environment for experimentation. We can't do tests if it's messy or dirty." Hugh walked over to a small cupboard and removed two full jugs of water.

Just the sight of them made the saliva in William's mouth turn into a paste, and his voice croaked. "I didn't realise quite how thirsty I was."

Hugh handed one jug to William and one to Matilda.

Although room temperature, the water soothed William's throat. As much as he wanted to drink the lot, he passed the half-emptied jug to Hugh and wiped his mouth with the back of his hand.

Hugh took a sip, sat down, and untied his boot laces. "Elizabeth and I had a blast on national service. I really got to know her well. She told me things she hadn't ever told anyone." He smiled, his eyes glazed. "She told me she loves me, and I love her too. We were planning to spend the rest of our lives here. She's smart enough to get in. Shame the city has fallen."

When Hugh removed his boot, the stench hit William like an uppercut. He covered his nose and mouth with the back of his hand and heaved, stepping away from his friend. "My god, Hugh."

A mixture of blood and pus had gathered in the hole in Hugh's foot. The wound weeped a pink, milky substance.

"It's okay," Hugh said while pouring water on it. "It's just a scratch."

No more than a glance between William and Matilda. As long as Hugh could walk on it, they didn't need to point out the obvious.

"It's a shame the labs have fallen." Hugh slid his sock back on, his tone light. "Elizabeth and I will have to find somewhere else to live."

Matilda drew a breath and William glanced at her. She paused for a moment before taking another swig of water.

"Anyway," William said, "I'd say it's about time we move on, yeah?"

Hugh drained his jug in three deep gulps, got to his feet, and clapped his hands together. "Follow me."

The same low-lying buzz of anxiety he'd had with him since they'd re-entered Edin, William walked with Matilda beside him, drawing his sword at almost the same time as her while Hugh took the lead. The stocky boy kicked the first set of double doors wide and led them deeper into the long wooden building.

The next room as empty as the one they'd left, Hugh reached the other side and kicked open the next double doors with another loud *crack!*

They moved from one room to the next, tracked by the diseased outside.

Another set of double doors, Hugh still hadn't drawn his sword as he strode ahead of them. William spoke so only Matilda heard him. "He might still think Elizabeth's alive, but at least he knows his way through here. As long as it's not doing anyone any harm, I say we let him believe whatever he wants."

The next room must have been the canteen. Clusters of tables and chairs dotted the place; it all looked very civilised compared to the dining hall from national service—that place had been a trough away from feeding time at the farm. His sword in one hand, William reached out to Matilda with the other, her warm grip responding to his. "How amazing is this place?"

Although she didn't reply, her scowl had left her, her jaw hanging slightly open as she looked around.

"We'll get to Artan, I promise."

She squeezed his hand before leaning across and kissing him on the cheek. "You were right about saving Max."

"Thank you. Although I didn't expect it to be this simple to get into the labs. Goliath has made our lives a hell of a lot easier. We'll get Max and then get the hell out of here." He smiled as he watched Hugh march towards the next door. "Hopefully the rest of our journey will go as smoothly."

CHAPTER 29

"The holding cells are on the other side of this door," Hugh said, the confidence of his swagger so infectious William let his own frame unwind a little. But could he really trust his friend? His actions had put them in jeopardy too many times already. What had he seen in the last few hours that had proven Hugh to be a reliable guide through anything? Although, the boy could fight; he still had that going for him.

Just as William opened his mouth to question their brash approach—the diseased still tracking them outside—Hugh kicked the door like he had all the others. It swung wide with a loud *crack!*

A much darker corridor than any they'd been in so far opened up before them. No windows—which at least meant no diseased beating to get at them.

So the door wouldn't close, William and Matilda halted, keeping them open to let the light in from outside. The hairs stood up on the back of William's neck when even Hugh stopped. He let go of Matilda's hand, wrapping a double grip on his sword's handle. The air had thickened, the sense of foreboding tangible.

Just as Matilda sniffed next to him, William also caught the scent. Rot. Vinegar. Disease. For a second time, he opened his mouth to speak. For a second time, he failed to get his words out.

The open door let in enough light to illuminate about thirty feet of the corridor before it turned ninety degrees to the right. The sound started quietly, distant as if it might not have been in the same corridor. Although, maybe that was William trying to kid himself; it was definitely in the same corridor. As it drew closer, the general hum gained definition. Snarls. Screams. Shrieks. A stampede of clumsy steps.

Matilda went first, spinning around and sprinting back the way they came. A second later, William followed, Hugh on his tail.

Matilda had always been faster than William, but when she reached the first set of doors, she stopped and held them open for him, and then Hugh a second later.

The diseased outside ran with William as he headed for the next doors. His turn to let his friends out, he pulled them wide, taking the moment's pause to recover. At least, he'd planned to. Matilda and Hugh were nowhere near him. Matilda lay sprawled on the floor, an upturned table in front of her.

Hugh closer than William, the stocky boy turned back and ran for Matilda. But he didn't stop. Instead, he charged at the double doors Matilda had held open.

"What are you doing?" William said. "You can't fight them all."

If Hugh heard him, he didn't show it.

"Hugh!"

The labs damn near shook with the diseased stampede bearing down on them. Hugh probably couldn't hear him over the chaos. William let go of the doors and ran to Matilda. His attention divided between his fallen love and Hugh, he caught up to her and reached down.

As William helped her up, taking her weight from where she couldn't stand by herself, Hugh took off his shirt. Like every jumped-up idiot William had ever met, Hugh appeared to be getting ready for a fight by baring flesh—like that would help save his life. Matilda had been right about him; he'd lost his mind and they couldn't get dragged down with his insanity.

William led Matilda away to the next set of doors, his love leaning on him as she limped at his side. "You're too slow with me," she said. "You need to save Artan."

"I'm not leaving you."

"You have to. We can't beat the diseased to the ladder."

Stumbling through the doors from where he supported Matilda's weight, William shook his head. "No."

A second later, Hugh joined them. Shirtless, he said, "I tied the doors shut. It will give us more time, but I'm not sure how much. I don't see that shirt holding for long." He then took Matilda from William and led her to the next room.

They got back to where they'd started, and Hugh took Matilda to the ladder before helping her climb.

After getting her to the roof, Hugh came back down, his muscular body exposed and glistening with sweat.

"What are you doing?" William said. The diseased hadn't yet broken through.

"Just get out on the roof. I'll be up in a minute."

They didn't have time to argue. William scaled the ladder and climbed out to safety. His entire body rose and fell with his deep breaths. He left Matilda rubbing her ankle and walked over to Goliath, the diseased whipping up at the sight of him. "Well done, boy. We'll be out of here soon." As he reached down to the creature, the horse leaned close and sent warm snorts against the back of his hand.

Back to the skylight and Matilda, William said, "Are you okay?"

She shrugged. "It's not much. Just a twist. I can feel it getting better already."

"Good job we had Hugh with us, eh? I wouldn't have ever thought to tie the doors."

Before they could say any more, Hugh emerged from the skylight dressed in a white lab coat. His face red, he cleared his throat as he looked down at himself. "It was the only thing I could find."

William and Matilda laughed.

"Thank you for saving me, Hugh," Matilda said.

"It was nothing." Hugh scratched the top of his head. "It looks like the labs didn't avoid the diseased, then. So how are we going to help Max?"

"Is there any other way to get to the cells?" William said.

Hugh shook his head. "The cell walls are lined with metal. They were made to contain the diseased, so the only access is through the cell door, which is locked with a special combination."

"And you know the code?" William said.

"As long as it hasn't changed."

"Seems like a gamble. Besides, we still need to access the cell by going in that corridor filled with diseased?"

"Yeah."

Matilda remained focused on her ankle, her cheeks flushing red. "I ... I hate to say it ... but I'm not sure we can help him."

Neither William nor Hugh replied.

"I mean, I need to rest my ankle, and as much as I want to rescue Max, Artan is still my main concern. Hugh, you want to get to James, right?"

Hugh stared at her.

"And, William, we need to go through agriculture. I worry

that it's suicide to try to rescue Max. It sounds awful, but someone needs to say it. Max *isn't* a priority. Besides, if—and it's a big *if*—we find a way to get to his cell without dying, who's to say Max is still in there? What if they've moved him already? What if he wasn't in there when the city fell? There are too many things we don't know." She looked up. "Am I wrong?"

William didn't have a counterargument, and if Hugh did, he kept it to himself.

CHAPTER 30

Once again, Goliath passed through the diseased as if he were invisible. William lay on his front, his hands sweating from gripping the leather reins. He had Matilda on his left and Hugh on his right.

Hugh said, "I think Max is still in his cell."

Matilda had been the one to make the point, but William wholeheartedly agreed. He'd backed up Hugh when they decided to go and look for Max; now he needed to back her. "I can't die trying to find that out," he said. "We don't know where he is. The risks are too high for us to fight our way through the labs to find an empty cell. We all have people relying on us."

If Hugh replied, William didn't hear it, his attention taken away by the person on the roof in textiles. "Olga?"

Both Matilda and Hugh lifted their heads, Hugh saying, "Well, I'll be damned."

A gentle tug on Goliath's right rein, William guided the horse and carriage across the wide road towards their friend from national service.

Olga's jaw hung slack as she watched their approach. "Holy shit! What are you three doing here?"

Deep, black bags beneath her eyes and her skin paler than usual, Olga glistened with sweat. "You look like you've had a rough morning," William said.

"You don't want to know. But, like I said, what are you three doing? Where are you going?"

Now they were close, Hugh sat up and held his hand out to Olga so she could step onto the carriage with them. Several diseased gathered around, their pallid faces turning up at them.

William shifted over, pressing up against Matilda so Olga had space. "You need to lie down. If the diseased can't see us, they forget about us."

Following his instruction, Olga said, "So, where are you all going?"

"Tailoring to see if we can find Hugh's brother. Agriculture for my parents. And the political district for Artan."

"And you think you'll find them?" Before anyone replied, Olga shook her head. "Sorry, I didn't mean to sound cold. It's been a rough morning. I've been on the rooftops for hours. There's not much left of the city."

"We have to see if they're okay," William said.

"And Artan's locked in a cell in the political district."

Olga raised her head so she could look over William at Matilda. "Artan?"

"My brother. It's a long story. My dad killed my mum several months ago, and Artan killed him in a fit of rage. They put him in a cell to evict him from the city when he got old enough, and … well, he never got old enough. I'm hoping the fact he was incarcerated might mean the diseased can't get to him."

"Max is in a cell too."

Olga's words silenced them, William's pulse quickening.

"What is it?" Olga said.

Matilda stared at the road ahead. "We went to the labs for Max."

"And?"

"We did our best, but we couldn't find him."

Tears swelled in Olga's eyes. She looked like she wanted to say more but couldn't. "Oh."

William pulled Goliath away from where they'd picked up Olga, and guided them back down the main road towards tailoring. Olga hadn't said she wanted to go with them, but she hadn't said she didn't.

Woodwork on their left, trails of black smoke rose from deep within the district. Maybe Hugh noticed him stare over, because he said, "At least woodwork's fallen. I hope the innocent families are safe."

After she'd drawn a stuttered breath, Olga said, "From what I've seen this morning, no one's safe."

His attention still on woodwork, Hugh said, "In that case, I hope the fire's taken the gangs down with it."

Olga wiped her nose with the back of her hand. "Me too."

CHAPTER 31

William leaned into Matilda, not through a desire to be close to her—despite that being a permanent need—but more due to his discomfort at his proximity to a grieving Olga. If they returned to the labs, they might find Max. If they returned to the labs, they might not come out again. Goliath swayed as he plodded down Edin's main street.

Ceramics on their right, woodwork and tailoring on their left. The fires in woodwork had spread, the district belching thick clouds of black smoke across their path. The acrid stench and thick air forced William to pull his shirt across his mouth as a filter.

As they drew closer to tailoring, Goliath following William's tug on the left rein, Hugh gasped. It took a few seconds for William to see why.

While watching them, Olga said, "I passed a few survivors as I made my way out."

There looked to be at least ten people gathered on the roofs in ceramics. William's heart sank to meet the traumatised stare of several children. As desperate as those they'd left in the national service area, but what could they do? It might feel like they were playing God by deciding who lived and who died, and maybe they were, but they couldn't fit everyone on Goliath's carriage.

Olga shrugged. "We can't kill ourselves saving others."

Matilda squirmed against William as they drew closer to tailoring and farther away from the group who needed them. Unlike Trent and his crew, no one called out.

Like with the entrance to the labs, the diseased packed the road leading into tailoring.

"At least seeing some survivors is a good thing," Matilda said.

Olga lifted her head. "How's that?"

"Well, if some people have survived, maybe the people we're trying to rescue have survived too."

Hugh—having said very little since they'd told Olga about Max—finally spoke. "Tell me what you've seen, Olga."

"I've seen a lot of devastation."

While they talked, William took directions from Hugh, which led them down tailoring's main street. The once clean shop windows and meticulously designed displays were in ruin, smashed glass now glitter on the cobblestones, and fabrics strewn across the road as if many of the shops had exploded.

"I know those who have survived are the lucky ones," Olga said, "and it was only luck that kept them alive. I hope all of your loved ones are in that number." Before anyone else spoke, she added, "I thought I had a connection to him."

"Who?" William said.

"Max. I felt like we were close on national service, and I couldn't stop thinking about him while I waited for my arm to heal. I was making my way over to the labs even before I knew the city had fallen. Maybe that's what saved me. When most people were at home, or focused on getting ready for work, I was outside and saw the creatures coming. It gave me the few seconds I needed to get to safety."

The clop of Goliath's heels. The moans from the diseased. The smell of smoke from woodwork next door. "For what it's worth," William said, "I think you and Max had a connection too."

The watery glaze returned to Olga's eyes. "You think?"

"Sure. Don't you remember the comments he used to make?"

"I thought he was being cheeky."

"He was ... because he *like liked* you."

Olga smiled as if reliving the good times. It damn near forced the truth from William, and from the way both Matilda and Hugh looked out across the district, they felt the same guilt. But they didn't know if he was still in the labs. It wasn't like they saw evidence of him being there and left. It would be suicide to try to find out.

Tears now streaming down her cheeks, Olga sniffed. "Thanks, Spike."

"William."

"*William?*"

"Spike was the name of a kid enamoured with the protectors. A kid who thought he lived in a city that would help him be who he wanted to be. My name's William."

Olga nodded. "I wonder how the city fell."

Although William had an awareness of Hugh looking across, he kept his focus on Olga. "It's a mystery. One of the politicians probably screwed up somewhere."

Hugh's features darkened, and for a moment William expected him to blurt out a confession. Instead, he pointed at a nearby street. "Down there."

A much narrower path than any they'd taken so far, the one-storey buildings were just a few feet away from them on either side. "The diseased might not be a danger to us," William said, "but we could be hijacked by survivors, so keep your wits. How far to your house, Hugh?"

After scanning their surroundings, Hugh pointed over to their right. "Just down the next street."

"I went back to my parents' house," Olga said. "Although, I don't know why. They died years ago."

"They were already dead?" Again William did all the talking, Hugh and Olga now lost in their surveillance of the fallen district.

"In their hearts they were. My sisters died when they went on national service."

"I remember you saying that to Bleach."

"I lost my parents that day too. They remained in body, but their hearts were broken beyond repair." The tracks on Olga's cheeks glistened anew with fresh tears. "I think they forgot they had one daughter still alive."

"So what did you find when you got there?"

"They'd been turned like pretty much everyone else in laundry. But anyway, life's depressing enough; what are your plans? Let's say we save your loved ones, then what next? Find a corner of Edin to rebuild from?"

Hugh wriggled and shifted before producing the map they'd found outside the city. He laid it out on the dark wood of the carriage's roof. "There's more than Edin out there."

"What's this?" Olga said.

"A map," Hugh said.

"Duh!"

"We found it on a diseased we killed in the ruined city. Looks like there's a whole world out there. Maybe they were trying to find out about Edin. Doesn't look like they knew much about the place."

"I don't know why they'd want to find out about this city." Olga squinted, the sun reflecting off the map's glossy surface. "It looks like they're much more advanced than us."

William frowned. "Why do you say that?"

Olga licked her finger and dragged it across the map. Although William gasped to see her attempt to deface it, the image remained.

"Whatever they've used to get these lines on the paper, it's better than anything we have. Were this a map made by someone in Edin, I would have been able to smudge it."

Even Matilda turned to look at the large sheet of paper. "I thought it was painted on there."

Olga shook her head. "I wonder how they did it."

When Hugh pulled on William's right arm, William guided Goliath down the next street. Even tighter than the one they were leaving, their ride became bumpy from where the diseased couldn't get out of their way. They ran over as many as they shoved aside. An already foul stench in the air, the reek of rot and vinegar heightened with the pop and crack of breaking bones.

Like with the main street, glass covered the ground, mixed with smashed wood from doors that had once been whole. The place had clearly fallen, but Hugh didn't need to hear that. They'd hold onto hope until they had none.

"It's that one," Hugh said, pointing down the street at a house that looked like all the others.

Although, with this one, the door remained in its frame and … "What does that sheet say?" William said.

Hugh sat up, the diseased around them all turning to face him. Mouths fell open, brows furrowed. "They've made a sign."

Not much wind, but enough to disturb the fabric so they couldn't quite read the embroidered message. Black thread on a pink sheet.

Then it settled and Olga read it. "Alive inside."

CHAPTER 32

They were just a few feet from the house, a house much like all the others surrounding it, much like many of the rickety houses in Edin. Their similarities lay in just how different they were. An eclectic mess of one-story residences. It made the luxury of the labs even more galling.

When Hugh stood up, the sounds of the diseased surrounding them lifted, agitated by the sight of the stocky boy. Goliath's hide tightened. William reached forward and patted the large stallion's warm skin.

Hugh stared at the sheet and shook his head. "Even now, when his life's in danger, Dad uses the cheapest offcut to make a sign."

The pink sheet danced in the weak breeze, only the top of it pinned between the door and frame. William said, "Maybe he knew this one would move the most so it could be seen from farther away."

A snort and then shake of his head, Hugh stepped from the roof of the carriage to the roof of his house. "He ain't that smart."

William handed Goliath's reins to Matilda. "Don't pull on

them too hard. He's a calm horse you can trust. Just reassure him." He then stood up—the diseased growing more agitated now they could see two of them—before stepping across to join Hugh.

A rickety roof made from slate and wood like many of those in Edin. The different shades of grey showed where it had been patched up over the years. Hugh peered down at the ever-increasing horde below. "How the hell are we going to get inside?"

"Go through the roof," Olga said.

Hugh nodded before reaching down to tear one of the pieces of slate away. While biting on his bottom lip, he threw it at the diseased in the street. It scored a direct hit, cracking one of them in the face and knocking it to the ground. William gave Olga a thumbs up and went to work with his friend.

It took them a minute or two—Hugh removing three times the number of tiles compared to William—but they opened a hole. It shone a light down on what looked to be Hugh's front room.

"Hello?" Hugh called. A few seconds later, a man appeared. He had long ginger hair, sleepy green eyes, and a slightly loose jaw.

Before the man spoke, Hugh said, "Where are they?"

The man scowled. "You not going to say hello to your old man?"

"Where. Are. They?"

Despite his initial terse response, Hugh's dad softened, his fixed features faltering. "Thank god you're here. I didn't think anyone would come. I thought I was going to die in this house. Thank you for coming back to me."

"Where are they?"

Hugh's dad glanced to his right, and before he said anything, Hugh made his way across the roof in that direction.

"I did all I could, Hugh. I tried my best."

If Hugh heard him, it didn't show, dropping down over another spot on the roof and tearing into it like a drill. William jumped back to avoid the slate he tossed aside.

It didn't take long to open a space over what had once been Hugh's kitchen. Two people were in there: a boy and a woman. The boy and the woman who'd come to visit Hugh after every trial. The boy William had seen Hugh hug like he'd never let him go. They both stared up through the hole. Like Hugh's dad, they looked like they were struggling with the bright sunshine pushing down on them. The glare of it glistened off their crimson eyes. Their mouths hung open as dark pits loaded with the disease, ready to be driven into someone with one hard bite.

Frozen, Hugh stared down at his family for what felt like at least a minute. He moved back over to the first hole, but walked straight past it.

At the edge of his house, directly above the front door, Hugh tore off another slate tile.

Hugh's dad continued to stare up through the first hole at William, who then left him there to join his friend. "What are you doing, Hugh?"

But Hugh didn't reply. Instead, he tore slate after slate free, throwing them through the first hole at his dad.

"Hugh," his dad shouted at him over the splashes of breaking tiles, "I did all I could for them, I promise."

The crash of more slate against the living room floor answered him, Hugh's hole growing larger by the second. The diseased by the front door shrieked and screamed at their desperation to get to the boy just above them. Matilda and Olga watched on from the roof of Goliath's carriage.

When one of the tiles clearly hit Hugh's dad, the man screaming in response, William grabbed his friend's thick arm to halt him. Hugh stood up and lifted his chest.

William held his ground. "What are you doing?"

"I'm getting to the front door so I can open it."

"But that's your *dad*. You're not thinking straight."

"I'm thinking straighter than I have in a long time, William. Now stand aside."

"You told me your dad was a good guy."

"I *lied*. He's an arsehole and always has been. I hate him and have since I've been old enough to hate. Another weak-minded man broken by the system and never able to find the emotional resources to pull himself back. Another family made to pay the price because of their patriarch's failing. He's a waste of space." His voice caught and his face momentarily buckled. "He couldn't even keep them alive."

"Can you blame him for that in this city?"

In a blink, Hugh drew his sword and held the point just inches from William's face.

Wide eyes, sweat glistening on his skin, Hugh said, "I will end you if I need to. Don't get in the way of this."

William showed Hugh his palms as if surrendering and stepped back several paces. He stood above the first hole, with a clear line of sight to Hugh's dad.

Hugh sheathed his sword and went back to work on the hole. His arms moved like pistons, tearing through the roof.

So he didn't get caught by the flying slate, and to get away from the whimpering man, William moved a step closer to Goliath and the girls. Maybe they should leave Hugh. The two concerned faces looking back at him from the carriage would have backed him up. But he didn't know Hugh's dad. He didn't know his friend's reasons for behaving this way.

The hole in the roof now large enough, Hugh drew his sword for a second time. He reached down with it and pushed the tip against the hinges running down one side of the door.

The ripping sound of wood and the chink of metal rang out as the top hinge fell.

Hugh's dad ran to the door and pushed against it. "What are you doing, boy? Are you trying to get me killed?"

A dark glaze covered Hugh's eyes. The glaze William had seen too many times already. The Hugh he knew had temporarily left.

Hugh tore another slate tile free, clenched his jaw, and threw it down at his dad. The man screamed like a diseased when the slate exploded on the top of his head. He ran back from the door.

With only one hinge remaining, the wooden door suddenly gave way, the bottom hinge too weak to hold the creatures back.

As the diseased flooded into the house, Hugh moved over to the first hole. A smile teased the edges of his mouth. He watched his dad through the loose focus of someone in a daydream.

Within seconds, Hugh's dad's scream stopped. Hugh then walked past William and patted his shoulder. The glaze had lifted from his features. He stepped across the gap onto the roof of Goliath's carriage and lay down next to Olga, who shifted a few inches away from him as if whatever he had was catching.

Under the scrutiny of the two girls, William followed Hugh, stepping onto the roof of the carriage before lying down between Matilda and Olga. He took the reins from Matilda and flicked them gently. None of them spoke as Goliath walked over the pink sheet with *Alive inside* embroidered on it.

CHAPTER 33

No one spoke for the next half an hour or so. Once or twice, William's eyelids grew so heavy he had to force them wide to stop himself falling asleep. The middle of the afternoon, they still had a lot ahead of them. No time for rest. That would come later—much, much later.

They'd left tailoring, moving at Goliath's slow pace as they ambled through the streets. How would they have ever managed without the large creature? Olga threw William a sharp glare every time he did it, but he reached forward and patted the horse anyway. Of the few diseased that noticed, they quickly got distracted by something else.

"I'm hungry and thirsty," Hugh said.

Matilda raised her head. "Me too. Surely we can find something in the city."

Just the thought of it made William's stomach rumble, and were he not focused on leading Goliath through the streets of his home district—every step moving them closer to his house—then he might have added to the conversation.

"Not seen many survivors here," Hugh said.

And they hadn't. The rickety roofs of agriculture stretched

out away from them, and so far they were clear of people. And thank god. Not that William didn't wish for survivors, he just didn't want to have to ignore them again. The survivors in ceramics … the rookies in the national service area … Max …

When Hugh laughed, it broke William from his thoughts.

"Lying on this carriage reminds me of sneaking out with Elizabeth in the evenings. Did you know we did that?"

"No," William said.

"Strange that. You always noticed if I went out for anything else, but when it was to meet Elizabeth, you slept like a baby. We'd lie on the roof of our dorm and watch the stars. We'd make plans for what we'd do when national service ended. Sometimes we'd lie there in silence, just holding each other's hands. I often think being able to share silence is what sets apart a good relationship from a great one."

"Why don't you try it, then?" Olga said, looking at the creatures below as if fearful of Hugh's words riling them.

Hugh laughed again. "Good one." After a moment, he said, "We need to get to woodwork."

William fought against the sinking feeling in his gut. "Whyyyy?"

The timbre of Hugh's laugh rang at a higher pitch than before. "To see if she's okay, silly. We need to make sure we get to her. She'll be worried sick."

Olga dropped a monotone bombshell, her patience clearly running out. "She's dead, Hugh. Like most people in this city."

Where Hugh had been smiling, his face fell slack. The light in his eyes dulled, his brow furrowing. In that moment, William saw the Hugh he knew from before. The unassuming and fiercely intelligent Hugh. The one who saw all the angles.

Another erratic laugh, Hugh nodded too many times and his cheeks reddened. "Of course." He laughed again and reverted to his withdrawn glaze. "I was joking, obviously."

As he'd been doing since they left tailoring, William guided Goliath down another street.

When Hugh spoke again, his words were loaded with uncertainty. It reminded William of when his grandma would forget everyone's name, like she was lost in the fog of her mind. "But what about tailoring?"

"Tailoring?" Olga said.

This time William let go of the right rein and rested his hand on Olga's shoulder. He shook his head at her.

"I need to see if James and my mum are okay. Look, I'll be honest with you, Spike—"

"Will …"

"Huh?"

William let it go. "Go on."

"I don't like my dad. Never have. He's a vicious man with a dark heart. But I need to see if James and my mum are still alive. I'm not sure what I'd do without them."

When Olga drew a breath to reply, William talked over her. "Don't worry." Like when he used to reassure his gran about trips she wanted to make to people long since passed, he reassured his friend. "We'll go to tailoring soon." They turned down a tighter street, now drawing close to William's house.

Where he'd been concerned for Hugh, the next turn sank cold dread through William. His house in front of them, the door hung open, the front room as populated with shambling diseased as the street outside.

Hugh and Olga had no idea where they were, but as they got close to his childhood home, Matilda reached forwards and held the back of William's left hand. The world in front of him blurred, and a lump swelled in his throat. He led Goliath straight past.

Although the carriage shook from Matilda shifting beside him, William didn't look at her. It took for her to hold the hummingbird hair clip in front of him to realise what she'd been doing. But he shook his head and cleared his throat. "Mum intended for you to have it. I'd like to honour that."

After she put it back in her hair, Matilda held William's hand again, the clop of Goliath's hooves taking them away from his childhood home and on towards the political district.

CHAPTER 34

Even Goliath seemed affected by recent events, moving slower than before as they made their way from agriculture. A blurred view of the world ahead, his eyes burning, William kept his focus fixed in front of them while Matilda continued to hold the back of his left hand, stroking it with her thumb. Like with her and the hummingbird clip, he still wore his dad's skull ring, the silver standing in stark contrast against his dark skin. The material gift—a vessel to carry good luck—against the genetic gift of pigmentation. Every time he looked at his own reflection, he saw his dad. What he'd give for one last trip with him to the back wall. For one last home-cooked meal with both of them.

"I'm still hungry and thirsty," Hugh said. "There must be somewhere to find food."

Olga nudged him with her elbow. "Hugh! Show some respect."

If Hugh knew what she meant, his dull eyes hid it well.

Before Olga could explain further, William shook his head. "It's fine. I'm hungry too. We need something to focus on. But where will we get food?"

"Did you have storage families in your district?" Olga said.

Matilda lifted her head. "What are storage families?"

"The families that held some of the rations above ground in their houses. Once the food comes up through the tunnels, it gets put in different houses to be stored and then distributed from there. Families would give over one of their rooms to the cause."

"I've spent eighteen years in Edin," William said. "How have I never heard of this before?"

Olga shrugged. "Edin's good at keeping secrets. I never knew about woodwork and the gangs until today."

From the way she lost focus, William nearly asked her what she meant. Instead, he said, "So how do you know about the storage families?"

"Our neighbours were one. When I got to know them, I started to work out who else was. The signs were always there, I just didn't know what I was looking for."

When no one replied, Olga elaborated. "They're always families who have lost someone in national service."

"So half of Edin?" Matilda said. "That doesn't narrow it down."

"No"—Olga raised her right index finger—"but here's the kicker. They've all lost someone, so they all have a spare room in their house. They're one of the families who didn't get relocated despite having an extra room. Every district has them, and every person complains about them. I mean, why should they have extra space when everyone else has to relocate. Luck of the draw, right?"

"Right," William said.

"Wrong!"

William nodded. "So *all* of them are storage families?"

"No, that would make it too easy. I think they let some people keep their larger houses as decoys. Like my family, for example. In fact, I'd say most of them aren't storage houses. But there's one more thing that marks the ration holders out from everyone else. Because they hold the rations, they get double the food for as long as they keep it secret. So they're always healthier, larger, and some of them are even fat. Every district has the families with fat little kids while all the other children are so hungry they'd eat grass if it helped."

The tears gone, William saw the world with more clarity than before. He let go of Matilda's hand and pointed over at a house on the left. "There! The Ratts. They had a little boy who was so fat you could barely see his features in his round little head. The older Ratt died on national service, and the mum and dad always looked healthy and strong. They fit the bill."

"But the door's open," Matilda said, a diseased standing in the doorway of the house. "So even if they do have supplies in there, there's nothing we can do to get to them."

The diseased in the street grew louder when Hugh raised his head, the boy instantly dropping it again. "How about we see if they have any food in there still? If they do, we can work out a way to get it."

When no one objected, William tugged on Goliath's left rein, the large beast nudging the diseased aside on his route to the Ratts' old home. As they pulled up next to it, he handed the reins to Matilda. "Do you mind waiting here with Goliath? I'm worried if we all go, he might walk off."

"Why don't you leave someone else behind?"

They couldn't trust Hugh, so William looked at Olga, who shrugged. "Sure. I need a rest."

Matilda led the way onto the Ratts' roof. The diseased offered their predictable response: angry, loud, and smelly. The carriage shook with their movement, and it took William a second to adjust to his surer footing when he stepped onto the roof of the house.

The diseased had already seen them, so there seemed little need for stealth. William called across to Olga, "Go for the spare room, yeah?"

She nodded.

Whether two or three bedrooms, most houses in Edin had a similar layout. The master bedroom first and then the extra rooms at the back. William led the way to what he guessed to be the first kids' bedroom.

Like they'd done on Hugh's house, William, Hugh, and now Matilda went to work on the tiles, tearing them free and launching them at the diseased in the street.

After a couple of minutes, they'd torn a hole wide enough in the roof, exposing the wooden ceiling boards beneath. William sat down on the edge of the gap and stamped one through.

Four diseased faces stared up at them. Both Hugh and Matilda launched tiles, knocking all of them down. Four more replaced them.

William stamped on the next ceiling board, the creatures unflinching as wood rained down on them. A better view of the room, he shook his head. "The supplies aren't in here."

As William got to his feet to walk away, the creatures in the room grew more agitated, biting at the air and reaching up as if their will could force the three of them to fall.

After several minutes of tearing a new hole, William's clothes stuck to the layer of sweat on his skin. He sat down again and kicked the boards through, two hard stamps driving one, and then the next, into the room beneath. "There!"

Only one open crate among many, it had bread and vegetables in it. Carrots, potatoes, swede … "Some of it needs to be cooked," William said. "But even if we leave that behind, it looks like there's enough for us to eat."

As several diseased shambled into the room—one of them

going down from a spinning tile launched by Hugh—Matilda sighed. "Now we need to find a way to get it out of there."

CHAPTER 35

Although Matilda remained beside William, Hugh walked off across the roof. "Hugh, what are you doing?"

When the boy didn't answer, William did his best to ignore Matilda's raised eyebrow and jogged to catch up with his stocky friend.

Close to the edge of the house, Hugh crouched down and tore several tiles free, launching them at the diseased in the street.

"Hugh, what's going on?"

But Hugh continued tearing the tiles away until he'd opened a large enough hole to kick the boards through. Like with the other rooms in the house, the gap revealed snarling diseased staring up at them. Splinters and dust on their faces, they fixed on Hugh.

A tight clench to his jaw, Hugh kicked at the ceiling boards until he'd bashed through a hole about two feet square.

"What? You're going to drop down there and fight them?" Matilda said.

While wiping his sweating brow, Hugh grinned. "That would be insane."

For the second time, William ignored Matilda's attention. They both knew Hugh had lost the plot. Why belabour the point? Although, it would help if he tried to understand his friend. "Then what are you planning on doing?"

"We need to get the diseased out of this house, right?"

William shrugged.

"So you and Matilda ride on the carriage over to the other side of the road and make a lot of noise. When the diseased run over to you, hopefully emptying this house in the process, I can jump into the front room, lock and barricade the door, and secure it so we can loot this place to our heart's content."

The plan seemed solid. But Hugh executing it? As much as Matilda had silently questioned many of Hugh's actions, she offered nothing.

"Sound good?" Hugh said.

"Sure?" William asked Matilda.

She shrugged.

While William and Matilda returned to Goliath's carriage, Hugh made his way to the hole at the back of the house: the room with the supplies in.

As much as Hugh's idea made sense, it was still Hugh's idea. His sense and William's didn't often align. Before stepping onto the carriage, William said, "How will you jump down into the front room if you're standing all the way back there?"

"I need to make sure they've cleared out of the back rooms before I jump down into the front."

Matilda spoke without moving her lips. "It all seems far too logical. I'm worried something will go wrong."

"You and me both."

If Hugh had any sense of their conversation, he didn't let on, smiling at William while he stepped across onto the roof of Goliath's carriage, holding his hand out to help Matilda deal with the transition to the moving surface. She looked at his hand, ignored it, and stepped across on her own. He should have learned by now.

Olga had clearly listened to the plan, guiding Goliath across to the other side of the road without being asked. Goliath didn't belong to him, but watching Olga guide the horse wound William tight.

A road packed with furious diseased gave them a chance to speak with more freedom. No way could Hugh hear them. "It seems like a solid plan," Matilda said.

Olga snorted. "From a fragile mind. I'm not sure I trust it."

Before she could say anything else, William said, "We're not asking you to trust it."

"Then what are you asking me to do?"

"Hold onto Goliath while we do what's required. You can do that, can't you?"

When they reached the houses on the other side of the road, Matilda stepped across first. Just before joining her, William turned to Olga. "I'm sorry. I shouldn't have just snapped then."

"It's okay. It's a stressful time." Her eyes had tightened into narrow slits, her face the antithesis of her words.

After joining Matilda on the roof, William ripped a tile free and sent it spinning into the face of one of the diseased. He scored a direct hit, and the creature went down beneath the surging crowd.

Matilda threw her tile with such force it embedded in the face of one of the creatures. She winked at William.

The street separating them and Hugh, William led Matilda and the diseased away from Goliath. "Come on then, you freaks." He threw another tile as Hugh, on the roof opposite them, moved away from the hole over the back room. It must have already cleared.

Matilda threw three tiles in quick succession. Every one

scored a headshot. William laughed. "You should swap your sword for a stack of tiles."

"I might just do that!"

By the time they were about ten feet from Goliath and still dragging the diseased with them, Hugh had moved over to the hole above the front room. He gave William a thumbs up. But before he jumped down, there was a loud *snap* as the roof gave way and he vanished from sight with a yell.

The creatures close to the storage house charged towards it. Three diseased vanished inside before the door slammed shut.

"He must be okay," William said just as several more diseased crashed against the door. It opened by a foot and then closed again.

"He's keeping it shut," Matilda said. "How many are in there already?"

William shrugged. "Three? Four?"

The pack outside swelled in number, the door opening and slamming shut again from where Hugh clearly fought against it.

"What shall we do?" Matilda said.

Before William could reply, Olga yelled and jumped from the top of the carriage. His heart beat treble-time as the short firecracker screamed like a banshee and sprinted to the other side of the main road. She took a diagonal path away from the storage house, dragging many of the diseased with her, including the ones trying to get through the door to Hugh.

Two diseased between Olga and the other side of the road, she punched one before ducking the clumsy swing of the other. Without missing a beat, she leaped, kicked off from the windowsill of the house she'd run at, and caught its roof before pulling herself to safety; the diseased caught up to her a second too late.

The front door to the storage house slammed shut, and a heavy thud of something fell across it. When the diseased tried to get at Hugh again, they met the resistance of a barricaded door.

"Shit!" William said. "Goliath!" The piebald stallion's eyes were wide, his nostrils flared. Although he high-stepped on the spot, his powerful body twitched with what looked like a need to bolt. The leather reins lay discarded on the roof of the carriage.

William closed the distance between him and the carriage and launched himself. Goliath moved forward by about two feet.

The slam of William's boots hit the carriage's roof, closer towards the back than he'd intended. Goliath jolted forwards, unsettling William's balance.

His stomach in his throat, William rocked back on his heels. The diseased in the road waited for him to fall. But then Goliath stepped back, moving the carriage the other way.

William slammed down on his knees before lying on his front, hugging the roof while he let his pulse settle.

A few seconds later, William reached out to touch his horse. "Thank you, boy. I owe you." A series of twitches ran across Goliath's hide.

Still out of breath, his pulse a kick drum in his skull, William led Goliath first to Matilda and then to Olga.

As their small friend stepped onto the roof of the carriage, taking William's offer of a hand, she said, "Just so we're clear, I questioned the plan, not the boy."

William accepted Olga's words with a nod, leading them back to the storage house. After a deep inhale, he handed the reins to Olga again. "Let's just hope he's survived this, eh?"

Matilda behind him, William got to the first hole, the one Hugh had fallen through. Three dead diseased lay on the floor on their backs. A large bookcase covered the door and formed a barricade against the creatures in the street.

The next hole showed the room beneath to be empty. William pushed through his reluctance and walked to the final one. Whatever lay in wait for him, he had to see it.

Sat on the pile of food, a loaf of rough bread in one hand, a jug of water in the other, Hugh winked at William and Matilda and toasted them with his drink. "You lot took your time."

Everything rushed out of William, his laugh going from zero to hysterical in seconds. He bent over double and rested his hands on his knees, Matilda also laughing beside him. It took at least a minute before he found the breath to talk. He shook his head at his grinning friend. "You know what, Hugh? You're a mad bastard."

CHAPTER 36

Every now and then William caught the stench of the diseased. Not that it hadn't been there all along, he'd just gotten used to the low-lying festering reek. It now took for a particularly foetid creature to stumble past for the foul aroma to register. Although, nothing would put him off his food. Still in the agricultural district, all four of them sat on top of Goliath's carriage and ate their picnic in full view.

William checked Goliath for what must have been the tenth time since they'd stopped. The large horse remained stoic and resolute. Maybe the reassurances helped; maybe Goliath had simply grown used to the presence of the diseased. "So you fought three of them off with kicks?" William said.

Several quick chews, Hugh swigged from his water jug before swallowing. "Yeah. What else could I have done? I had to keep them at bay and hope you'd get the others away from the front door." A nod at Olga. "Thanks again."

Olga looked at William when she said, "You're welcome, Hugh. We're in this together, right?"

"They're pretty dumb anyway," Hugh said, clearly oblivious to Olga's undertones. Such a sensitive boy when they'd started national service, he now lived in his own world. "It didn't take much to drive them back. Thankfully there were only three of them."

William chewed the rest of his carrot, the loud crunch amplified through his skull. When he'd finished, he bit into the small sweetbread he'd been saving, the sugary taste swelling through him. While staring at the treat, he smiled. "This reminds me of my eighth birthday. We'd had an awful harvest that year, so rations were tighter than usual. I didn't expect much that day, but it turned out my mum and dad had been saving some of their food in the weeks leading up to it. They'd given me the normal rations so I wouldn't find out."

"They must have been starving," Olga said.

Heat flushed William's cheeks and his throat locked. He nodded and coughed through it. "Yeah. I couldn't believe it when I woke up to a table filled with food. There was more sweetbread than I could eat. I think I ate more that day than I had in the two weeks preceding it. It sounds greedy, and maybe I would have refused the gesture as an adult, but even as a kid I saw how much joy it gave them. They said it made their year. It was their way of showing how much they—" He stopped, his eyes burning. He rubbed his face and looked out over Edin.

Another bite of the sweetbread, his eyes now watering, William smiled again. "Every time I eat, especially sweetbread, it reminds me of that day."

A deep breath, William then looked at Matilda to see her eyes red and swollen, her lips buckling out of shape. "They were special people," she said.

"They were."

As the damp weight of his parents' loss eased, William took in his home district. The fields stretched away to the large wall encircling the city. The carriage shook from where Goliath stepped forward and back a few paces, although it seemed more from boredom than agitation. And who could blame him? Maybe an hour had passed, maybe more. Although spring, the evenings were still short, the sun having passed its zenith several hours previously.

A surprisingly observant Hugh started packing up one of their wooden boxes. They'd taken three from the storage house and filled them with food they could eat without cooking. "I reckon we need to move on if we're to get to the political district before dark."

Stomach full, his thirst sated, William helped the others as they followed Hugh's lead, packing up their feast. They had enough to last them a few weeks, longer if they rationed it.

William had eaten so much it almost hurt to lie on his front. The others on either side must have shared his discomfort. They all lay on their backs.

Returning to the main street, the gentle clop of the large horse tapped into William's post-feast drowsiness. They passed laundry on their left, the arena in the distance on their right. Then Hugh said, "Oh shit!"

Hugh's tone sent a tight clamp through William's full stomach, and he looked in the same direction as his friend. They hadn't been there moments before, but now, on the roofs, close to the road, stood about ten to fifteen boys and girls. All of them carried blades: some knives, some swords. A small army, they were ready to go to war.

Olga called it out. "The boys and girls from woodwork."

William tugged Goliath's right rein to give the gang a wide berth. "We just need to keep going. The road's wide enough to avoid them, and they'd be insane to get off the roofs."

One of the taller boys walked closer to the edge. "You've been making quite a noise with that horse of yours. We want it."

Although none of them replied to the boy, Matilda sat up,

the diseased on the road responding to her. "What the hell is that?" she said.

The squeak of wooden cartwheels announced the appearance of a carriage similar to the one they were on. No horse, it had two boys with swords on it. Several gang members on laundry's roofs used long poles to push it out in the road.

More squeaking from their right, another carriage got shoved out in front of them. It also had two armed passengers and butted up to the first carriage, blocking the road.

"They've got us surrounded," Olga said.

William looked back to see the same behind as in front: two carts with four passengers. "Shit!" What had started as about ten to fifteen kids on the roofs around them had now doubled. Two more carts appeared on their right, blocking access to agriculture.

"They clearly want us to go down there," Matilda said, nodding at an alley on their left.

"Do we have any other choice?" William said.

If any of them had ideas, they didn't offer them. William tugged on the left rein. "Goliath can get us out of here." His grip tightening, he said, "Hold on." A sharp flick of the reins, it was enough to tell the large stallion what he needed. Goliath charged at the alley into laundry, and William did his best to aim him down the middle of the road, giving them as much space on either side as possible.

But the gang didn't try to use their blades. They had rocks and stones in their hands. Too busy controlling Goliath, it took for Matilda to shove a box over William's head, blinding him, before he realised what they were doing. "You've just thrown the food away?"

A rock destined for his skull crashed against his impromptu wooden helmet, his ears ringing from the loud *boom!* Coupled with the sound of the runaway cart, if Matilda replied to him, he didn't hear it.

Trusting in Goliath, William held on, his body bouncing on the roof of the carriage like a bean on a drum.

A few seconds later, William removed the box in time to see they were on a collision course with a wall. A tight clench to his jaw, he pulled hard on the right rein, forcing a ninety-degree turn from the stallion.

Goliath made it around. The cart didn't. As the horse tried to drag them with it, the carriage tilted, the right side of it lifting before the whole thing tipped. William, Matilda, Olga, and Hugh flew from the roof, made weightless by the speed of their sudden sharp turn.

CHAPTER 37

The planet shook as William slammed into the dead-end wall. He hit the ground, the impact damn near realigning his skeleton. Surrounded by the shattered wood from Goliath's carriage and their spilled supplies, the ringing in his ears nearly deafened him. But nothing could mute the shrill call of death closing in on them. The diseased descended from all sides.

Legs barely able to support him, William stood up, one hand on the wall. It took two clumsy attempts to reach his sword handle and unsheathe it. The coppery taste of blood in his mouth, he spat crimson. To his left, Hugh and Olga dispatched the diseased with their usual deadly efficiency, Hugh with his sword, Olga with a baton. They'd need help soon. The diseased might have had inferior fighting skills, but the numbers were well in their favour.

William hadn't yet seen … "Matilda!" A pair of still legs poked from beneath the wrecked carriage. Several diseased charged up the road they'd ridden Goliath along. They must have seen her too.

Two wobbly steps, William found his stride before leaping the part of the carriage Matilda lay beneath. He headed straight for the diseased, leading with the tip of his sword, his momentum burying his blade in the front runner's chest. As he landed, his foot twisted on a piece of wood, and he only just held his balance, finding his footing so he stood ready to fight the others. Where one diseased fell, several filled its spot.

Before they got to him, William reached down and pulled the box from Matilda's head. He then spun around, bringing his sword in a wide arc before burying it into the neck of another diseased.

Two more strikes dropped two more diseased. It bought him a moment. Matilda remained on her back, staring at the sky through glazed eyes. Blood ran from her nose, covering her top lip. A line of it trickled from her right ear. William waved in case she couldn't hear him and enunciated his words as clearly as possible. "We can't stay here. You need to get up."

The Matilda he knew returned, clarity pushing through her daze as she nodded. William dropped another diseased before jumping back over the wrecked carriage. It partially blocked the road, giving him enough time to help Matilda to her feet.

Matilda stared towards Olga and Hugh. And why wouldn't she? The two of them together were a sight to behold. But what she said next rocked William's world more than the skeleton-jarring collision with the wall. "Goliath!"

He hadn't checked his horse. Goliath lay on his left side, what remained of the carriage still attached to him as he kicked out with his right front leg. It had snapped halfway down, the bottom of it swinging loose.

William navigated the debris to get to his horse. Goliath's nostrils flared. His wide ribs rose and fell with his quickened breaths. Although he knew Olga, Hugh, and Matilda were fighting the diseased, he only had eyes for his horse. They'd buy him the time he needed.

As William rested his palm against the side of Goliath's

sweating face, he whispered, "There, there, boy. Everything's going to be okay." Even as he said it, his clamping throat threatened to take his words away. Goliath's dark brown eyes fixed on him, a depth of understanding unlike any he'd seen before. The horse couldn't be lied to.

"*William!* We've got to move. We won't last long here." Maybe Hugh had said it several times already, his tone frantic, his sword swinging at the onrushing diseased.

Then William saw them. The front runners from woodwork had caught up, their blades glinting.

His hands shaking and damn near blinded by his tears, William unhooked Goliath's carriage and shoved the wooden bars free. Hacking, slashing, stabbing around him. A smell of the disease stronger than ever before. The metallic tang of blood mixed with rot and vinegar, the true curdling of an organism. But he needed to get Goliath out of there.

William ran back to his horse and pulled on its neck. "Come on, boy."

Goliath didn't move.

"*William*"—Olga this time; she cracked several skulls with her baton—"we need to get out of here."

"Come on, Goliath, get up."

Still Goliath remained on his side, a pool spreading out beneath him from where he let his bladder go.

"*Get up!*" William screamed, drowning out the cries around them. "Get up, you dumb beast."

Goliath closed his eyes, his large frame relaxing.

"No! Don't give up. We can get you out of here."

When someone touched his shoulder, William spun around as if to fight them. Matilda. She didn't say anything. She didn't need to. Instead, she stepped towards Olga and Hugh, who were moving off in the direction of a nearby alleyway. But she waited. She wouldn't go without him. Even if that meant death.

William's voice cracked. "I can't leave him."

"Look at him. He's done. He knows it."

Tittering laughter over the top of diseased's cries, a rock crashed down next to William from the gang on the roof. Matilda dropped two more diseased, blood spraying away from each of them in a wide arc.

A deep inhale, William stood over Goliath as more projectiles crashed against the ground. His entire body shook like he had hypothermia. "I'm sorry, boy. I shouldn't have made you turn so fast. I'm so sorry." He wiped his vision clear and looked into the deep brown eyes of his horse. The most noble being he'd ever met, he saw both pain and acceptance as if, even now, in the darkest moment when he should be looking after Goliath, Goliath was protecting him.

"*William*," Matilda said, rising panic in her tone.

His yell tearing at his sore throat, William screamed and drove his sword, tip first, into Goliath's head. The creature's skull more resilient than the many diseased he'd ended, it gave with a deep *pop*. A series of spasms snapped through Goliath before he fell limp.

Matilda had already set off after Olga and Hugh, more rocks and stones crashing down around them.

It was like he'd been slammed into the wall all over again. William's legs barely had the strength to carry him, but he pushed on, following his friends as a stampede approached from behind. The boys and girls from woodwork cackled like monkeys, trying to keep up with them as they tracked them from the roofs.

CHAPTER 38

Although Olga and Hugh streaked off ahead, Matilda moved at a slower pace to give William the chance to find his stride. His grief had turned his legs bandy, and he fought his lack of co-ordination with every step. As his tears dried, his view of their route cleared. Hugh and Olga led the way, the bulk of the diseased behind them and the woodwork gang stalking them from the roofs.

Like every district, laundry had a residential sector filled with one-storey houses. They zigzagged with no apparent direction. A maze that would have been easy to get lost in if they didn't have Olga. At present, they had to remain on the ground. Their lead over the diseased horde was a safer option than fighting the small army on the roofs.

But who knew what lay in wait, and the pack behind was drawing closer. William didn't need to turn around again to see how close. The thunder of steps grew louder. The heavy breathing. The screams.

Even over the furious diseased and cackling laughter of the gang, Matilda managed to send her voice towards their friends about twenty feet ahead. "We're running out of time, Olga."

A raised hand from Olga and nothing more. They needed to trust her.

His chest still tight from losing Goliath, no matter how many times William inhaled, he couldn't catch his breath. It didn't matter how much he trusted her, his body would give out soon.

Olga's plan suddenly unfolded in front of them as both she and Hugh, and then William and Matilda, burst out onto a wide street. Cobblestone like many of the main roads in Edin, it stretched at least twenty to thirty feet wide and ran away from them in both directions. Troughs of water lined the centre of the road, some of them serving as baths for diseased corpses.

Olga and Hugh moved fast, cracking and splitting the heads of the closest diseased. Their aggression and pace caught the creatures unawares, and they reached the other side of the road before scrambling up onto the roofs.

William ran one way around a trough in the middle of the road and Matilda the other while diseased closed in. The cobblestones uneven underfoot, stars swam in William's vision from where he still hadn't caught his breath.

But before they reached the buildings opposite, three narrow alleyways in front of them belched a stream of diseased. Hugh and Olga must have drawn them out.

Their way in front blocked, the diseased who'd chased them burst out behind. The ones on the right were close, the ones on the left closer. Matilda said, "Shit."

When Hugh pointed to their right, William and Matilda took his advice and ran. Only then did William see there were no alleys to run down and the houses that way were taller. Too tall.

Olga and Hugh tore across the rooftops and soon overtook them.

Hugh—now several houses ahead of them—lay on his front

on one of the rooftops. Olga crouched over the back of his legs as an anchor while he reached down with both hands.

The diseased behind were so close William could almost feel their hot breath on his neck. They had about a thirty-foot gap to the creatures ahead. The gang tracked their progress from the roofs on the opposite side of the road.

"You need to go up first," William said.

Matilda didn't argue. She climbed faster. She'd clear the route quicker like she did on their way to the gym's roof. She sped up, opening a small gap between them.

Matilda used Hugh like a rope, climbing to the roof in two fluid movements. William next, he grabbed his friend's hands and let Hugh drag him up.

His lungs tight, William fell on his back and panted at the sky. After a few seconds, he sat up, his entire body shaking. About thirty boys and girls from woodwork stood on the other side of the road. They remained armed, although knives and rocks had zero effectiveness with the gap separating them.

When Olga flipped them the bird, William stood up and did the same. He then turned his back on the gang and followed the fierce girl from laundry across the uneven roofs of her home's residential area.

CHAPTER 39

⁂

For about the next half an hour William and the others followed Olga's lead across laundry's rooftops. The setting sun in their eyes, they travelled at a manageable pace. It helped William to keep moving because every time they slowed down, thoughts of Goliath caught up to him. The diseased packed the main streets and had a presence in the narrower alleys. The creatures were everywhere, but the deeper they'd travelled into the city, the less densely they populated it. Had Goliath crashed in agriculture or woodwork, they wouldn't have made it out alive. They were yet to see the gangs from woodwork again.

Another check around, William said, "Do you think we've lost them?"

Although the other three also checked, none of them replied. Who'd want to say for sure?

Olga stopped on one of the buildings. It looked much like the others, another canted roof in the rickety sea. But it stood slightly taller than those surrounding it.

Her hands on her hips, her tanned skin glistening in the

fading sun, Matilda breathed heavily as she said, "What are we doing here?"

Instead of replying, Olga walked to the edge of the roof, dropped down to her knees, and lowered herself backwards off the building. A loud *crack* and she disappeared from their sight.

When William got to the edge, Olga looked back up at him from what appeared to be a loft. "Come down," she said.

Hugh went first, then Matilda. His body still weak, the rough tiles were tricky to hold on to, but William managed it, hanging down from the roof, his stomach turning backflips as his legs dangled. Someone then grabbed his belt and pulled him in. When he felt solid ground beneath his feet, he let his grip go and stepped into the open space.

White sheets, towels, and curtains everywhere. Before William could ask, Olga said, "This is one of the fabric storage houses where we keep freshly washed garments. Unless you know the district, you don't know they're here. They're amongst the few buildings that have lofts."

The only light came in from the small hatch Olga had kicked open. Matilda stood closest to it. "Why is this door here?"

"Two reasons," Olga said. "Ventilation for if the garments are still slightly damp, and sometimes it's easier to access the fabrics from the ground than to go through the building to get to them." After she'd used her feet to shuffle some of the sheets into a small mound, Olga fell onto them and lay on her back.

Matilda remained by the hatch. "So why are we here?"

Olga sat up. "It's getting late. We need to rest."

"What about Artan?"

"We need to rest. Besides, we can't create more sunlight. Give it another hour or two and it'll be dark out. I'm not confident I can find a better place than this in that time."

Matilda's cheeks had reddened and she shook her head. "We're too vulnerable here."

"As opposed to the streets outside?"

William felt Hugh's attention on him as if in a silent plea. If anyone could persuade Matilda to see reason, it was him.

Matilda shook her head. "No."

"No?" Olga stood up again.

"I'm not staying here. If Artan's locked in a cell—"

"Then he's safe," William said. All three of them turned his way, but he kept his focus on Matilda. "If he's in a cell, he's safe. The city only fell this morning, so he won't have been on his own for long. He'll be okay for the night."

"What about the state he's in?"

A flashback to when he'd been to see the boy, William scratched his head and sighed. "I'm not sure one extra night will make things much worse. Olga's right." His voice caught in his throat and he swallowed several times. "We don't have Goliath anymore. We can't move through the city as easily as we did. Here, we're hidden. We're away from the diseased and the gangs, and we have blankets in case it gets cold. We'll go first thing, but for now, we all need a rest—including you. Fatigue will make all of us sloppy."

No matter how he empathised with her current state, when Matilda fixed her narrowed eyes on William, it ran straight to his heart. She moved away from the hatch to the darkest corner of the loft. If she had to wait here for the night, she wanted to be left alone!

William moved over to the opposite corner, hiding in the shadows as he laid his sword on the floor before sitting down and pulling several sheets around him. Hidden from the others' sight, he ran through Goliath's last moments. Such a noble creature, his deep brown eyes had begged him for release and given him the permission to do it. It took for a tear to fall from his chin before he realised he was crying. The dark loft a blur around him, he let it all out.

CHAPTER 40

The hard rain woke William with a start, a knot like a hot coal beneath his left shoulder blade from where he'd leaned against the wall all night. The murky glow of a new day spread through the loft, a strong breeze filling the space with cool and fresh air. Matilda remained in the corner she'd picked the previous evening, Olga nearby. Both of them were still asleep.

Despite the weather, it didn't mask the steps on the roof above. "Hugh?" Olga stirred. Matilda remained motionless.

With slow movements, William pulled the sheets back and slipped from his impromptu bed, rolling his shoulders as if the action would be enough to rid his exhausted body of the aches inhabiting it. But they'd been driven deep into him, the collision with the wall enough to alter his posture for months.

The loft hatch opened inwards. It had made it much easier to access from the roof and allowed them to leave it gaping all night. Their only threat came from above, and if the gangs from woodwork couldn't see a hatch swinging away from the building, then how could they possibly find them?

The rain fell so hard it stung William's face. He opened his mouth to catch some of it. A muddy taste, but it would have to do, seeing as their supplies had hit the wall as hard as he had, and were no doubt now mashed into the wet ground surrounding Goliath's corpse.

Although he hadn't heard them over the rain, the sight of the diseased quickened William's pulse. A harsh reminder of what they still had to face. But at least they now only had the rest of laundry and then the square between them and the political district.

William reached up for the rough tiles. They were wet but coarse, so they wouldn't turn slick. He clamped his jaw against the stabbing beneath his left shoulder blade and kicked off from the loft, pulling himself up to see the roof. The second he did, he damn near lost his grip.

His legs swinging, the diseased giddy below, William pulled through his aches and reluctance, dragging himself onto the tiles.

On his feet, William walked towards Hugh, who stood in the centre of the roof. The short and powerful boy hadn't yet turned his way. Keeping out of his reach, he called to him, "Uh, Hugh?"

Seven bodies in total lay scattered around them. When Hugh finally lifted his face, his eyes were red and puffy, his mouth open a little.

Seven corpses were bad enough, but what Hugh had done to them sent a shudder through William. One of them, a boy who must have been several years younger than them, had been splayed like a butterfly pinned to a board. His arms and legs stretched wide; he'd been cut open along the centre of his body. His intestines had been dragged across the tiles.

Hugh's shaking hands were as covered in blood as his white lab coat. His hair soaked, rainwater dripped from the end of his nose.

Another body nearby, it took William a few seconds to identify the headless corpse as a girl.

When he looked up, William balked to find Hugh staring at him. His sword in his right grip, Hugh trembled. He finally closed his mouth, his teeth clamped shut, his jaw widened from the tight clench.

Loud enough to be heard over the rain, but desperate not to startle him, William said, "Hugh, what's going on, mate?"

Prior to Elizabeth's death, the Hugh currently on the roof had been a stranger to William. But as the days went on, Hugh's alter ego became more prominent. A stronger personality than the mole of a boy they'd met when they first arrived on national service. His glazed eyes sat somewhere between fear and fury.

In the face of such volatility, William held his hands up to urge calm. "Put your sword down."

Hugh's face buckled again and his voice broke. "Why?"

"You're scaring me, Hugh. Just put the weapon down and then we can talk, yeah?"

Clearly battling against himself, Hugh finally opened his hand, the sword hitting the wet tiles with a loud *clang!*

With slow, deliberate steps, William focused on his friend rather than the surrounding carnage. When he got close enough, he wrapped Hugh in a tight hug.

Hugh shook more than before. "I should have been there for Elizabeth. I should have been there when the woodwork gangs got her."

"But you didn't know her then."

"I should have. I should have known what the gangs were doing and done something about them. I lived in the district next door. I should have known."

"None of us knew about it, Hugh." The rain continued to drive nails against the top of William's head. "What happened? Where did these people come from?"

"I heard them in the night. They were a few roofs away. Maybe they didn't know where we were, but I didn't want to take the risk. It was dark enough for me to get onto the roof unseen. But I don't know who did this to the bodies afterwards, Spike, I really don't."

Before William spoke, Hugh took a sudden step back. The glaze returned as he spun on the spot to take in the carnage. "*I* did this. I can see that now. I killed my dad, I mutilated Sarge, *and* I let Elizabeth die."

"You *didn't* let Elizabeth die."

"But you know what scares me the most?"

William waited.

"Apart from Elizabeth, I've enjoyed it. The act isn't the worst part. It's when Hugh comes back to face what I've done."

"Who's here when Hugh's not?"

Hugh's eyes turned darker as he said, "The devil."

William fought to both remain on the roof with his friend and to get his words out. "You'll get back on track. A lot of people come back from national service with things to work out. And we've lost almost everyone."

"Thanks to me. *I* created this. *I* left the gates open. Nearly everyone in Edin is dead." He looked at the hellish massacre at their feet. "And then we left Max. Who are we to decide who we save and who we don't? The kids in the national service area and then Max? He's still in the labs; I know it."

A glance back to where he'd come from, William relaxed to see no one there. "You need to be quiet, Hugh. Olga can't find out what happened. It's suicide to try to get Max, and there's no guarantee he's still there anyway."

"Doesn't she have a right to know? Wouldn't you want to know if it was Matilda?"

"Know *what?* We don't know *anything* for certain."

"Wouldn't you want to know?"

"Look, all we can do now is clean you and this mess up. We were going to be attacked in the night and you saved us, that's a good thing. The girls don't need to see what you've done to the bodies, do they?"

Hugh frowned and looked around while scratching his head. The glaze had left him again. "Oh dear, I've really done this, haven't I?"

"Come on." William reached down and picked up a severed arm and leg before walking across the roofs of several houses to a small alley. The diseased looked up in time to get the body parts in their faces. When Hugh threw the headless corpse of the girl off after him, William said, "Hopefully this will serve a purpose."

"How?"

"If the gangs see it, they'll think twice about following us. Now take that lab coat off."

Hugh did as he said and tossed the coat into the alley.

Of the bodies around them, William found one of a similar build to Hugh. The boy lay on his front with his rear end in the air. It took all he had not to look at where Hugh had shoved the machete. He rolled the boy over and removed his top. He couldn't look at Hugh as he handed him the garment. How long would it be before the devil returned? And when it did, would it turn on them?

∼

AFTER ABOUT TEN MINUTES, THEY'D CLEARED THE BODIES FROM the roof. The rain had done a good job at washing most of the blood away. William rubbed his hands on his trousers as if wiping them would somehow remove the experience from his psyche. A machete in his hand, he showed it to Hugh. "At least Olga has a better weapon now." They just needed to make sure she didn't know where it had been. "Are you ready to go back to the girls?"

Hugh frowned, his eyes red from crying. He then nodded.

"Right, we'll tell them you saved us, because you did. You killed several people, and now we need to move on."

When Hugh didn't reply, William said, "Right?"

Hugh nodded. "Right."

William went first, kneeling down on the roof and sliding off it backwards, letting his legs hang down until his feet found the floor of the loft below. Hopefully, Hugh wouldn't feel the need to talk about his guilt surrounding Max and the labs. On top of everything else, that was the last thing they needed.

CHAPTER 41

The rain had stopped, the sun breaking through the dense grey clouds. Not quite a jog, but they'd been on the move for about twenty minutes, their pace quick enough for William to be sweating beneath his clothes. They spoke little, all of them on high alert for the gangs from woodwork. As of yet, none had shown themselves. They'd known about Goliath, so hopefully they'd used that same ability to spy on them to witness what Hugh had done. If that didn't keep them away, nothing would.

Hugh set the pace, jumping alleyways as he moved from roof to roof. Although William, Olga, and Matilda followed, they were at least thirty feet behind. Far enough back for Olga to speak freely. "What are you not telling me?"

"Huh?" Had Hugh told her about Max? William looked at Matilda. "Uh … what do you mean?"

"Come on, we can see Hugh's lost the plot again. What did he do to those kids from the gangs?"

Even as the memory of the massacre flashed through his mind, William relaxed. A grisly thought, but better than admitting the truth about Max. It didn't matter how often he told himself the lie, the chances were Max was still locked in a cell in the labs. Were he back there now, he'd do more to free him, but they were too far away to do anything to help.

"*Well?*" Olga said. "What did he do?"

"Whatever it was, you think they didn't deserve it?"

"Oh, no, I'm sure they deserved it. My concern isn't for them. It's obvious that Hugh's losing the plot. Who knows what he'll do in his current frame of mind. What if he turns on us?"

"He won't."

"You know that?"

"I promise you he won't."

"How can you make that promise?"

"I trust him."

"That's not a reason for us to trust him."

"*Us?*"

"Matilda agrees with me."

An apologetic wince, Matilda lifted her shoulders with a slight shrug. "At what point does he become too much of a liability?"

"Shit," William said and halted. He then drew his sword. "We should have been paying more attention."

At least fifteen boys and girls from woodwork blocked Hugh's way. William jogged to catch up with him. One of the boys stepped forward. A tall lad with a shaved head, the sun bounced off his pale scalp. His blue eyes glared almost as bright. "We saw what you did to the others."

"They shouldn't have followed us," Hugh said, the slow ring of steel as he drew his sword.

Olga and Matilda caught up, Matilda with her sword drawn and Olga gripping her machete.

The tall and bald boy held Hugh's glare, his tone flat. "Well, *we've* followed you."

"I thought the threat was implicit in my response," Hugh said.

A vacant wash travelled across the boy's face before Hugh sighed. "You've enunciated the point I was making. It seems like I need to be more direct with you. Spell it out and maybe speak using words with fewer syllables. *You* shouldn't have followed us because you saw what happened to those who did. Do you understand now?"

The bald boy's face twisted and he charged, the gang rushing forward with him. Before William or the girls reacted, Hugh ran to meet his attackers. Fast and with deadly accuracy, he slashed his sword across the throat of their leader, dragging a line of blood away from the bald kid's neck.

As the boy fell, rolling over when his momentum continued to carry him forwards, Hugh took two more down, predicting their moves like they were as easy to read as the diseased. The gangs had been bullies for their entire lives. They didn't understand combat, and it showed.

By the time William, Matilda, and Olga had moved forward to join the fight, Hugh had taken down nearly half the gang, and the others had backed off. And why wouldn't they? Especially when Hugh had ignored the very real threat of those still standing and went to work on those he'd already dropped. He hacked and slashed, removing hands, feet, and heads, even from the ones who'd clearly passed. While he did it, he shouted, "This is for you, Elizabeth. These gangs won't be able to harm anyone else."

Nine members of the gang left, by the time he'd finished mutilating the fallen, Hugh backed them towards the edge of a roof at laundry's perimeter. A drop of several feet to the ground below, William heard the diseased waiting for something to feast on.

"Please," one of the nine said. "We'll go. Just let us go."

The drop from the roof landed in the square, the only thing between them and the political district. It took for them to get this close for William to see the wooden wall where there hadn't been one before the city fell.

His sword pointed at the kids from the gang, Hugh stepped towards them. He shook when he shouted, the diseased below falling momentarily silent at the loud outburst. "On your knees and drop your weapons."

Whatever had happened to him when Elizabeth died, it gave him a drive unlike anything William had seen. It had turned him almost superhuman. The gang fell to their knees.

"Now drop your weapons."

The clang of several machetes and knives hit the tiles.

"Over the side, you morons."

All nine of them—the once brave thugs of the gang—were reduced to subservient pets in the face of Hugh's rage. They all threw their weapons over the side.

"Now hands behind your heads."

One of the gang members Hugh had already dropped lay nearby. Still just about alive, she groaned as she tried to stand up on her one remaining leg. Olga hacked a deep cut into her neck.

Closer to Hugh, William again took in the square stretching out in front of them. The cage in the centre of it, rotting heads of the diseased on the spikes in the middle. The benches the lovers sat on. A lump lifted in his throat. Mr. P didn't deserve that treatment. If he ever saw Robert Mack again ...

"How are we going to get across?" Matilda said.

There were as many diseased in the large square as anywhere else. Too many. As William traced the route from one side of the square to the other, he sighed. "There's nowhere to hide from them, and what's that wooden wall about?"

Olga pointed across the main road at the structure in the distance. "What about the arena?"

"What about it?" William said.

"It might be a better route to the political district."

"How?" Matilda said.

"We might be able to use it to get over the wall. It's right next to it."

Matilda shook her head. "But how will we get there?"

"Hugh?" Olga said.

The same glaze William had seen too many times fixed on Olga. A distance in his dark eyes. The devil had returned.

"Can you get these clowns over to the main road?"

"They'll do whatever I need them to."

"Okay," Olga said, "I have a plan."

"You heard her," Hugh said to the gang, directing where they should go with a flick of his sword.

The gang stood up and walked off in single file. William spoke to Olga from the side of his mouth. "Good job we had Hugh to help us then, eh?"

CHAPTER 42

About ten feet from the edge of the roof, William stood with Olga and Matilda while Hugh moved closer to the street and lined up the woodwork gang. He made them kneel and face the main road as if they were about to be executed. The diseased grew louder at the sight of them.

"Please," one of them said, a short girl with blonde hair, "I have a baby brother who needs me. His name's James."

William's heart sank and he turned away as Hugh kicked her in the back. The excited diseased below smothered and then silenced her screams.

The girl now one of them, the diseased quieted while Matilda muttered, "If she'd have said any other name ..."

Hard to tell from where he stood, but William expected to see the dark glaze in Hugh's eyes. They might have been a gang, and they might have done horrible things, but they were still people. The Hugh he'd met in the dining hall would have made that distinction.

The eight remaining captives knelt with their heads bowed, and many of their shoulders bobbed with their tears.

"Okay," Hugh said. When he turned to Olga, his eyes were so dark, William stepped back a pace. "What now?"

Her hand raised to implore patience from the short and stocky boy, Olga said, "Not yet, but in a minute we're going to throw them off."

The girl's scream still echoing through his mind, William said, "*What?*"

"You think they deserve better? They're bullies and rapists. I'm not one for capital punishment, but they came with the intention of *killing* us. They killed Goliath."

"So we play God and kill them?"

"Look around, William. You think God lives in this place? If she does, she'd best show up soon. Until then, I think we need to make the decisions. We can't leave them alive because they'll come after us again, so we might as well use their deaths to serve a purpose."

"What purpose?"

"You haven't worked it out yet?"

Matilda cut through their conversation and pointed at the arena on the other side of the road. "While the diseased are focused on them, we can make a break for it."

"You agree with her?"

"I think it's the best plan we have."

One eye on his prisoners, Hugh stepped closer to William and the others. His face blank, his eyes dark, he spoke in monotone. "I'll do it."

Although he didn't look directly at her, William couldn't avoid the smugness emanating from Olga. "We're fighting for our lives and you're happy about scoring points?"

"I just think it's the best plan. I'm happy the majority agrees."

The fire died in William. He could hardly claim democracy only when it suited him. "Fine, but there's no way Hugh's doing all the dirty work. Not again." The mess on the roof above the loft flashed through his mind. "We'll all do it."

Throwing the girl over the side had left them with two prisoners each. William stood on the far left between two, Matilda next to him, Hugh farther along, and then Olga on the other end. The girl who claimed to have a brother now bled from her eyes. She'd become just another rancid freak in the crowd.

"Now, this can play out two ways," Olga said. "You either jump down of your own free will and try to outrun the diseased, or we shove you down. Whatever happens, you're all going over the edge so we can get to the arena. Wha—"

Before Olga finished, one of the kids from the gang jumped from the roof. Landing in the mosh pit of snarling diseased, he threw punches and shoved several creatures as he bolted in the direction of the arena, dragging the ravenous and uncoordinated crowd with him. Although quick, the diseased were quicker. He lasted just three paces before he vanished beneath a scrum of writhing bodies.

"Well," Olga said, "I think your friend there just showed us you can't be trusted—"

"We can." The girl in front of Olga looked up, her nose running, her eyes puffy. She had dirty brown hair and acne. "Just give us a—"

The girl screamed as she fell, driven from the edge of the roof by Olga's hard kick. The diseased jumped on her when she hit the ground.

Matilda cried as she kicked her two off, William and Hugh following suit.

"Remember," Olga shouted while sprinting off across the roof, "they came to us with the intention of doing much worse. Think of the suffering those gangs have caused. They wanted to hurt us."

Olga led them away from the carnage below. She maintained her pace, the first of them to jump down to the cobblestone street. Hugh, Matilda, and then William followed her over.

The gang had bought them seconds, no more. The instant Olga hit the ground, the creatures around them yelled. The kids from woodwork already dealt with, the mob now turned their focus on William and his friends. As much as they'd worked together to get to this point, they were now on their own until they reached the arena.

Olga in the lead, her machete proved more useful than a sword when on the run. She dealt with several diseased without missing a beat.

One of the vile creatures charged William from the left. He avoided its snapping jaws, shoving it in the chest. The impact drove a foul stench from the beast's lungs, but sent it stumbling backwards.

Half a mind on Matilda, William fought to keep his attention ahead. The road no wider than forty feet, it felt like they had miles to cross.

Because they had to dodge and weave on their way to the other side, the pack they'd whipped into a feeding frenzy closed the distance on them.

Still ten feet or so from the arena, William saw the doors and fought to get his words out. "It's locked!"

Olga, as the leader, altered their course slightly. They'd have to head to agriculture instead. If they got on the roofs, they could reassess.

"Wait!" Hugh pointed at the arena.

Although the main gates were closed, a gap had been smashed through the top of them. Large enough for them to fit and at least ten feet from the ground, so the diseased couldn't follow.

Olga reached the doors first, kicking off the wooden barrier before diving through the hole. Who knew what waited on the other side, but with the creatures behind them, they had to take their chances.

Hugh reached it next, but he turned, yelled, and dropped three diseased in quick succession as Matilda followed Olga into the arena.

Were Hugh not smiling, William would have waited, but he knew he'd meet resistance from his friend if he tried to help. The gate boomed as he kicked off it, and he too pulled up and then dived through the gap.

Where William expected the landing to drive the wind from his lungs, he fell on something soft, several strange faces looking down on him before a large man dragged him out of the way. Hugh landed where he'd been only seconds before.

The man who'd dragged William clear had long curly black hair, bulging arms, and a grin filled with stark white teeth. They were all the whiter in contrast to his deep brown skin. Yet, despite his sunny demeanour, it stood in stark contrast to the sword he'd levelled at William's face.

CHAPTER 43

"Stay there, boy." If anything, the large man's winning smile broadened. The tip of his sword hovered just an inch from William's nose. "Now, while you're lying there, I'd like to welcome you to one of the last diseased-free spots in Edin. As long as you don't turn, we can offer you sanctuary."

"T-turn?" William said. Matilda, Hugh, and Olga were also held at sword point, Hugh still on the mattress, the others dragged free like William had been. The shiny tip so close to Matilda's face quickened his pulse, driving his response. "What the hell are you talking about, and what do you want with us?"

But the grinning man didn't answer. A more level head in that moment than William's, they both needed him to settle the situation.

About five minutes passed before a bell rang and the grinning man pulled his sword away. He offered William his hand.

The ease with which the man brought him upright tamed what remained of William's fury. Not only did the brute have a sword, but he had the kind of strength that would break William's neck should he have the inclination. William walked over to Matilda. "Are you okay?"

The woman who'd held a sword to Matilda's face backed off several steps, and before anyone else spoke, the smiling man clapped his hands once. "Right, now we can get off on a better footing. My name's Samson. I'd like to welcome you to the arena. Like I said earlier, this is one of the last places in Edin that isn't infected with the disease."

Samson walked towards the ring, and they followed, William and Matilda holding hands.

Upon entering the circular fighting area, William's mouth fell open and he spun on the spot. The stone seating stretched up and away from them in all directions. The amount of times he'd imagined himself here ...

Matilda's grip tightened, pulling William back into the moment. He found Samson still grinning at him and said, "I never thought I'd get to be in this spot. I mean, as a kid, I dreamed about it every night, but with everything that's happened ..." The words caught in his throat and his eyes burned with his tears. After rubbing them, he let go of a hard sigh. "This certainly wasn't how I expected it to play out."

The touch of Matilda's hand against his back lifted William, and he filled his lungs, wiping his eyes again. "Sorry, it's been a long few days."

Samson raised an eyebrow. "Hasn't it just."

Several people approached the group with cups of water and chunks of bread. William's hand shook as he took a sip, and the bread caught in his tight throat when he tried to swallow.

Seeing them drink and eat appeared to lift Samson's already buoyant mood. "Your arrival makes ninety-six of us now. Four more until one hundred."

"And what then?" Olga said.

Samson laughed. "Dunno."

The dark glaze remained in Hugh's eyes. "How can you be so happy?"

"I'm alive." Samson slapped Hugh on the back, the short and stocky boy remaining rooted to the spot where many would have stumbled. "That's got to count for something, right? Again, sorry about how we just welcomed you. We set the gates up so only the uninfected could get in, but we had a few who brought the disease in with them and then changed. We nearly lost everything because of it, so we put all new arrivals through a five-minute quarantine to be sure they're okay. How have you still survived? I was starting to lose hope in anyone else getting here."

As William opened his mouth, Samson cut him off. "You know what? I'm sure it's a long and stressful story that you don't need to be recounting right now. All in good time, eh?"

The touch of Matilda's hand left his back, and William watched her step closer to Samson. "Look, we're here on our way to the political district."

"Then you're about as shit out of luck as the rest of us, young lady."

"What do you mean?"

"Come with me."

Samson led Matilda towards a set of ladders leading up to the seating area.

Samson's booming voice called out around the arena for everyone to hear. "So why do you want to get into the political district?"

"My brother's in there."

"Still?"

"Yep."

"How can you be so sure?"

"He was in prison when the city fell."

"Oh."

"Yeah. He killed my dad."

"Wow. Look, you don't have to tell me …"

William knew everything about what had happened with Matilda's family. As she explained it to Samson, it was probably the first time she'd been able to run through it from start to finish and process what had happened to her. From the way Olga watched her, she was taking it all in too, probably piecing the story together from the fragments they'd given her during the chaos of trying to stay alive.

At the top of the arena, Matilda out of breath from talking all the way up, William finally stood next to her and held her hand again. She squeezed back with a trembling grip.

Several rocks had been placed at the foot of the back wall. They stepped up on them and peered over. Olga said it best. "Shit."

They'd seen the wooden wall from laundry, but their new vantage point showed them the second one behind it. There was a gap of fifteen to twenty feet between the two. The gap was filled with at least two hundred diseased. And hanging over the first wall—

"They've had this defence plan for years." A woman's voice, William turned to see the receptionist from the justice department building. "They were worried the city would fall, so they built the first wooden wall to stop the diseased getting through. They were also worried about woodwork rioting, so they built the second one. The first blocks the diseased, the gap between the two keeps the people back. The only way to open and close them is from inside the political district."

At any other time, it would have thrown William off to see the receptionist, but he couldn't take his eyes off the first wall, and more specifically ... "Why have they—?"

"Hung people over the side?"

About every six feet, a diseased hung down from the first wall. Women, men, and children. They had nooses around their necks, twisting and turning, grabbing at the ropes as if they could work them free. "Hung diseased over the side," William corrected.

"They weren't diseased when they were thrown over." The receptionist had a scarf around her neck. When she pulled it down, both Matilda and Olga gasped. Angry rope burns, each one at least an inch thick. "That was the part of the plan the political district kept from us. They wanted to drag the diseased close to the first wall as quickly as possible, and what better way than to use bait?"

"But why them? Why you?" Olga said.

"Because we weren't one of them. Politicians look after their own. They'll throw anyone else to the dogs in a heartbeat if it elevates themselves. Cleaners, cooks, receptionists, we were nothing but cannon fodder to them."

Matilda's jaw hung loose. "How did you get away?"

"They didn't tie my rope properly." The receptionist laughed. "Guess I was one of the lucky ones, eh? There were easier pickings, so I managed to get away and into the arena while the diseased were preoccupied."

"How did we not know about this?" Hugh said.

"The walls are retractable so they were easy to hide."

Matilda this time. "And where are the controls for the walls?"

"The justice department building."

The large building backed up against the wall closest to the political district. William had been there several times already. "You remember me, right?"

The receptionist nodded.

"The boy I came to visit a few times, he never got evicted, did he?"

She shook her head.

"Is he still in there now?" Matilda said. "He's my brother."

The woman's face softened. "I'd imagine so. As far as I

know, they didn't let any of them out. They saw them as dangerous criminals. It was easier to keep them locked up."

"Well, that's something at least," William said. "Are you going to try to get back into the political district?"

The receptionist shook her head. "Hell no, my family are from woodwork."

"My god," William said. "We've heard a lot about that place in the past few days."

The woman lifted her shirt to reveal a star-shaped scar, the damaged tissue white against her brown skin. "Working for the politicians was the only way out. It was only a slight improvement, to be honest, but I was safe."

"Damn. I'm sorry."

"You didn't do it."

A slight lull in the conversation, William said it without thinking. "I'm not a homophobe, you know?"

The receptionist dipped a nod at him before walking away from the group. Although William felt the attention of the others, he didn't elaborate. What the receptionist thought of him hardly mattered.

"So what are we going to do?" Olga said. "There's no way we're getting through that lot. Climbing the walls won't be a problem, but none of us will make it through that mob to the second wall."

The same glaze in Hugh's eyes, William saw he was about to drop them in it and spoke first. "We could go through the tunnels?"

Olga shook her head. "The tunnels are compromised. I saw hundreds of diseased chasing people into them in agriculture."

"Besides," Samson added, "part of the political district's plans were to collapse the tunnels so nobody could get through. You need someone who can walk amongst the diseased."

William's heart sank, and before he could say anything,

Olga shrugged. "Max is the only person I know who can do that."

Both Hugh and Matilda fixed on William. A few seconds later, Olga looked at him too.

His stomach dropping to his knees, William pulled down a dry gulp and said, "Olga, there's a chance Max is still alive."

CHAPTER 44

The second he said it, William stepped back from Olga. Her face puce, her fists balled, her words trembled when she said, "What the *hell*?" The large arena amplified her fury.

Heat flushed William's cheeks and he did his best to ignore the onlookers. Because he'd been the one to say it, he faced the full force of her wrath. "Look, we don't know for sure, but there's a *chance* Max is still alive. But we don't know."

"What? Why?" Spittle sprayed from Olga's mouth and she threw her hands up in the air. "Just tell me what's going on."

The wind blew stronger because they were at the top of the arena, so William had to speak loudly enough for everyone to hear. "It's *possible* Max is still in a cell in the labs."

"Why am I only finding out about this now?"

Matilda stepped forward. "We thought we were protecting you."

"By *lying* to me?"

When Hugh put his hand on Olga's shoulder, she shook him off and glared at him. Even he stepped away. "I know the labs well. The cell they have Max in is lined with metal. The only way in is through a locked door."

"So we unlock it."

William this time. "The locked door is at the end of a tight corridor filled with diseased. None of us could make it through there without getting turned."

"But now you need to get to Artan, and you need Max for it, suddenly you can do it?"

"It's not like that," Matilda said.

"It sounds very like that to me."

"When we were in the labs," Matilda said, "we saw how hard it was to get to Max. Hugh still hadn't checked on his family, William hadn't checked his parents, and I needed to get to Artan. We'd not seen Max to confirm he was in the cell—"

"Although you had a pretty good idea he would be?" Olga said.

"Maybe, but like with the people in ceramics, and like with the rookies in the national service area—"

Olga's face had grown redder as she leaned towards Matilda. "Rookies in the national service area?"

Still the closest of the three to her, Hugh sighed and ran a hand over the top of his head. "There were some rookies on the roof of a dorm in the national service area. They needed help, but we left them because we couldn't take them with us."

"The point is," Matilda said, "people have died in this city. *Lots* of people. People we know. And there are people we can or could have saved, but to do that would be to jeopardise the lives of those we love. We care about Max, of course we do, but—"

"He's not as important to you as your loved ones?"

Matilda shrugged. "You know what? I know it sounds cold—"

"Stone cold."

Tears stood in Matilda's eyes. "It's hung over us since

we've left him, but my main reason for being in this *damn* city is to get to Artan. *Nothing* can get in the way of that. Nothing."

"So why didn't you tell me when you met me? Why did you lie?"

"To save you—"

"What? From myself? To stop me doing something stupid? Don't patronise me, Matilda."

Tears now ran freely down Matilda's cheeks. "No, to save you from having to live with the guilt of leaving Max in the labs. The same guilt we've had to live with. If you'd have gone back on your own, which you would have done because we needed to move forward and wouldn't have come with you, you would have reached the same conclusion and walked away. You didn't need that burden."

"Or you would have died trying," Hugh said.

"Well, maybe I'm smarter than you lot and would have found a way."

Preoccupied with the argument, William had stopped noticing the people in the arena until that moment. Samson and the lady from the justice department close by, a lot of the other survivors had closed in around them too.

Where Olga had been fully committed to her rage, her face slightly softened, her eyes pinching as if she could see into Matilda. "So what's changed?"

"What we've seen over there." Matilda pointed in the direction of the political district. "It's changed everything. We need Max to free Artan. We now have to take the risk to save him, no matter how dangerous it is. I'm not sure how it'll work out, and I'm not sure we'll all come away from it alive, but he's our only hope."

Despite the muscles in Olga's face contorting, she accepted Matilda's comments with the slightest of nods. "So what are we waiting for?"

CHAPTER 45

One of the tallest structures in Edin, the arena still had nothing on some of the collapsed buildings in the devastated city beyond the walls. William fixed on the wrecked civilisation on the horizon. It seemed like a lifetime ago when he'd been a wandering madman, killing diseased in the ruins on the hill while calling his lover's name. The creatures on the road below snapped him out of it, shambling around as they bumped into one another. They were oblivious to anything beyond their own torment. They wouldn't be oblivious for long, not when William and his friends tried to get to the roofs in agriculture.

Samson had dropped a rope ladder over the top of the arena. It lay flat against the rough wall and ran all the way to the ground. The political district behind them, they were about to head back the way they'd come. They needed to return to the labs.

Although he'd tied the ladder, Samson held it with a tight grip as if to offer them reassurance. "You ready?"

Instead of replying to him, William looked over the edge again, his stomach turning backflips. They had a descent of about twenty feet. One slip and the cobblestones would shatter their bones like they were ceramic.

Again, Samson took the lead. He'd done this before. "You need to hide so the diseased don't see you."

William and the other three dropped down, Samson crouching and sitting on the ground with them. One of the ninety-four survivors stood in the ring, awaiting Samson's instruction.

After a final look at William, Matilda, Hugh, and Olga, Samson nodded and raised his thumb. The woman in the ring passed the gesture on to an unseen survivor down the tunnel by the gates.

The sound started low on account of it being so far away. The rattling of metal: pots, pans, cutlery, and even weapons. A cargo net of noise, they'd shown it to William and the others before hanging it out through the hole in the gates they'd used to enter the arena.

Shrieks and screams were drawn to the sound, but as William went to stand up, a strong grip dragged him back down again. Were it anyone else but the permanently jovial Samson, he might have been more put out, but he accepted the man's greater strength and experience.

A smile as large as any William had seen, Samson said, "Sorry to pull you down like that, my man, but you need to give the diseased a moment to get out of the way before you show your face. If just one of them sees you, it'll take a lot longer to get you out of here." A slight pause, he went on, "Also, I wanted to say good luck. I hope we see you again. You're always welcome back here." A few seconds' pause, he nodded. "Okay"—he squeezed his grip on William's shoulder—"go and get your friend back."

William stood up first and peered over the side. The road now empty of diseased, the shambling beasts were all flocking towards the front of the arena down the main road on their right. Why had he chosen to go first? But he couldn't back out now. Fighting his shaking limbs, he climbed over the top and hung his legs down. The rough stone scratched his stomach as he lay across it and let his feet swing until they found a ladder rung. The small wooden bars made poor footrests because they lay against the wall of the arena. They stuck out an inch or two at best, but they were all they had.

As William descended, he focused on his grip, the ladder pinching the backs of his fingers between the wooden bars and the rough wall.

Slow progress, cuts ripping where skin met stone, William made it to the ground, drew his sword as quietly as he could, and waited while more diseased tore down the main road just thirty feet away.

Matilda joined William next and also unsheathed her weapon. Olga followed her. They hadn't said as much to Hugh, but they wanted him on the ground last so he didn't start a one-man crusade against all the diseased in Edin. The boy could be trusted to fight, but not to make any judgement calls.

The rattling rush of metal continued to distract the diseased, the gap between the arena and agriculture still free of the creatures.

Olga led the way and, as the last one up, William let Matilda and Hugh drag him onto the building's roof. While fighting against his quickened breaths, he looked up at the beaming Samson and raised both thumbs. "Well, that was much easier than I expected."

"I'm not sure we'll be saying that again," Olga said.

They all waved their thanks at Samson before setting off across the roofs of agriculture at a jog.

CHAPTER 46

Olga stood with her hands on her hips, staring across the main road in agriculture, her chest rising and falling from where the run had left her breathless. They'd been on the move for about an hour. "Are you sure there's no other way?"

"Certain," William said. The road was too wide to cross without going to ground, but they had no better options. The main road running through Edin stretched wider than the one in front of them. In the other direction, they had the fields of agriculture, which were as populated with the diseased as anywhere else, and the open space gave them nowhere to hide.

Before anyone spoke, William moved to the edge of the roof, inciting hatred from the mob below. If he looked hard enough, he'd recognise some of the faces.

When Matilda approached William, he raised a halting hand at her. "Stay back. I'm going to distract them. When I've pulled enough over to me, drop down into one of the alleys and sprint across, okay?"

Matilda moved away from him and back to the others.

"You horrible bastards," William said to his sea of fans. "You disgusting cretins. You're revolting, you know that?"

Maybe they knew what he said, but more than likely, their impassioned reaction came from their desire to drive the disease into his system.

William had no chance of completely clearing a path for the others, they knew that, and as much as he would like to tell them when they should go, they were better equipped to decide when to risk their lives. They could see the road well enough to make their own choices.

But instead of dropping into an alley like they'd planned, Hugh ran at the edge of the roof and jumped off, landing on the cobblestone road, the slap of his feet calling to the diseased.

William cupped his mouth with his hands. "Hugh! What the hell are you doing?"

Olga and Matilda followed the stocky boy, dropping to the main road and running after him. Why didn't they wait? "You should have let me distract them again!" But William's calls were drowned out by the diseased seeing their new targets.

Where Hugh had already crossed the road and ran down an alley, the diseased following him closed that option off to Olga and Matilda. Instead, they vanished down a different path. William lost sight of them, his heart on overdrive.

First Hugh appeared on the roof on the other side, and then Olga. But no Matilda.

Still no sign of his love, William saw the road was about as clear as it would get from where the creatures had followed his friends. When Olga waved him across, he hesitated. But staying put wouldn't help anyone. William leaped down from the roof, his sword ready as he took off towards the one-storey buildings on the other side.

The first alarm went off, a diseased spotting him and letting the others know. The gap from him to the wall no more than six feet, he sheathed his sword as the creatures closed in on him. If it came down to a fight, he'd lose. He jumped for the roof of the next building.

Hugh's strong grip reached down and took a handful of William's shirt before dragging him up.

Still no sign of Matilda, William shoved Hugh, who stumbled back several paces before falling on his arse. "What the hell? Why didn't you wait for them?"

Although Hugh stared up at William, he said nothing, tears in his glazed stare.

When Olga—several roofs away—bent down and pulled up Matilda, William sprinted over to the pair. The uneven tiles made his feet twist and turn.

He wrapped Matilda in a tight hug. "Are you okay?"

Still out of breath from her escape, Matilda squeezed him, leaned into his neck, and pressed the softest kiss against it. "I'm fine."

CHAPTER 47

William grabbed Hugh by the tops of his arms and leaned in to force eye contact.

His friend looked anywhere but at him. "What are you doing, William?"

Were his eyes darker than usual?

"You're freaking me out."

There seemed little point in trying to second-guess Hugh's madness unless William wanted to go down with it. He had to take the boy at face value and give up trying to predict the unpredictable. "We nearly died the last time we tried this." They'd moved across the roofs from agriculture to textiles and now stood directly opposite the labs, Edin's main road between them. "We're going to leave you behind to attract the diseased so we can cross. When we get to the other side, we'll distract them so you can make a break for it, okay?"

"I *was* there the last time, you know?"

"Were you?"

"What's that supposed to mean?"

William searched for the dark glaze before he let go of a hard sigh. He turned to watch woodwork burn, thick smoke billowing into the air. "When I say we nearly died last time, what I mean is *you* nearly screwed it up for us."

"*I* pulled you to safety."

"But by jumping off the roof before the others, you jeopardised Matilda and Olga's chances. Do I really have to explain that to you?"

The devil had jumped from the roof, not Hugh. William watched the realisation of it play across his friend's face in his slackening features. His brown eyes fell to the dark slate tiles at his feet. "I'm sorry. I'll make sure it doesn't happen again."

Although William wanted to reassure him, what could he say? Don't worry, you're losing your mind, but hopefully it's not permanent? Hopefully you won't get yourself and us killed in the process?

The girls had watched the conversation, both of them frowning. When Matilda tilted her head to the side to question their choice, William nodded. They could trust him—at least he hoped they could. "Right, Hugh, when you're ready—"

Hugh let go of a call so loud William instinctively went for his sword. The short and stocky boy stamped his feet, cracking several tiles as he marched away, clapping his hands as he went. Veins stood out on his neck, his face a glowing beacon of crimson. He shook with the effort of driving his words out. "Come over here, you diseased pricks. Come and taste my sweet blood if you can get me."

It worked, the calls and cries from the packed main road rising in volume. Vacant expressions with slack jaws followed the boy's progress across the roof.

William, Matilda, and Olga were standing far enough back to remain out of sight, but as Hugh led the beasts away, William stepped forward for a better look. They had a relatively clear run across the thirty feet of cobblestones. After that, they needed to get into the corridor created by the lab's wooden fences and far enough down to get on the roof of the building. A more ambitious run than any they'd tried before, but what other choice did they have? No Goliath this time, and they needed to get Max out of there.

With Matilda beside him and Olga beside her, William held Matilda's hand and squeezed. Best to keep the noise down, he looked at the two girls. Both of them nodded, so he drew his sword, Matilda doing the same, and Olga keeping a tight grip on her machete. He held his hand up, using his fingers to count down. Three … two … one …

Several feet of tiles between them and the edge, William sprinted across the uneven surface. He leaped from the roof and landed on the cobblestones below. The diseased close to them yelled, but most of them were in the pack following Hugh over one hundred feet away.

As much as William wanted to check on Matilda, they were in this for themselves until they made it to the other side. He needed to give her the same respect she gave him. She'd make it. She had it in her. As Matilda opened up a lead on both him and Olga, he nodded to himself. Of course she'd make it.

William swung his sword at the first diseased to get too close. The tip of his blade sliced its throat. It went down screaming. He slammed his right forearm into the chest of the next one and shoved it away.

A dense cloud of black smoke from woodwork cut across their path. It momentarily suffocated William, but he pushed on, his lungs tight, his legs moving on autopilot. Bursting out the other side of the dark fog, he entered the entrance to the labs, chasing his breaths to fill his lungs again.

Several steps into the tight corridor, William slowed down. A horde larger than the one Hugh had dragged away charged at him. They weren't going to make it. At least, he wouldn't make it.

Matilda passed the end of the tall wooden fence, reaching the building they'd climbed on previously. She jumped and kicked off a door handle to propel herself onto the roof. Olga followed her a few seconds later. William came to a halt as the wall of diseased entered the corridor, closing down his option to follow them. The smoke hid those behind, but their galloping steps told him they were coming.

The wooden fences on either side were only a few inches thick and at least twelve feet tall. Even if he did get onto them, he had nothing to stand on.

Thundering steps. Deep growls. Snarling hisses.

Nothing else for it, William sheathed his sword and charged at the fence closest to the labs, kicked off it, and reached up to catch the top. The wood cut into his grip, and the whole thing swayed when the fastest of the diseased slammed into it below him.

William dragged himself to the top, threw his right leg over, and dropped down the other side. He fell in stages, trying to land on his feet before his legs gave out and he folded into a heap. Pinned between the wall and the labs, he lifted his head in time to see the diseased had come around the other side of the wall and flooded into the tight space.

His knees sore, his legs weak, William scrambled to his feet and turned his back on the creatures. The lab on his right, the fence on his left, he sprinted away, running around the end of the long wooden building.

The gap between the wall and the lab was much tighter, and it took William back to the protectors' trials. Clear of diseased for the moment, he had no idea what waited for him around the other side. A better choice might not come up.

His hands shaking, his lungs ready to burst, William removed his boots, throwing them onto the lab's roof. A scream responded above him, and Olga's red face peered over the side, Matilda joining her a moment later.

After tearing his socks off, William stuffed them into his pocket, jumped, and made a star, his feet pressing against the window on one side and the wooden fence on the other.

Fatigue turned every movement sluggish. William gritted his teeth and grunted through the pain as he braced his feet against the walls on either side before raising his hands higher. He then braced his hands to lift his feet. The first of the diseased appeared around the side of the building.

The front-running diseased jumped at William as he lifted his feet again. The creature stumbled and fell flat when it missed him. He took a moment to catch his breath as the crowd gathered below. They knew they couldn't reach him, but they'd be ready when he fell.

Both Matilda and Olga offered William words of encouragement.

"You're nearly there."

"You're doing so well."

"Another foot higher and we can drag you up."

Covered in sweat, William's right foot slipped an inch, squeaking against the glass. The girls gasped. The diseased roared.

Shaking with fatigue, William braced himself with his hands and readjusted his feet. They held, but for how long? One final test of his feet's grip, he blocked out the sound of the beasts below and focused on the girls' dangling hands. If they didn't catch him, he'd be screwed. If he didn't jump, he'd fall.

Pushing as hard as he could against the window and fence, William used what strength he had left in his legs, leaped, and reached up.

CHAPTER 48

The girls worked with the synchronicity necessary to save William's life, both of them grabbing one of his wrists at the same time and dragging him onto the roof.

The screams below him roared in frustration as William rolled onto his back and stared up at the bright sky. He used his entire being to breathe, his ribs swelling and relaxing with his heavy gasps.

When Matilda leaned over him and kissed his forehead, he managed a smile, a few seconds later forcing out, "Thank you. Thank you both."

"I should think so too," Olga said while rubbing her forehead with one hand and holding one of his boots in the other, "especially after you damn near knocked me unconscious."

Laughing on his exhale, William shook his head. "Sorry."

"What are we laughing at?"

"Hugh?" William sat up too quickly, his world spinning, stars flashing through his vision.

Hugh walked towards them across the roof, his shirt soaked with blood.

"How? What? How?"

"I ran across after you. I don't know if you noticed or not, but the diseased seemed somewhat preoccupied, so I took my chance."

William fell flat against the roof again, laughing as he said, "You're a mad bastard, Hugh."

Hugh snorted a laugh. "I love you too."

∼

THEY WAITED FOR WILLIAM TO GET HIMSELF TOGETHER, AND although his body still trembled, his muscles aching from the run, he found it in him to walk over to the skylight they'd left open on their previous visit.

Because Olga hadn't seen the building before, she hung inside to look.

William glanced at where Goliath had waited for them, his breath catching in his throat.

When Olga reemerged, she pointed towards the far end of the lab. "There's clearly someone in the cell down there."

"How can you possibly know that?" Matilda said.

"The diseased are down there."

"That doesn't tell us anything," William said. "If we can't see him, they certainly can't."

"Maybe he's been banging for someone to let him out? He's probably worn his fists to stumps by now."

William, Matilda, and Hugh fell silent. Like they didn't feel bad enough for leaving him. Olga then tutted and walked off down the roof.

They stopped about ten feet short of the end of the building before Olga reached down and tore a tile free. She threw the slate from the roof like a Frisbee. Several diseased's shrieks suggested she'd scored a direct hit. Two more tiles, she sent them the way of the first. As she removed the next one, the others helped until they'd exposed a patch about three feet square.

Olga sat down at the edge of the hole and slammed her heel against the wooden ceiling. On the second blow, a creaking rip ran through the boards.

Several kicks later and Olga's foot went through the roof. The creatures inside roared at the intrusion.

All four of them tore the gap wider to reveal the corridor below.

"That's the cell," Hugh said, pointing at the large metal door.

Olga raised an eyebrow at him. "No shit."

"All right, I was just trying to be helpful."

"Being helpful would have been saving him the first time around."

"So how are we going to get down there?" William said. Many of the diseased in the corridor wore lab coats. "There's too many of them."

"Where's the key?" Olga said.

Hugh pointed. "In a box locked with a combination."

"And you know the combination?"

"Zero, eight, five, two. They never change it. The only problem is, that's the box."

A scowl dominated Olga's face as she tried to look where Hugh indicated. It took a few seconds. "That box near the floor?"

"Yep."

"So how are we going to get to it?"

"That's what I mean."

"I thought *you* were the smart one."

Hugh shrugged and he lost focus. "I don't know what I am anymore."

"You're Hugh, no one else." Not the devil.

The others looked at William.

The diseased both inside and outside calling up to them, Olga finally said, "How about Matilda and I go inside? We could stand by the double doors you tied and try to bring the diseased towards us. Someone can then slip in to get the key."

"Why don't *you* jump down and get the key?" William said. "It's suicide to go down there."

Before Olga could reply, Hugh said, "I'll do it."

Both William and Matilda turned on him. "*What?*"

"I'll do it. I can get down there and open the door in time."

"What about going down there and blocking the door from this side so the diseased can't come back in? We could trap them between two locked doors."

Hugh shook his head. "There's nothing to block the door with, and I won't be able to tie it because it's a single door. But if I wait for them all to leave, it should close behind them. Even with the small window in it, I'll be too hard for them to see."

Olga patted Hugh's back before tugging on Matilda's arm. "Let's do this, then."

But Matilda shook her off and stepped close to Hugh. "Are you sure you're okay with this?"

The dark glaze had returned. Although the malice had gone. Maybe the devil had left. It had already broken Hugh, what more did it need to do?

After hugging him, Matilda followed Olga across the roof towards the skylight. She glanced back several times, her brow furrowed.

"This is madness," William said. "We'll find another way."

Despite the distant glaze, Hugh's eyes shimmered behind his tears. "I'm done, William. I've had enough." His brown eyes were first magnified and then rippled before he cried freely. "My head's gone. I'm a liability. How long will it be before I get you and everyone else killed? You've as good as said it yourself."

"But you're getting better."

"Just because you want that to be the case, it doesn't mean it is." While knocking his skull with a closed fist, Hugh cried even harder. "Every moment is a battle for me. I'm putting you all in danger. I've killed an entire city; I can't have the death of my best friends on my hands too. Max is an asset to your survival. I'm a hindrance."

"You *didn't* kill everyone in the city, the disease did."

"I let it in."

"It was an easy mistake to make. We could have done it when we were leaving for the night." Although Hugh looked like he wanted to reply, William cut him off. "We'll get through this together. We're your friends. We're here for you. We *need* you. Look at how far you've come. Remember that awkward boy who was petrified to be on national service and talked too fast for anyone to understand?"

Smiling through his tears, Hugh wiped his nose and nodded.

"And now look at you, you're a machine. You fight like you were born for it. Like a protector. You fight better than any of us. We'd be lost without you."

"Maybe you need to take another look at Matilda. She's a warrior. And Olga taught me everything I know."

"I won't let you go down there if you're not coming back out again. We'll find another way. We'll leave Max. If Olga wants him so badly, let *her* go."

When Hugh didn't reply, William said, "If you're going down there, I need you to promise me you'll come back out again."

"I can't do that."

"Yes, you can. *Promise* me."

Once he'd removed the map they found outside the city

from his pocket, Hugh handed it to William. "I promise, but take this just in case."

The map in his hand, William watched Hugh remove his sword and lay it flat on the roof. "You might need that."

"If I get to the point where I need it, I'd say it's game over already."

The start of tears burned William's eyes. "Promise me you're coming back."

"I promise." The glaze had gone, the compassionate boy he'd met in the dining hall returning. "I lost myself for a moment, but I'll make sure I get back out. And I'll bring Max with me. I promise."

"Okay." Trying his best to remain hidden from the diseased in the corridor, William walked towards the hole and peered in. "Now we have to wait for the girls to call them away."

CHAPTER 49

Still keeping his distance, William peered through the hole at the diseased in the corridor. A waft of smoke from woodwork then blew across his face, the start of a cough tickling his throat. He backed away, the creatures on the outside of the labs screeching when they saw him, his coughing drowned out by their raucous reaction.

The black smoke from woodwork continued to rise straight up, the wayward cloud an apparent anomaly. When William returned to the hole and stood beside Hugh, the diseased were shuffling away from Max's cell and heading towards the banging noise against the double doors deeper in the building.

As William removed his shirt, Hugh looked him up and down. "What are you doing?"

First William tied a knot at the cuff of one arm before wrapping the other end around and securing it to his wrist. He tested the strength with a tug. "I'm going to hang this down through the hole for you to grab on to. As soon as you've opened the door with the key, I'll be ready to pull you out."

Hugh wrapped William in a tight hug. "You've done all you can, Spike."

Checking for the dark glaze, William said, "William."

Although Hugh smiled, his eyes didn't. "Not really the time for jokes, is it? You've been the best friend anyone could hope for, William."

"You're coming back out of there, even if I have to follow you down and drag you back out myself."

"I will; I just want you to know you've gone above and beyond. No one has been as kind to me as you. You've been the best friend I could ask for. It's important for me to say thank you."

Goliath, his parents, the entire damn city, William's voice trembled when he said, "Shut up, Hugh. You're wasting time. Get down there and come back up as soon as you've unlocked that door. You hear me?"

If Hugh heard him, it didn't show. The boy moved to the edge of the hole and hung his legs down. He then turned around and lowered himself in, holding onto the tiles for a second, fixing William with his teary glaze before he let go, the tap of his feet hitting the floor inside.

The wind crashed into William, bringing with it another dark cloud of smoke. This time he held his breath, shifting from one foot to the other, spending his impatience while he waited for it to clear.

When he looked into the corridor again, William saw Hugh crouched next to the locked box. While entering the code, Hugh threw glances in the direction of the mob. The girls matched the creatures' fury with their own hammering blows. Hopefully, it would be enough to keep them preoccupied.

The box fell open and Hugh pulled the key out. He remained crouched while he reached up and unlocked the cell door with a gentle click.

William, shirtless, lay on his front against the tiled roof. His right hand throbbed from how tightly he'd tied the knot at his wrist.

"Hugh?" Max's voice. Croaky and weak, he repeated himself. "Hugh! How did you get in here?"

From his current vantage point, William could only see Hugh, who smiled. "Hi, Max." A pause as he appeared to look at someone else in the cell. "We've come to get you out."

"We?"

"Me, William, Matilda, and Olga."

"Olga's here? What's happened?"

"Edin's lost. The entire city has fallen. Only a handful of us have survived."

A conversation they could be having on the roof, William hung his shirt down into the corridor and swung the knot towards Hugh to get his attention.

"My god," Max said. "The whole city?"

"Nearly all of it. The political district managed to lock themselves down. Although, I don't know what the damage is there; no one can get in."

His jaw clenched against his need to shout, William poked his head into the corridor to check for diseased. The single door at the end of the windowless stretch had closed like Hugh had hoped. Its slim rectangular window showed him the mob and the girls banging against the double doors to keep their attention. They were still winning, but it only took one to notice Hugh.

Again, William waved the knot in Hugh's direction. With Max still in his cell, only Hugh could see him. Was he ignoring him? "Hugh!"

Max stepped through the door, fixed on William and waved. "Spike, how are you?"

And why should Max know to keep his voice down? Before William could tell him, the diseased in the other corridor yelled.

The swell of a stampede. "Hugh! Get the hell out of there now!"

As the diseased descended on Hugh, the stocky boy stared at them before he looked up. His lips bent out of shape as he cried, "I'm done, William. I've been done for some time. I'm sorry I just lied to you, but I'm *not* coming back up. There's no coming back from where I've been."

"No! *Hugh!*"

The single door at the end of the corridor smashed against the wall, and chaos shoved it open.

Hugh raised his voice over the insanity. "If I don't go now, I'll lose it out there again. I can't cope with anyone else dying because of me."

Tears running freely, William's voice shattered when he yelled, "Max, do something!"

As Max ran in front of Hugh, the woman they'd found outside the walls when they were on national service stepped from the cell. Where Max held his ground to shield Hugh, the woman walked headlong into the diseased.

The corridor was narrow enough for Max to slow them down, but for how long?

A thud in the room between the dark corridor and the girls. Before William could work out what caused it, one of the glass walls shattered. The woman must have decided she wanted out. More creatures rushed forward.

"Hugh! Get out of there now!"

Max fell to the flood of diseased. Hugh vanished a second later.

Although William scanned the chaos for his friend, he'd gone. The next time he saw him, he'd have the bleeding eyes of a diseased. Nobody needed to see that. Rolling onto his back, he clapped his hands to his face and let go of a throat-tearing scream.

CHAPTER 50

Other than to sit up, William hadn't moved, Matilda beside him with her arm around his shoulders. "We've lost so many people already," he said. "Why did he have to do that? I could have gotten him out."

Olga hovered nearby, but remained at a safe distance and stared out over Edin.

Despite William's blurred view of the world, when Max appeared through the skylight, he had to do a double take. He rubbed his eyes. The Max who'd been holding back the diseased just minutes before looked stronger. The boy had always been slim, but now he looked positively skeletal. He walked as if it caused him pain. His shoulders were higher than usual, his skin so pale it had turned almost translucent.

But Max didn't return William's attention. Instead, he used their elevated position to take in the drastically changed city. The already shattered boy slumped as he turned several slow circles. The woodwork district still burned, black smoke rising from the scores of wooden buildings, scenting the air around them. There were diseased everywhere. "What the hell's happened?"

As the most composed of the group, Olga explained everything, Max's already pale face turning paler with every gruesome detail.

It took a few seconds after Olga finished for Max to close his jaw. He shook his head as if it would somehow shift the reality of what had happened into some kind of order he could process. "What caused it all?"

While Olga said, "We don't know," William and Matilda shared the briefest of glances. Maybe that secret should die with Hugh.

"Look," Olga said, turning her back on the others while she spoke to Max, "the quickest route out of here's through national service."

Tension balled in William's abdomen before the words exploded from him. "You snake!"

Still armed with a machete, Olga tilted her head to one side, lifting the weapon slightly away from her body. "What did you call me?"

"You heard me."

Olga returned to her conversation with Max. "You need to know the truth of what's gone on so you can make the right decision for you."

Before William could even think about standing up to continue the argument, Matilda pressed down on his left shoulder. And maybe she was right. Max deserved to know.

"William, Hugh, and Matilda came past the labs yesterday and chose to leave you. When they met up with me, they kept it a secret until they decided they needed your help. They're only here because of what you can do for them."

Skin so pale the bright sun damn near turned Max into a mirror, the glare of his confusion dazzled William. "Okay,"

William said, "you want to know the truth of it? We *did* come here. We came here and we crept into the labs to try to get to you. Then we met a corridor filled with those *things*."

"And what did you do after that, William?"

William ground his teeth. "Look, Olga, I like you. I admit, we made a mistake not telling you about Max, but"—he turned back to Max—"the reason we didn't try to save you is because we thought it would kill one or all of us."

Olga's taut features settled. Although she opened her mouth as if she had a reply coming, she clearly thought better of it and let it die. A second later, she dipped a nod at William. "I'm sorry. I can see it wasn't an easy choice to make. With the state of this city, we've all made some hard decisions. We're expected to play God by deciding who lives and who dies."

While scratching his head, William released a long sigh. "Look, Max, I'm so sorry we didn't come up with a better way to rescue you before this. I also think it's important you know the reason we've come back is because we need your help like Olga said. That changed our decision. We decided it was worth risking our lives for. I'm sorry that sounds callous, but it's the truth. I mean, look around, you can see what the world has changed into since you've been in that cell." The itch of tears spread across his eyes. "Olga was right to tell you, but please know we didn't make the decision lightly. Will you help us?"

Instead of replying, Max turned his back on the three of them and returned to the skylight, disappearing into the labs. The lack of the creatures' reaction screamed louder than their fury ever had.

After a few seconds Matilda said, "Where's he gone?"

CHAPTER 51

"At what point do we accept he's not coming back?" William said. They'd waited for at least ten minutes, watching the skylight as if Max would emerge from it at any moment.

"We don't." Olga's face lit up as Max reappeared. He had blankets, a jug of water, and a cloth bag filled with something.

The bag had apples and some bread in it, which he passed around. "I want to help you, whatever it is you need. I don't care how or why you got me out, and I recognise the sacrifice made to rescue me. Were it not for you, I would have starved to death, so for that I'm grateful. I'm not making a judgement on any of your previous decisions. But before I do anything, I need to go to construction to see if any of my family are still alive." The wind tossed his hair as he faced his home district. "I'm not holding out much hope, but I need to check." After a moment's pause, he nodded at the folded map poking from William's pocket. "What's that?"

William pulled out the map, holding down two corners to prevent the wind from blowing it away. Max crouched in front of it and held the other two.

After studying it for a minute, Max traced the line separating the top two-thirds of the map from the bottom. "It makes more sense now."

When no one replied, he said, "The woman I was in the cell with."

"Where is she now?" Matilda said, and then added, "So much for that glass being hard to smash."

"I don't know. She was immune like me, so my guess is she's left Edin. Why would she stay?"

The day they took her in had unsettled everyone on national service: a feral woman speaking a language none of them recognised. Where William had been a naïve child before, that day showed him just how ruthless Edin's rulers could be. It would have pleased Hugh to know he'd contributed to her freedom. "Did you manage to understand her?"

Max shook his head. "Not really, but there were a few things we worked out between us. She talked about a wall. About war. About weapons. I'm not really sure what a lot of it means, but this here"—he tapped the map—"must be the wall. If she didn't prove it already by arriving and talking in a language no one understood, I think this map shows us there's a lot more to this world than just Edin."

The conversation alone drained some of William's already depleted energy. "We've got a long road ahead."

"That's for sure." Max stood up again. "I will be back, I promise. I got the food and blankets so you have something. Besides, I'm sure you all need the rest."

William knew Matilda as well as he knew anyone. If arguing with Max would get them to Artan sooner, she would have done it, but the boy stood strong and resolute. He hadn't asked their permission.

"Give me an hour or two at the most. I promise I'll be back. And thank you again. I don't care how it came about, the fact is, you freed me. Whatever happens moving forward, we're in this together. All of us. See you soon."

As Max turned to walk away, William said, "Max?"

The boy halted.

William held up Hugh's sword and sheath. "Hugh would have wanted you to have this."

For a moment, both boys held the sword at the same time. William then let it go, withdrawing into himself while he saw Hugh's kind face in his mind's eye.

CHAPTER 52

True to his word, Max returned, poking his head through the skylight. Maybe two hours had passed, maybe longer, but despite his stomach locking in anxious knots, William had managed to keep his head straight and put faith in his friend from national service. Max had asked them to trust him, and after the decisions they'd made with his life over the past few days, they owed him that. Besides, they hardly had a choice.

While waiting for Max, they'd eaten all the food he'd brought up, drank all the water, and did their best to keep the conversation light. They were all tired and stressed, and if the others felt anything like William, one spark could erupt into an argument. And he couldn't blame Olga for what she'd said to Max. He deserved to know. Maybe, with time, he'd be grateful to her for getting it all out in the open. Maybe.

It took for Max to climb out onto the roof before Olga said, "Damn, what's happened to you?"

Dripping in blood, Max moved closer, his steps slow and lethargic. "I thought I'd thin the herd, you know?"

"You look like you've slaughtered the entire city," Olga said.

"If only! But I think with my immunity, I have a responsibility to chip away at the numbers when I can."

The roof shook beneath Max as he slumped down. He ran a hand through his blood-soaked hair. While fixing on the tiles in front of him, he cleared his throat with a wet cough. "I killed one of my brothers. I went to my family home. I should have walked away the second I saw it. It looked as wrecked as all the other homes in the district. I didn't need to see any more. But then a diseased stepped out. It came at me like it knew me. To every other diseased I've been invisible, but I'm certain this one recognised me. It was Drake. He was the youngest of my four older brothers and the one I was closest to. He …"

Max stared off into the distance and heaved another heavy sigh. "The way he looked at me … he *knew* who I was. I hadn't killed any diseased until that moment. I stabbed him through the chest and kicked his head until I didn't recognise him anymore. Those creatures have no right wearing his face."

As Max talked about what he'd done, William noticed the chunks of flesh and white flecks of bone on his boots. The blood on his face had cracked from where it had dried, and parts of it flaked away like old paint.

"I left soon after," Max said.

Olga shifted closer to Max and put her arm around him. "I'm sorry you had to go through that."

"We've all lost people, right?"

A moment's pause, Olga said, "I always liked Hugh."

Were it not for the touch of Matilda's hand on his leg, William might have reacted.

"It wasn't ever about me not liking him," Olga went on. "It's more that he scared me. A lot. When I trained him, I could see how damaged he was. We rarely spoke. Well, I spoke." She laughed. "I shouted at him frequently. But he never said anything in return. At the end of every session, he didn't even say thank you. Instead, he'd hug me, squeezing me so tightly it almost hurt. And he'd hold on. Not to the point where it felt uncomfortable, but just long enough to share his vulnerability with me. I came to cherish those hugs. They were an intense squeeze of humanity in a situation where we'd all nearly lost ours. But I didn't see that Hugh anymore." She looked out across the city. "Every time he came close to me, I yearned for one of those hugs. Just a sign to know the boy I'd trained with remained."

While Olga talked, Matilda moved closer to William. He relaxed because of her proximity. "Thank you for telling us that, Olga. He was a great friend. One of the best." The attention of the others burned into him as he focused on the hole his friend had gone through. "Just before he went in there, he told me he was done. He had no fight left in him and he didn't want anyone to die because his actions were putting people at risk. I made him promise me he would come back up again; otherwise, I wouldn't let him go. I said if he remained down there, I'd jump down to save him—and I nearly did—but I knew it would kill us both."

Matilda shook her head. "If only he knew we were all here for him. We would have helped him through."

"I told him that. But he'd had enough. I could see that. He couldn't keep the crazy at bay anymore. I always thought suicide was selfish, but I suppose it's selfish of me to want him to stay alive for my sake. He was done." The world blurred in front of William. "He was done."

Maybe a minute passed before Max looked up, tears having cut two tracks through the blood on his cheeks. "So what do you think? We have maybe two to three hours of daylight left. I'm not confident we'll achieve much moving through the city at night. So do we try to get to the arena or stay here until the morning?"

"I can't wait any longer," Matilda said. "Artan's been in that cell for months already, and I don't know when he was last fed or given water. The wait is driving me insane. I appreciate we've all lost people and you can't make a decision just for me, but if you can see any way of at least getting to the arena today, then I'd like to try."

William nodded while she spoke, and it didn't take long for Max and Olga to follow suit, Olga adding, "Even if we just get closer to the arena, that's something, right? But if we're going to go, we need to do it now."

When they'd entered the labs earlier that day, they had to run into the district to get past the tall wooden fences. Now that they were leaving, though, they headed to where William had climbed up where the fence and the end of the labs were closest together.

While staring across the wide road, the diseased everywhere, Max said, "This has to be the best place to jump off. It gives us a shorter distance to travel."

"I'll make the noise for the diseased," William said. "Are you okay chaperoning the girls, Max?"

William was as good a candidate as any of them to wait behind, and maybe they saw that, because neither Olga nor Matilda argued with him. He kissed Matilda, and when they pulled away, he stroked some of her hair behind her ear from where the hummingbird clip hadn't caught it all. "If anything happens, meet me in the arena."

"Why would anything happen?"

"I'm sure it won't," William said, "but in light of what's already happened, I'd say it's better to plan for the worst."

They were all far enough back from the edge of the roof to be hidden from the diseased. Before Matilda said anything else,

William clapped his hands and made loud noises as he marched to the spot where they'd made Goliath wait the first time they came into the district. To imagine his horse standing there robbed him of his voice, but he swallowed his grief and shouted again. It wasn't the time to be thinking about the noble creature.

Open mouths, bleeding eyes, snatching and snapping arms below, William continued to yell while he reached down and ripped several tiles free from the lab's roof. When he had a stack of them in his left hand, he lifted the first one with his right and threw it like a Frisbee. The stone rectangle smashed into the face of one of the diseased. The creature swayed, stunned from the contact.

As Matilda, Olga, and Max vanished off the edge of the building, he shouted louder than before and threw the next tile harder than the first.

∽

WILLIAM HAD BEEN THROWING THE TILES FOR AT LEAST FIVE minutes, and once he'd found his rhythm, he couldn't miss, nailing diseased after diseased with the spinning projectiles. Another armful of them, he wound back for his next throw. But then he stopped. And a good job too. The only face free of disease in the mob, he waited for Max to pass beneath him into the labs before he spun the next tile into the baying crowd.

A minute later, Max appeared at William's side. "What are you doing?"

"What else am I going to do? Like you said earlier, we might as well thin the numbers a little. Oh, and next time you might want to carry a white flag."

"Why's that?"

"You nearly got a tile in your face."

"You would have missed."

William smiled. "How are the girls?"

"They're fine. They're on the other side of the road, making as much noise as they can."

"And getting them across worked okay?"

"How fast can you run?"

After throwing his armful of tiles from the roof, William walked with Max to the end of the labs and stopped a few feet from making himself visible. Large gaps had opened up in the road, most of the creatures over to the right at the feet of Matilda and Olga. They'd dragged them in the direction of the national service area, away from the arena.

"You should go first," Max said. "If you lead, I'll catch up and follow. Although they're not interested in me, they're interested enough to notice when I land in the street. We don't want to prime them for you jumping down."

"Okay." They'd done this a few times already, and it had to be easier now they had Max's help. They'd made it every other time, so why not now? Little point in dwelling on it, William took off, stepping from the labs to the top of the fence before dropping to the cobblestones.

William's legs buckled when he landed, throwing him to the ground. No time to dwell on the shock to his body, he jumped back up again and took off towards textiles directly opposite.

About halfway across the road, Max a few steps behind, a mob of about two hundred diseased spewed from one of the large alleyways in front, creating an impenetrable wall between William and safety. It was like when they'd followed Hugh and Olga in laundry all over again.

"Where the hell did they come from?" Max said.

William changed direction, running away from the mob and the girls. The mob followed.

Max now beside him, William gritted his teeth and dug deep. They sprinted down the centre of the road, the small one-story buildings of textiles on their right. If they could get close enough, he could drag himself up. But more diseased appeared from more alleys. The girls' crossing must have alerted them. They should have waited longer before he jumped down.

"Shall I try to hold them back?" Max shouted.

"There's no way you can. There's far too many."

"What, then?"

The conversation dragged more air from William's lungs. "We keep going."

Now William ran with the creatures beside rather than beneath him, their roar and stench dealt an almost tangible blow.

As more diseased burst from textiles and then ceramics, they kept William in the centre of the main road. With woodwork on fire, he couldn't go there. A roar then exploded from the burning district. More diseased appeared on their left. "We're screwed, Max."

Before William could come up with a plan, Max shoved him. He stumbled towards textiles and into one of the storage basements lining the road. Max slammed the doors shut behind them, throwing them into complete darkness.

Both of them fighting for breath, William wiped his sweating face. "What are you doing?"

"You think we had a better option?"

"*You* do! You can go where you like."

"So you should be doubly thankful that I've saved your arse *and* decided to come in here with you."

"There are *diseased* down here."

"I don't know if you saw, William, but there are diseased up there too. Hopefully we can get through these tunnels and come up somewhere safer. Somewhere closer to the arena. The fact that this place is a labyrinth should work in our favour."

"The diseased will be as lost as we are? And what about Olga and Matilda?"

"They'll meet us at the arena like we planned."

His heart beating so fast it felt like it might burst, William's entire body turned to gooseflesh when he heard the hellish shriek of the diseased. "Shit!"

"It looks like our grace period has ended," Max said. "Let's go before they find us."

"That sounds like a solid plan, genius! All we need now is to work out how to see in the dark."

CHAPTER 53

Another scream flew at William through the tunnels, and he spun on the spot as if it would somehow help in the disorientating dark. The only sense of his bearings came from the diseased in the street outside as they hammered their frustrations against the closed doors. Were there not so many of them crowded around the hatch, daylight might have revealed cracks, giving them a sliver of illumination to guide their way. But there must have been hundreds of them in the street. How long before the doors collapsed beneath their weight?

"What do we do, Max? You brought us down here, so what's the plan?"

"*You* were going to die if we'd remained outside."

"So you want me to thank you?"

An arm caught William in the face, throwing him off balance. As he raised his fists, Max placated him. "Sorry, that was an accident."

"Somehow I doubt it." Max shuffled around in front of William, who then said, "What are you doing?"

A few seconds later, William flinched again as Max first touched his face, shoulders, and then patted down his arms until they were holding hands. He fed a piece of cloth into William's grip. "Here, hold this."

The banging behind them louder than before, the screams closing in on them from somewhere in the tunnels, William's throat hurt to shout over the noise. "What are you doing?"

"This is my top. I've tied it around my waist so you can hold on to it. It makes sense for me to lead because I can bump into the diseased and not get bitten."

"But you still can't see anything."

"No, but I'm more useful than you."

"All right, no need to rub it in."

"Oh, and, Spike—"

"William!"

Although Max replied, a chorus of shrieks from somewhere in the tunnels drowned him out, so he tried again. "Does it really matter right now?" Before William replied, he added, "Your sword needs to be sheathed."

"*What?*"

"You need to make sure your sword's away. I can't have you swinging it when you're no more than a few feet behind me. So are you ready?"

"No."

"Will you ever be?"

"No."

The slack in Max's shirt pulled taut as he moved off, and William—despite every desire—let the boy lead him. Each step in the darkness sent a flip through his stomach in anticipation of a fall.

They started slow, leaving the reek and hammering of hundreds of diseased behind as they delved deeper into the rich, earthy dampness of the tunnels.

Max quickened the pace and William tugged against it.

Then another diseased's wail barrelled through the darkness and he yielded. If they were too cautious, they'd die.

Nowhere near a sprint, but they quickened to a jog, every step blind, every step loaded with the potential to throw them to the ground.

The first William knew of Max stopping came when he crashed into the back of him. "What's up?"

More diseased's screams.

Several seconds of heavy breathing, Max finally said, "They're getting closer. What shall we do?"

William held his breath and listened to the slap of steps. "It sounds like just one of them."

"Shall we let it come to us?"

"Yeah. I need to draw my sword though. If we stay back to back, it'll be safe."

"Okay."

William dropped Max's shirt, drew his sword, and backed into his friend. He pushed away thoughts of when he'd done the same with Hugh near the gym. Neither spoke as the steps closed in on them. The cries sounded almost human as if the thing tried to articulate words it once knew.

The footsteps mirroring his heartbeat, William battled his short and rapid breaths while tightening his grip on his sword's hilt. Max shifted behind him, his turning feet scratching as he clearly widened his stance on the gritty ground.

The approaching diseased rounded the corner and came at them. Slathering, rattling, phlegmy breaths, it drew closer. An awkward and uneven gallop, William held his sword out, tip first, inviting the creature to skewer itself at full charge.

It sounded about ten feet away. Eight feet. Six feet. Two feet ...

But nothing crashed into them, the steps flying past as if they belonged to a ghost.

"What the hell?" Max said.

After a few seconds to be certain the steps were definitely running away from them, William shook his head. "It must be in another tunnel." He felt the touch of Max's hand as he passed him his shirt again. He sheathed his sword before giving the sleeve a tug. "Let's go."

Where one set of footsteps had passed them, twenty pairs took its place, diseased sprinting through the tunnels, coming at them from every direction.

The speed they'd moved at before the ghost of the diseased had nothing on their current pace, William hanging on to Max's shirt while fighting against his own tense reluctance to run. But they needed to get out of there.

A flash of light then punched through William's vision as he slammed nose-first into the back of Max's head. A ringing in his ears, he stumbled back, letting go of Max's shirt and hitting the hard ground. His eyes watered and the coppery taste of his own blood ran down the back of his throat. He sat up, his lips damp with his nosebleed.

"William, are you okay?"

William reached out and grabbed Max's leg. He felt the touch of his friend's hand, who pulled him to his feet.

"I hit a wall. Are you okay?" Max said.

Several nods, William spoke in a nasally tone. "Yeah, although I think I've broken my nose."

Another furious scream crashed through their conversation.

"Can you still run?"

"As long as you don't hit a wall again."

"I'll try not to. Let's go."

Before setting off, the sound of the creatures approached from behind. More than one this time. "What do you want to do?" Max said. "Stay and fight?"

Adrenaline sent a violent shake through William. "How many do you think there are?"

"I've no idea."

"If they catch us, I'm not confident we can fight them off."

The slack in Max's shirt pulled taut again, so William followed him, running blind with the horde on their tail.

They were slower than the diseased, the creatures getting louder with every step. Shouting to Max wouldn't help anyone, but William guessed they had thirty seconds at most before the beasts were on them.

William then crashed over the top of Max, his forearms slamming against the edges of several stairs. In spite of the sharp sting from his fall, he scrabbled to his feet. "Max, are you okay?"

The diseased drew closer.

"Stairs have to be a good thing, right?" Max said.

William scrambled up them, smashing his head against the wooden barrier of closed doors. When he pushed against them, the metal frame felt hot to touch. They had fifteen seconds at the most before the diseased reached them. The air had already curdled with their rancid vinegar reek.

A clenched jaw, sweat and blood running down his face, William pressed his palms to the warm wooden doors and yelled as he shoved one of them with everything he had.

The *crack* of the door fell wide, and the muted daylight dazzled William. He clambered from the hatch, falling against the ground. Just one door open, he fought to breathe in the smoky air while Max scrambled free.

A wall of diseased on their tail, the second Max burst from the hatch, William slammed the door shut to the satisfying crunch of the lead runner's skull.

William put his weight against the doors to hold them back, and Max shoved a thick metal pin at least two feet long through the handles. It was attached to the doors with a chain, clearly used for locking the tunnels from the outside. Although the diseased opened the doors by a few inches, the pin prevented them from shoving them any wider.

His hands on his knees, William battled his own fitness and the thick black clouds around them. Hot from his run, his surroundings were like a furnace. They'd come out in the woodwork district.

After a heaving coughing fit, Max stood up and nodded at the doors they'd just clambered through. He then squinted to take in their surroundings and shook his head before he said, "Out of the frying pan …"

CHAPTER 54

Now they were in daylight—albeit muted daylight because of the thick clouds of smoke—William got a clear sight of Max with his shirt off. Every one of his ribs were visible, and his stomach looked like it had been sucked in. He wore the neglect of a prisoner of the state—and that was someone in a luxury prison; what would Artan look like? Would he even be alive when they finally got to him?

The doors rattled and slammed shut repeatedly from where the diseased continued to push against them.

Max sheathed his sword, untied his shirt from around his waist, folded it, and then fastened it across his nose and mouth. William followed suit, removing his sheathed sword from his back so he could take his top off to make a mask.

Although William breathed more easily, the impromptu filter did nothing for the thick smoke in his eyes, tears streaming down his cheeks as he blinked against the noxious clouds.

His words muffled, Max said, "At least the diseased are held back."

"Yeah, but that door won't be anywhere near as effective when it's on fire."

The air alive with pops and crackles, a deep creaking ran through a tall building on their right. As William turned towards it, the structure failed, dropping as if the bottom of it had been obliterated. It fell straight down, thrusting out hot air. The burning embers died just a few feet from them. As more of their surroundings creaked, he said, "Let's go."

Almost as blind above ground as they were beneath it, William led their escape this time. Black clouds, bright explosions of fire, and the wind thrusting stinging fireflies at them added to their dilemma.

Yet another building creaked on their left, so William led them right as it fell.

They reached a dead end, a wooden fence at least eight feet tall; it was aflame like everything else in the damn district. William's shoulders slumped. "Shit."

A tight grip clamped on William's left arm before Max dragged him through a dark cloud. They were back in the tunnels, blind and with William trusting his friend's lead.

The other side of the cloud showed them another path, albeit one with flaming beams in their way. Despite the heat, his inability to breathe, and the chance of a mountain of fire collapsing on them from any of the towering infernos on either side, William would take this over the tunnels any day. Limited visibility always won out over no visibility.

As they drew closer, what William had initially taken to be a hunk of wood turned out to be the charred remains of a person. The whites of their teeth revealed them as human. Hopefully, it had been a diseased.

Max stopped first and William caught up to him. Another burning dead end. The pop, crackle, and roar of fire around them, Max didn't try to speak. He didn't need to. They were screwed.

This time William took the initiative, kicking the wall as hard as he could. The flaming fence panel toppled, opening a way through.

Several more twists and turns, William tripped as he made it into tailoring, stumbling several paces before he fell to his knees. Max joined him a second later. There were no diseased nearby. Although they were far from safe. If the monsters heard or saw someone to infect, their caution would undoubtedly abandon them.

The moisture leeched from his body, William gulped, but it did nothing to sate his thirst. "Are you okay?"

Before Max replied, a shrill scream cut through the air. But not the scream of a diseased … the scream of a child.

After he'd pulled his shirt away from his mouth, Max said, "Was that a diseased?"

As much as William wanted to lie, to pretend they hadn't just heard a cry for help, he couldn't. The child screamed again, and this time he saw her. "Look."

Max looked where William guided him. "Shit."

The girl was trapped on what looked like the roof of a factory at the edge of the district, surrounded by flames. William shook his head. "And she nearly made it."

"She still could."

They'd left plenty of people behind already, what made this girl so different? "What do you mean?"

Max's turn to point. "The building next to the one she's trapped on looks relatively stable."

"By relatively stable, you mean only about sixty percent on fire rather than ninety?"

"That's forty percent we've got to work with. If we can get up next to her, we can persuade her to jump across."

"Are you insane?" As William said it, the girl screamed for her mum, her voice tearing with her grief, fear, and no doubt pain as she got slowly roasted.

When Max didn't reply, William shook his head. "I've got to get to Matilda in the arena. We need to rescue Artan. We've left people before; why should this girl be any different?"

"Were the others you left about to burn to death, or did they still have a chance of surviving?"

If he'd had an argument, he would have given it. For the first time, he made eye contact with the girl. Wild and wide, her pure terror stood out on her soot-stained face.

Max said, "She can't be any older than nine or ten, and one thing we know for sure is if we don't help, she'll burn."

"Damn it." William stumbled back towards woodwork. "Come on."

The building beside the warehouse had rungs much like the steps to get to the roof of the gym. It was such a simple addition that William imagined most of the wooden structures in Edin had them. It gave them easy access for maintenance.

On the roof of the building, the entire structure swaying as if it could collapse beneath them, they managed to get to within about six feet of the girl as the flames began closing in around her. William pulled his mask down so she could hear them. "You have to jump."

The gap between the buildings stretched two feet at the most, but even though the girl stepped forward, she halted before she reached it.

"Come on," Max yelled. "You have to jump now."

The girl's blonde hair had the same soot stains as her face. Her mouth hung open. William locked eyes with her. "Jump! *Now!*"

"She's not going to do it," Max said.

The flames were closing in. "Jump, you idiot," William

said. "You'll die if you don't." Where he'd had the girl's attention, he lost it in that moment. The same glaze he'd seen in Hugh, she'd stopped listening.

While still fixed on him, the girl remained perfectly still as the flames blocked off her exit. She then vanished behind the shimmering orange wall.

The heat forced both William and Max back, but they both stayed on the roof as if the girl might somehow burst through.

William said, "There must be a way to help—"

The scream of a child burning to death cut through his words.

At least a minute of wailing and crying, screaming and shouting, the girl finally fell silent.

The building William and Max stood on swayed. As much as William wanted to mark the girl's passing, they had to get the hell out of there.

Max backed off the roof first, descending the ladder they'd climbed up. The woodwork district roared and spat like a giant beast.

His eyes streaming, William took extra care to find his footing before he followed, the toe of his boot missing several times before he caught a wooden rung. A short climb and he reached the reassuring stability of solid ground, taking off after Max and leaving woodwork for a second time.

CHAPTER 55

It had taken them several hours to get from woodwork to the edge of tailoring. The death of the girl had kept them silent for at least an hour of their journey before William finally talked to Max about the apprenticeship trials, giving him a full account of what had happened. While they spoke, they remained on high alert for any sign of the gangs. The onset of night made the task increasingly difficult.

Now, as they stood with the main road between them and the arena, the bright moon highlighting the heads of the shambling masses, Max shook his head. "It's too dark to cross; we need to wait until morning."

Near ready to drop, his eyes burning, his muscles aching, and the scream from the girl in woodwork still echoing through his skull, William said, "Maybe you've got a point, and were we all together right now, I'd agree with you."

"But?"

"That road's thirty feet wide at the most."

"It's not the width of the road you should be worried about, it's the scores of diseased on it."

"But surely the dark will hinder them too? They didn't find us as easily in the tunnels."

Although Max opened his mouth to no doubt deliver an argument, William cut him off. "I *need* to see them, Max."

"You need to see *her!*"

"What's wrong with that?"

"Everything if it means you're going to take stupid risks."

A cock of his head to one side, William raised an eyebrow at his friend. "It's a little too late to be talking about that now, wouldn't you say? We've come back into the city after all. Besides, Olga will be glad to see you. And what good will waiting here do when I'll spend the entire night awake and worrying about whether they've made it back or not?"

"You're not thinking straight, William. Matilda's a big girl; she can wait for you until the morning."

"But *I* can't wait for her. Besides, you don't need to make the decisions for me here. It's not like my actions can cause you any harm."

"No, but you need my help. Without it, you're not getting across. I don't think you're making a reasonable judgement. As a friend, I'm trying to intervene."

"And I appreciate you being candid with me."

Before the conversation could go any further, William moved to the edge of the roof in two steps and jumped off, his arrival amongst the diseased met with their usual hellish wails.

Max called after him, "You should have at least let me go across and check they were there first."

It seemed so obvious now. Obvious, but a little too late for William to do anything about it. At other times, he might have drawn his sword, but if he stopped to fight, he'd die. He shoulder-barged the first diseased, the creature's arms windmilling as it fell backwards and hit the ground.

No more than a third of the way across and he already had a

pack behind him, but those ahead hadn't yet wised up to his presence. Shoving, kicking, and running with all he had, he weaved through the busy main road with only the moonlight to guide him.

His attention on the gates to the arena, William put everything he had into his pumping legs.

The slam of William's boot against the arena's large locked gates went off like a thunderclap, the diseased responding with their own explosion of sound. As he pulled himself up to the hole at the top of the arena's gate, he searched for Olga and Matilda. He shouldn't have paused.

Several pairs of hands wrapped around his legs and tugged hard. His head cracked against the gate on his way out into the street. His back slammed against the hard stone ground. The small amount of light from the moon vanished as the diseased piled in.

CHAPTER 56

The foetid stench of the diseased caught in William's throat. Closing his eyes, he waited for the searing burn of teeth to sink into his flesh. But it never came.

When William opened his eyes, he found Max standing over him. "Get up now!"

William stood on shaky legs and leaped at the small opening for a second time. The blood from Max battling the things to keep them at bay sprayed his back and turned the gates slick. His feet were slipping, and his arms were on fire from having to support his weight.

"Hurry up, William!"

William's feet slipped again before he finally found purchase then pushed and dived through the hole. What sounded like an army of diseased slammed against the locked gates as he hit the mattress, gasping to fill his tight and still smoke-irritated lungs.

But before he could recover, Max appeared above him. As William rolled aside, his friend landed on the mattress.

The arena floor was nowhere near as soft, but it would do.

William let his body fall limp and continued to look up into the dark sky. A second or two passed before his view of the stars got blocked by Matilda's smiling face.

CHAPTER 57

Although Max threw several harsh glares William's way, he saved the lecture. They both knew William's mistake; there seemed little point in dwelling on it. After all, they'd made it across the road and they were both still alive —just.

They now stood at a table in the middle of the arena. It had a handwritten note on it. Written all in capitals, the words were only just visible in the moonlight. "So we've finally got to one hundred. It might have been an arbitrary target, but aren't most goals? The important thing is we're going through with our plan to leave. We hope one hundred will be enough to fight our way somewhere safe. Maybe even close the main gates so we can try to take Edin back. I hope you found Max. We've left enough water for the five of you, and some bread too." As he read the last bit, Matilda passed him and Max both the water and bread mentioned in the letter.

William took a bite of the loaf and sip of water before continuing. "William, Matilda, Olga, and ..." After a pause to clear his throat, William managed, "Hugh, we wish you all the best. And welcome, Max. Give those bastard politicians everything they deserve. The world will be a better place without them. Good luck and much love. Samson."

Matilda held up a small bag and a flask. "They left us one flask and we found this bag for the bread. I thought we could use it to take Hugh's rations to Artan?"

She didn't need to ask William, but Max nodded, speaking with his mouth full. "Of course."

"What were the tunnels like?" Olga said.

Max shook his head as he chugged down his bread. "Labyrinthine, pitch black, and filled with diseased." A smile utterly devoid of mirth, he raised his eyebrows. "They were positively delightful."

"Although, it was a toss-up over which was worse, the tunnels or the fact we surfaced in woodwork," William said.

The clap of Matilda's hand slapped across her mouth. "My god. What was it like in there?"

William replied quickly, sharing a look with Max. "Hot." Even as he said it, the memory of the girl's screams rang through his skull. From the wince on Max's face, he undoubtedly had a similar experience.

"Can I see what's going on with the political district?" Max said.

Matilda had clearly been waiting for him to say that, responding on the heels of his question. "Are you sure? You don't want to wait until morning?"

"Best to see what we're dealing with now, eh?"

William remained at the table to take another sip of water before jogging to catch up with the others.

Before William reached them, Max had peered over the edge of the arena. "My god, what have they done to those people?"

"They used them to bait the diseased so they could trap them between the two walls," Matilda said.

"They used kids?"

When William reached the top, he flinched. His memory had somehow muted the reality. About two hundred diseased between the two walls, and the ones who'd been turned while having a noose tied around their neck still hung at regular intervals. They continued to tug at the ropes as if they could get them off. The only way free of them would be decapitation.

"Maybe I'm off here," Max said, "but I feel like the politicians have planted their flag. They're now the enemy, right? You say the prisoners are still in their cells?"

"That's what we believe," Matilda said.

"So they're safe whatever happens to the district?"

"That's what we believe."

While scratching his face, Max's eyes narrowed as he studied what lay below them. "I suppose the best time to go in there is now, while it's dark and hopefully most of them are sleeping."

Matilda practically bounced on the spot. "Are you sure you want to go now?"

"It'll make it harder for the people in the political district, and that's what we want, right? To cause panic and chaos between them so we can get Artan and the other prisoners out."

"I worry about what state Artan's in. I'd like to get down there and be the one to let him out of his cell if that's possible; I think I should be the first person he sees."

William moved close to Matilda and held her hand.

Max nodded. "We'll make sure that happens."

Olga had watched quietly until that moment, hooking a thumb in the direction of the opposite side of the arena. "I'll go and get the rope ladder. It has to be the best way in."

As the short girl walked off, the butterflies in William's stomach became frenzied. They'd had a difficult path through the city, but something about their next step felt like it would be the hardest yet.

CHAPTER 58

William stood with Olga on his left and Matilda on his right. All three of them watched Max descend the rope ladder down the side of the arena's stone wall and over the first fence into the trench of diseased.

"It doesn't matter how many times I watch him walk among them," William said when Max reached the ground and moved like a ghost through the foetid mob, "it still puts me on edge. We know those he's encountered so far don't want to bite him, but how do we know they're all like that?" What would Hugh think? Had they ignored the scientific method and jumped to a conclusion about Max's invulnerability too soon? Although, they hardly had the time to test him against every diseased they encountered.

Olga kept her focus on Max. "Well, we won't know until it happens, so I guess there's no point in worrying about it."

Most of the hung and still-writhing bodies thrown over the wooden fence were no more than a foot or two from the ground. A couple of the children were slightly higher. Max approached a woman whose shirt had been torn from her. The moonlight revealed the bite marks on her exposed chest. He cut her down.

The rope the woman had been hung from was now a perfect height for Max, who reached up, grabbed the frayed end of it, and used it to pull himself over the first wall.

After Max had vanished over the fence into the political district, Matilda exhaled hard. "I suppose all we can do now is hope he'll be okay."

∼

ALTHOUGH THEIR ELEVATED POSITION AFFORDED THEM A DECENT view of the political district, the darkness made it hard to track Max's path. William hadn't seen him since he'd vanished over the wall, and the others hadn't said anything either. "I hope he doesn't have too much trouble finding the wall's mechanism."

Olga blinked against the darkness, her gaze locked on the mob trapped between the two walls. "And hopefully he'll open the right wall. He might end up having to guess if it's not that clearly labelled. If he lets in the chaos from the rest of Edin, it will flood the political district with diseased."

As if he'd heard them, a loud clacking noise rang out. It took a few seconds of watching the gates to see he'd got the correct one, a crack opening down the centre of the wall closest to the political district. It slowly widened. By the time it had opened to just a few feet, most of the diseased had already charged into the district beyond.

The silhouette of Max appeared through the gap, spun around several times, and then vanished back into the political district.

As the wall started to close again, Matilda said, "What's he doing?"

"I think he's trying to make it safe down there for us."

∼

A FEW MINUTES LATER, MAX CLIMBED BACK OVER THE WALL and lowered himself to the ground with the gentle slap of his feet touching down. Several diseased remained in the space between the two walls, which he quickly dispatched before waving for the three of them to join him.

"You go first," William said to Olga. "I'll watch the rope ladders and make sure they hold."

∼

AT THE BOTTOM OF THE LADDER—MATILDA AND OLGA HAVING already climbed down before him—William wrapped a tight hug around Max. "Thanks, man."

The shrill calls of furious diseased charged through the district on the other side of the wall. Pausing as if to highlight what lay in wait for them, Max shook his head. "Don't thank me yet. We still have a lot to do. I was saying to the other two that the gap between the wall we're about to climb over and the justice department building is small enough for you to be able to jump it. The building has plenty of glass windows. We can smash one and climb in. I'll clear the diseased out and secure the place, and then, if Artan's inside, we'll be able to focus on saving him."

"What would we do without you?" Olga said, her eyes alive.

Not even the darkness could hide Max's blushes. "Anyway," he said, "let's do this."

As part of his clear-up while they were descending the rope ladder, Max had both killed and cut down the women and children used to bait the diseased. It left several ropes, but as William wrapped his hands around one, Max pointed at the end of the wall. "This fence is too thin to climb along, so you all need to use that rope down there. That'll take you over close to the justice department building. Let me lead the way."

While pulling on the rope, Max walked up the wooden wall to the top before vanishing over the side. Like with the rope ladder, Olga followed him, Matilda next, and finally William.

∽

BY THE TIME WILLIAM JUMPED FROM THE TOP OF THE WOODEN wall to a window ledge on the justice department building, Max had already smashed the window and slipped inside. The glow of the moon cast a silver light over the district in front of them, the screaming diseased audible but hidden from sight. He shuddered. "Something about this is too easy."

"Don't say that," Matilda said.

"Sorry. It's just, nothing has gone according to plan since we came back into the city. I just …"

Both Olga and Matilda glared at William. He raised his hands in submission. "I get it. Shut up, right?"

Neither replied because Max's voice echoed through the cavernous building. "It's all clear and locked. Come in."

∽

AS THEY'D DONE WITH EVERY OTHER STAGE OF THEIR PLAN, William arrived in the building last. Too dark to have noticed it from the window, when he landed, he saw Max had someone with him. The person remained dead still, the point of Max's sword just inches from their throat.

It took for William to get closer to recognise the ratty face. "Robert Mack. Well, well, how did I know you would have survived? I wonder how many people you've sacrificed on the way. I wouldn't mind betting those hanged kids and adults had something to do with you."

The politician pressed his lips tight as if fighting the urge to argue.

"I've got him here; we can deal with him later," Max said. "I think you three should go and find Artan."

Having been here several times before, William led the way, heading to the now empty receptionist's desk and moving through the door directly behind it.

The stench of sewage in the tight corridor had a tangibility that made William's eyes itch, and he retched several times as he acclimatised to the reek. From the sounds of the girls behind him, they both had similar reactions.

A small amount of light emanated from the windows in the main building. Olga remained by the door, keeping it held open to let the glow in. It helped William see the keys lined up for all the cells. Fortunately, they were numbered.

Number one being the closest cell, he took the key and opened the door with a deep *clunk!* Olga remained at the door while Matilda stood beside him. The strong reek of waste flooded out of the dark space, but despite his desire to step away, William squinted to peer into the shadows. They revealed nothing ... until the darkness came to life. The large form of something more than human exploded from deep within the room, driving both him and Matilda back.

Olga's distance from the cell must have given her a moment to think. While William and Matilda stepped away, she charged the figure, and despite being half its size, punched it on the nose and knocked it out cold.

Even unconscious, it took all three of them to drag the prisoner from cell number one back into her locked room. After locking her in again, William said, "This isn't going to work."

"Artan?" Matilda shouted, her word falling dead as if the shadows feasted on it.

"Artan?" Still nothing.

"Art—" A double thud against one of the doors halted her mid-shout.

"Artan?"

The thud responded.

With Olga back at the exit holding the door open to let in what little light she could, Matilda ran down the corridor, William remaining by the key rack.

"Artan?"

Thud. Thud.

"Thirteen, William. He's in thirteen."

At that, several more thuds slammed against their cell doors —they were a bit too slow on the uptake. William liberated the key from the number thirteen hook and ran to be with Matilda.

This time, William unsheathed his sword as Matilda slid the key in the lock.

A loud *snap*, and the hinges on the door creaked when she pulled it wide.

"I have a sword," William said. "If you rush us, I'll assume you're hostile and cut you down. We're hoping that's you in there, Artan. Come out slowly."

Too dark to know who came forward, but they were cautious in their approach. About the same height as Artan, the person had long and scraggly hair, and looked several stones lighter than the boy they both knew. But he continued to emerge with gradual steps, taking Matilda's hand when she offered it to him.

William stood aside to let him exit the cell and walked behind them, his sword still drawn as Matilda led the boy back towards Olga.

"Is it him?" Olga said, squinting as she took the figure in.

Matilda gasped and sobbed, the back of her free hand pressed to her nose as she nodded furiously.

Following the two girls and Artan out into the main building, William sheathed his sword, flinching when the moon showed him what had become of Artan. It took all he had to keep his thoughts to himself. If he had nothing nice to say ...

"Is it him?" Max said, his voice echoing in the large space.

"Yes," Matilda said, hugging her brother. "Yes, it's him." She sat him on the floor, dropping down with him, and handed him the bread and water from the arena, her hands shaking as he unscrewed the cap from the bottle of water. Although Artan took the offerings, biting a chunk from the small loaf, he still said nothing.

Matilda stroked her brother's lank and greasy hair away from his face and whispered, "I'm so glad you're alive. You won't believe what it's taken to get here."

"What number was he in?" Max asked.

"Thirteen," William said. "Why?"

"You have the key?"

"It's in the door."

Rougher than he needed to be, Max pulled Robert Mack to his feet and dragged him in the direction of the cells. "Looks like there's an empty room for you."

"Please, please don't do that to me. Please."

The *crack* of Max's fist against Robert Mack's chin snapped through the large space, the politician turning limp from the blow. The scrape of Robert Mack's flaccid feet left the foyer with Max, Olga following and holding the door open for him like she had for Matilda and William.

"It's time to eat and rest now," William said, reaching forward and rubbing Artan's bony back. "We'll get out of here in the morning."

CHAPTER 59

"Are you sure you want to handle this?"

William nodded at Max. "Yeah, I've got a plan."

"Why does that worry me?"

"Just draw your sword." He looked at Olga and Matilda too. Despite it now being morning, Artan having had the time to eat, drink, and be around his sister, he still had a distant glaze like Hugh used to get. Although, unlike Hugh, Artan would be more of a hindrance to himself than anyone else. From the frown on Matilda's face, she read William's pity for her younger brother.

They were behind the receptionist's desk in the justice department's building. Light flooded in from the windows in the roof around them, just one of them smashed from the night before. William opened the door leading to the prison cells, bracing against the stench before it hit him.

Door number one. The cell with the lady they'd knocked out and dragged back inside. Hopefully, she'd recovered. William unhooked the key for the door and Olga gasped. "Her?"

"I think so."

"Do you know what you're doing?"

"Not entirely, no. But I think it'll work."

Before any of the others questioned him, William slammed the side of his fist against the large wooden door. The loud booms elicited groans and cries—not too dissimilar to those made by the diseased—coming from many of the locked cells.

When he got no response, William raised his hand to knock again, but a voice on the other side halted him. "What?"

"Look," William said, "we're sorry about what happened."

"About your little mate blind-siding me with a sucker punch, you mean?"

He scratched his face, Olga's jaw tightening at the comment. "Yeah, that."

"It'll take a bit more than sorry."

"Maybe you want to consider the situation we're currently in," William said.

"Huh?"

"I have the key to your cell in my hand. I also have four friends with me, and we're all armed." They'd found more swords in the justice department building, Olga abandoning her machete, and Artan taking one for himself too. Or rather, Matilda strapping the sword to her brother. Whether he'd use it or not, William couldn't tell. Before he'd given them the swords, William checked they were put together well. He saw the tear in Matilda's eye as she'd watched him do it. He'd never be as adept as Hugh with maintaining their weapons. "We mean you no harm."

"Which is why you punched me and have now come back with swords?"

"I can see how it looks. And we had swords last night, but we chose not to use them."

A loud slam against the door forced them all back a step. The woman panted on the other side.

"Look, we really don't want to walk away and leave you in

there, but there's very little motivation for us to do anything but that at the moment. We don't want a fight."

The same ragged breaths, it took William back to his dad dealing with some of the bulls in agriculture. He'd seen him take several of the younger ones by the horns and overpower them. That wouldn't work here.

Bang! The sound exploded along the hallway. "So what do you plan to do with me?" Several more slamming blows as if she could smash the door down despite it already standing the test of time.

Max, Olga, Matilda, and even Artan watched on. Max gently shook his head at William, who turned back to the door, raising his hands as if the woman inside could see him. "You need to calm down."

"That's easy for you to say. Do you even know what it's been like to be in this cell for the past several weeks?"

Artan's long and greasy hair covered one side of his face, his skin pale, his lips cracked.

"No, I don't, but I can imagine it wasn't fun. You don't know what it's taken for us to get here either. We've had to travel from one side of Edin to the other."

"*So?*"

"Edin's lost."

"What?"

"The diseased got in. The entire city's fallen."

The woman's heavy breaths ceased.

"We battled from one side of the city to the other to free a prisoner. Most of our families are dead; we've lost people on the way and seen many more die. The person we came to rescue didn't deserve to be here, so we're making that assumption of you. We want to let you out, but you're not giving us any reason to at the moment. Despite what happened last night, you need to trust us. It was dark, we've been fighting diseased for days, and we're all at our wits' end. If anyone runs at us like you did, we'll fight to defend ourselves. We didn't get here by cowering away from violence."

The woman continued to listen.

"When we let you out, you need to be careful. The political district is in a much better way than most of Edin, but the streets are still filled with the diseased. As long as you're not a threat to us, we'll open the door."

Silence.

"Are you a threat to us?"

"No."

"Now I'm guessing you're still pretty pissed off?"

"Of course."

William hadn't told the others of his plans because he didn't want their opinions on it. If he didn't run it by them, they couldn't say no. "What would you do if we told you Robert Mack is also in one of these cells?"

Several of the others gasped and Olga said, "You can't do that."

As William opened his mouth to argue with her, Matilda turned to Olga. "The man who killed people for being gay? Who believed in punishment, punishment, and more punishment. Who is responsible for the deaths of many of Edin's citizens when he himself is more abhorrent than most of the people he's punished. You think he deserves better?"

The prisoner sounded calmer, filling the silence left by Olga's lack of response. "I'd ask you which number he's in?"

"That's for you to find out. Open all the doors and you'll find him eventually."

"Why are you toying with me?"

The looks from the others seemed to be asking William the same question. "Believe me, I'm getting zero pleasure from this. Who do you think the prisoners will react better to when their doors are opened? You or us?"

"So you want me to free all the other prisoners?"

"Wouldn't you have done that anyway?"

"Okay, fair point."

"Think of Robert Mack as the prize. Are you ready to be let out?" The others tensed around William, raising their swords. Artan leaned against the door, letting the light in.

Clunk! The loud snap of the lock, William turned the handle and pulled the door open.

At least six feet tall, the woman had broad shoulders, thick red hair, and freckles on her pale skin. Like when they'd opened Artan's cell, the reek of waste flooded out with her. William did his best to stifle his reaction.

After blinking repeatedly, her eyes red and swollen, the woman took in William and his group, her gaze settling on William at the front. Her broad shoulders rose and fell with her deep breathing, and her brow furrowed.

William tightened his grip on his sword. Where he'd negotiated her release with confidence, his voice now shook as he said, "The keys are there." A shaking finger at the end of his outstretched arm. "Good luck when you get out of this building, and be careful going out the front door. There are diseased everywhere."

A slight softening of her features. "You're for real, aren't you?"

"Absolutely. We really don't mean you any harm."

The woman's broad shoulders relaxed. "Thank you."

"Of course." He stepped aside. "This is Artan. We came here to rescue him. I can only imagine how hard it must have been in there."

"You've no idea. So, are you going to tell me where Robert Mack is?"

"And spoil the hunt? The more of you there are, the more punishment the vile creature will get. After all, he's Mr. Punishment himself, right?"

The woman's face completely changed with her smile. "Fair enough, but you know what, we might just leave him in there to be forgotten about. I'm sure he planned to do the same to us, and I wouldn't mind betting most of these prisoners don't have violence in them despite what the city's propaganda machine tells its residents."

"Maybe they didn't before they were locked away," William said.

They left the woman in the corridor and walked across the foyer to the main doors. "I expected that to be harder," Olga said.

"Oh, don't worry," Matilda replied, "we've still got to get out of Edin."

CHAPTER 60

Only a few minutes had passed since they'd released the prisoner from cell one. The *thunk* of doors being unlocked called from the back of the room. William, Matilda, Artan, and Olga hovered around the front door.

"We've not really thought this through," Olga said.

William saw he wasn't the only one watching the door behind the receptionist's desk.

Olga continued, "We might have just made peace with that one prisoner—and I'm not even convinced we did that—but what about all the others? There must be twenty of them down there. And maybe I'm out of line for making this assumption, but some of them must be locked up for a reason."

Matilda opened the front door a crack before pushing it shut again. "I can't see Max."

While tying her hair in a ponytail, Olga chewed the inside of her mouth. "I think we all have to agree that if Max isn't back by the time they come out of there, then we run anyway, right?"

"Right," Matilda said.

William shrugged. Neither option seemed ideal, but he had nothing to add.

The door then opened in front of them, and Max slipped inside, pushing it closed behind him again. His clothes were slick with blood, the splash-back on his face too. "Right, it's clear for now. I reckon if we sprint and keep the noise down, we can get through most of the district. You all read—"

A scream from the back of the room, they all turned to look. William said, "I'm guessing they've just opened cell thirteen. Come on, let's get out of here while we still can."

Max led the way, all of them following him out into the street as Robert Mack begged for his life. The prick deserved everything he got.

Tall buildings lined the main road running through the political district. It might have been the most direct route from the city, but they had nowhere to run to if any diseased appeared. William caught up to Max. "Are you sure this is the best route?"

"No, but with the time I had to make a decision, it's the one I've come to. We want to get out of Edin, right?"

"Sure."

"I think this is the quickest way of doing that."

Even now, the smoke William had inhaled in woodwork still restricted his breaths. Maybe Max felt the same because they moved fast, but they could have moved faster. At least, William, Matilda, Olga, and Max could have moved faster. Their progress looked to be causing Artan physical pain, his face twisting and squinting, his skin almost yellow in the bright glare of a new day.

Other than the sounds of their steps against the cobblestones, they kept the noise down. The houses on either side of the street stood taller than most and would be hard to climb. The doors were closed on many, and once or twice

William saw a silhouette in a window. They were closed for a reason.

Two diseased then appeared ahead of them. But two diseased they could cope with. Until Artan screamed like his skin had been set alight—like the girl they watched die in woodwork. William's heart sank. A reaction like that could turn two diseased into twenty. They should have thought about his fear sooner. They should have seen it coming.

Max stepped forward and dealt with the two, Artan still screaming and shouting.

Even after Max dropped the creatures, Artan's hysteria continued.

"Matilda!" Olga said. "If you don't shut your brother up, I will."

William stepped between the two girls. They didn't need to be fighting each other. His back to Olga, he forced Matilda to look him in the eyes. "Can you calm him down?"

But they were too late. It started in the distance: the shrill call of a mob answering Artan's cries.

Matilda pointed at a house on their right. "That's our best option."

One of the only buildings in the penned-in street that had something to climb on. A lip of brickwork about ten feet from the ground protruded from the building by two to three inches. Another lip about five feet higher would help them hold on. They could use the window ledge below it to get up there.

It took a shove in the back from Matilda for Artan to move off, the glaze gone from his eyes as they fixed on the mob now at the end of the street.

Max ran towards the diseased as William and Matilda boosted Artan onto the brickwork ledge. Olga had already gone up before him and helped him higher. Once they were happy Artan wouldn't fall, they climbed up after him.

CHAPTER 61

By the time Max had taken down what turned out to be seventeen diseased—William counted because he had nothing better to do as he clung onto the side of the building; also, it took his mind away from the fact he could fall at any moment—William shook, cramps running through his hands from his tight grip, his legs shaking from where his toes had to support his weight.

More diseased blood dripping from him, his shoulders rounded, Max's mouth hung wide. "You can come down now."

William nodded in the direction of the scaffolding at the end of the street. "I think we need to get there and rest. But we need to make sure the diseased can't follow us. Can you smash the ramp leading up to the first level? We can still climb up, but they won't be able to."

"I'll come with you," Olga said, but before she could jump, another diseased's scream called down the street at them.

A similar amount of the vile things, Max sighed before readying himself to fight.

When the pack reached the house, they fixed on William and the others out of their reach. Max made his way slowly through them. His movements were clumsy as he used his sword. If William didn't know better, from watching the boy he would have assumed the weapon weighed three times what it did. Sure, he had nothing to fear from the diseased, but slaying so many of the creatures looked like hard graft, like digging holes all day.

A window then flew open close to where the four of them clung on. A man in his late forties to early fifties stuck his head from the building. A puce face and puffy blond hair that yielded to the wind, he sneered. "Get off my building, you plebs."

A second later, he produced a stick with a metal hook as if it had been designed for removing the poor from their spectacular abodes. Did they all have one in the political district? He went for William first, hooking his waistband and then tugging.

It ripped William's bottom half away from the wall, his toes slipping from the ledge, his legs hanging down. Burning streaks ran along his fingers, challenging his ability to hold on.

Max stopped killing the diseased. His slack features tightened when they fixed on the man. He charged the house with renewed energy, hitting the door with a shoulder barge. The tear of splintering wood, the slam of the door flinging wide and hitting an internal wall, and then he stood aside as the remaining diseased charged into the house.

Bright blue eyes alive with malicious intent suddenly lost all their spark. The man dropped his prodding pole and pulled back into his home. His screams were silenced a few seconds later. William found his footing and slammed the window shut so the diseased couldn't try to get to them that way.

Max emerged from the house with a large key. He pulled the door shut and locked it before scratching something into the door that William couldn't read from his current position.

"That was easier than killing them all," Max said.

William smiled at his friend. "Thanks for the save there, buddy."

"Are you all okay if I go and prepare the scaffolding? From the look of this street, I'm not sure there are better places to hide between here and there."

"We're fine," Matilda said, sweat running down her red face. "Just please be quick."

Max nodded and took off.

CHAPTER 62

Max smashed the ramp leading from the ground to the first floor of the scaffolding at the back wall just in time, because William had to let go. He'd spent the last ten minutes using every drop of strength he had left, a pack of diseased banging against the window he'd just kicked closed.

William landed by the front door. Max had carved a large *X* into it and the words *diseased inside*.

Olga landed on the ground next, Matilda and Artan following suit.

"Part of me thinks we should open all these doors," Olga said. "Let the diseased take these scumbags before they can cause us any more harm."

"We can't make that choice," William said. "We let them in here to save ourselves; that's enough. We can't decide who lives or dies beyond that."

"Unless it's Robert Mack." Olga cocked an eyebrow. "Or Max."

"And there's the prisoners," Matilda said before William could rise to Olga's provocation. "We know nothing about them, but they might decide to live in this district, so let them choose how to manage the residents."

William smiled. "Somehow I think the time of fat men in smart suits is over. I'm sure they'll get exactly what's coming to them."

The street quiet again, William tugged on Matilda's sleeve. "Let's get on the scaffolding before another mob arrive."

Their route to the scaffolding remained clear, the climb to the first level as easy as William had anticipated. As of yet, they hadn't attracted the attention of any more diseased.

Before they could climb any higher, William saw Max staring back down the street. "What are you looking at?"

"Wait here." Max jumped from the scaffolding and disappeared into a nearby house where the front door had already been smashed off its hinges.

∼

A FEW MINUTES LATER, MAX EMERGED WITH WHAT LOOKED LIKE a tablecloth, the corners clung together to turn it into a bag bulging with goods. In his other hand, he carried a large jug of water. William dragged in a dry gulp as he drew closer.

With Max back on the scaffolding and all of them having sated their thirst, William finally led the way up the large wooden structure. "This is the first time I've walked up here without it being packed with people. If only Dad could see it this quiet."

As they climbed to the next level, Matilda and Artan directly behind him, William paused. "Sorry to show you this, Artan, but as you can see: Edin's gone."

Black smoke rose from the ashes of woodwork, many parts of the district still on fire and tailoring now ablaze next to it.

The diseased looked tiny from this far away, but they were no less numerous. Edin now belonged to the virus.

They climbed the rest of the structure in silence, Max handing out bread sweetened with apple. Every bite sent a sugary hit swelling through William's mouth, who leaned on the rough wall when they got to the top, the overgrown meadow and large lake beyond. "There seems to be about the same amount of diseased out there as always. I reckon if we partly open the gates, we can funnel them so they're easy to kill. We could take the lot of them down before going outside."

"I need a rest first," Max said.

"Of course, you've been a star. Thank you for everything."

"Hear, hear," Olga said, holding Max's hand. "I'm glad we got you out of that cell."

If her glare was meant for Matilda, it fell flat because she had most of her focus on Artan. Little had changed in the boy's demeanour, but at least he ate and had drank some water. As long as he moved when they needed him to, then he could have all the time he needed to get himself straight again.

The wind crashed into William like it always did this high up. He returned his attention to the lake on the other side of the meadow. His words caught, burning his throat, but he pushed through them. "I used to come here all the time with Dad. It was our chance to catch up. The number of people we saw evicted … I even knew one of them."

The diseased's blood had dried on Max's face, flakes falling away with the persistent wind. "Who was it?"

"Someone Matilda and I knew. He ran a restaurant in ceramics."

"And what did he do?" Olga this time.

"He was gay."

Matilda pulled away from Artan for a moment. "Robert Mack deserves everything he got back there."

"And then some," Olga said.

Despite the rough surface, William continued to lean on the wall. "I can't believe how much has happened in less than three days. Mum and Dad gone. Hugh. The girl in woodwork ..."

The focus of Olga and Matilda turned on him. Artan still looked like he hadn't registered much of what they'd said.

"We haven't told you about her yet, have we?"

"Uh ... no," Olga said.

"When Max and I were leaving woodwork, there was a child trapped on a burning building." A deep sigh to help him push on. "We tried to save her."

The touch of Matilda's hand against William's back allowed him to stop. They didn't need to hear any more if he didn't want to say it. "But anyway," he said, "I'm sure there will be plenty of time to talk about loss in the future. For now"—he held up the piece of bread he'd been eating and looked at the sky—"to Hugh. We wouldn't have gotten here without you. Rest well, my friend."

The others held their bread up, Olga crying as she chewed her next bite.

A few minutes of silence passed where they watched the long grass and the twenty or so diseased shambling through the meadow. Max then said, "So what now?"

William had plans, but before he could voice them, Matilda said, "Uh ... you lot."

Close to twenty of them, all of them carrying weapons, all of them covered in blood, they were led by the woman from cell number one, and they were heading straight for them, marching up the main road. They were ready for war.

Olga voiced the group sentiment. "Shit!"

CHAPTER 63

Because she walked at the front of the mob, William watched the prisoner from cell number one, and she stared straight back. They were too far away, but he was still careful to barely move his lips so his words couldn't be read. Although, drawing his sword probably said everything it needed to. "We have the advantage."

"How do you work that out, genius?" Olga had her sword ready. "We're outnumbered at least four to one."

"They have to climb up here. We can defend from higher ground."

"Or they can just wait for us at the bottom."

"But the diseased are down there."

Maybe Max saw their conversation was going nowhere, because he interrupted them. "I suppose we'd best get down there and see what they want."

The prisoners reached the broken ramp between the first floor and the ground and waited, their attention on the five as they descended the wooden structure. When they stopped, William nodded at the woman at the front. "Number one."

The large ginger woman, her face fixed in a scowl, suddenly smiled. "You can call me Liz."

From storm to sunshine, William's shoulders loosened and he smiled back.

"What?" she said. "You expected a different reaction from us?"

"You didn't look friendly on your approach. I'm pleased to see you all got out okay. We heard screams. I'm guessing you found Robert Mack?"

A slight wince and shake of her head. They didn't need to talk about him. "I told the others what you did for us, and we've come to thank you. To see if you need any help?"

While holding up the bag of food he'd scavenged, Max stepped forward. "We're out of water, but if you'd like to share some of this bread with us?"

∽

AFTER THOSE FROM THE CELLS IN THE JUSTICE DEPARTMENT climbed up on the scaffolding so they could safely enjoy their meal, William repeated what Liz had spent the past ten minutes discussing with him. "So you're definitely staying here?"

The bread had a thick and stodgy consistency, which Liz clearly struggled with as she ran her tongue around the inside of her mouth. She looked around at the part of the political district visible to them. "It makes sense. It's already fortified. There aren't many diseased here—"

"Probably more politicians," Max said.

A wicked grin spread across Liz's face. "We call that sport."

William suppressed a chill. Whatever happened to them, the politicians deserved it.

One of Liz's gang, a man shorter than even Olga but as

stocky as a bull, spoke in a deep baritone. "I think it's about time we did some of our own evictions. See how they like it."

There were many worse ways to punish someone. They should think themselves lucky to be given a chance. And what more fitting way than being evicted?

"We might move out from here," Liz said. "Reclaim Edin a bit at a time."

Most of her attention had been on Artan, so when Matilda spoke, everyone listened. "Just please don't bring back national service."

The frame of a warrior and a heart of a leader, Liz reached across and placed one of her large hands over the back of Matilda's. "The reclaiming of Edin will be entirely voluntary. There are no protectors here now. No politicians. No one calling the shots and forcing others to do what they don't want to. In Edin, you now have choice. Choice over where you work, where you live, and who you love."

While staring into the distance, Matilda reached across and held William's hand. "If only we'd grown up in that Edin."

"You still could," Liz said.

William spoke first. "I can't make decisions for anyone else, but Edin has too many bad memories."

"Then where will you go?"

The map had taken a battering in William's back pocket, but when he opened it and spread it out on the wooden boards, several of those from the cells gasped, and even Artan peered over. "It's a map."

"I can see that," Liz said. "But of where?"

"This uncharted territory here"—William circled the space above the ruined city with his finger—"we think is Edin."

The short and wide man who'd spoken about the evictions leaned over the map. "So there's a lot more out there?"

"It looks that way. And I'd like to find out what it is. Of

course, what the others do is on them, but if Matilda chooses to stay, then I'm staying."

Matilda's cheeks reddened as she stared at the map. "I'm ready to move on."

"Me too," Max said.

Olga nodded. "And me."

Although they looked at Artan, he didn't comment.

"I'd like to see what these other places are," William said.

Liz raised an eyebrow. "They say curiosity killed the cat, you know?"

"They do. But what do they say about living a life without answers? Is that the slower, more painful death?"

"We can't talk you out of this, can we?"

"No."

"So what's the plan? How are you going to get out of here?"

William pointed at the wall directly behind him. "There aren't many diseased out there. Twenty or so at the most. I think if we open the doors a little to restrict the flow of them coming in, then we can leave through the back gate after we've slaughtered them all." He turned to the rest of his group. "You don't need to come with me, but I made a promise to a group of rookies in the national service area that I'd return to free them. We left them on the roof of a hut three days ago. I need to go back to see if they're still there."

The past three days had clearly taken it out of everyone, Olga paler than William had ever seen her. Even paler than she'd been when she broke her arm.

"How about just Max and I go?" William said.

Max shrugged. "I'm up for it."

"But how are we going to get back to the national service area?" Matilda said.

"We'll walk back around the front of the city."

"What about the diseased?"

"I can't leave them to rot on that roof!"

A nasty twist took over Olga's face. "But you were happy to leave Max in the labs?"

"We made the wrong choice."

"Because it turned out you needed him?"

"Initially, yes, but also it taught me that if I have any agency over whether someone lives or dies, then I should exercise it."

"Yet you're happy to leave the politicians here?"

"You want to save them?" William said.

Olga shrugged. "I'm just trying to find the magnetic north of your moral compass."

William's heart quickened, the attention of the group burning into him. "Politicians aren't people."

A smile lifted one side of Olga's mouth. "That's a compass I can follow."

∼

A PILE OF DEAD DISEASED LAY IN THE GATES' NARROW OPENING, William's clothes clinging to his sweat-soaked body. Eighteen in total.

Just before leaving, William turned to Liz. "Thanks for your help."

"Thank you, William Johnson. You saved our lives. I hope those kids in the national service area can say the same. When Edin remembers their protectors, yours will be the first name they think of."

The woman stank from where she'd spent time in her cell, but William hid his reaction as she wrapped a tight hug around him, his back cracking from her constrictor's grip. She hugged the others—save Artan, who clearly didn't have human contact in him yet. One of the people from the cells gave William a bag filled with bread. While they were fighting the diseased in the gates, a few of them had gone back into the political district at Liz's whispered orders.

William leaned down to grab one of the diseased bodies, but the short bullish man said, "Leave them. Let us do it."

William led the way out through the gates into the long grass in the meadow beyond. The bright sun dazzled him and his eyes watered. He let his tears out, mourning the path he'd now never take. In Edin, he left behind a life. A home. His parents. Mr. P. The girl in the woodwork district. And his dreams. Whatever else happened, he'd never be one of Edin's protectors. Whatever else happened, he'd never see Hugh again.

END OF BOOK FOUR.

Thank you for reading *Collapse - Book four of Beyond These Walls*.

∽

Support the Author

Dear reader, as an independent author I don't have the resources of a huge publisher. If you like my work and would like to see more from me in the future, there are two things you can do to help: leaving a review, and a word-of-mouth referral.

Releasing a book takes many hours and hundreds of dollars. I love to write, and would love to continue to do so. All I ask is that you leave a review. It shows other readers that you've enjoyed the book and will encourage them to give it a try too. The review can be just one sentence, or as long as you like.

∽

If you've enjoyed Protectors, you may also enjoy my other post-apocalyptic series - The Alpha Plague. Books 1-8 (the complete series) are available now.

The Alpha Plague - Available Now at www.michaelrobertson.co.uk

Or save money by picking up the entire series box set at www.michaelrobertson.co.uk

THE ALPHA PLAGUE
THE COMPLETE SERIES
MICHAEL ROBERTSON
THE ALPHA PLAGUE 1
THE ALPHA PLAGUE 2
THE ALPHA PLAGUE 3
THE ALPHA PLAGUE 4
THE ALPHA PLAGUE 5
THE ALPHA PLAGUE 6
THE ALPHA PLAGUE 7
THE ALPHA PLAGUE 8

ABOUT THE AUTHOR

Like most children born in the seventies, Michael grew up with Star Wars in his life. An obsessive watcher of the films, and an avid reader from an early age, he found himself taken over with stories whenever he let his mind wander.

Those stories had to come out.

He hopes you enjoy reading his books as much as he does writing them.

Michael loves to travel when he can. He has a young family, who are his world, and when he's not reading, he enjoys walking so he can dream up more stories.

Contact
www.michaelrobertson.co.uk
subscribers@michaelrobertson.co.uk

READER GROUP

Join my reader group for all of my latest releases and special offers. You'll also receive these four FREE books. You can unsubscribe at any time.

Go to www.michaelrobertson.co.uk

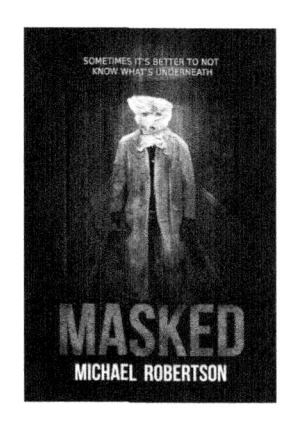

Michael Robertson

EDEN

**A Short Story
About The Zombie Apocalypse**

RAT RUN

A POST-APOCALYPTIC TALE

Michael Robertson

ALSO BY MICHAEL ROBERTSON

THE SHADOW ORDER:

The Shadow Order

The First Mission - Book Two of The Shadow Order

The Crimson War - Book Three of The Shadow Order

Eradication - Book Four of The Shadow Order

Fugitive - Book Five of The Shadow Order

Enigma - Book Six of The Shadow Order

Prophecy - Book Seven of The Shadow Order

The Faradis - Book Eight of The Shadow Order

The Complete Shadow Order Box Set - Books 1 - 8

∽

GALACTIC TERROR:

Galactic Terror: A Space Opera

Galactic Retribution - A Space Opera - Galactic Terror Book Two

∽

NEON HORIZON:

The Blind Spot - A Cyberpunk Thriller - Neon Horizon Book One.

Prime City - A Cyberpunk Thriller - Neon Horizon Book Two.

Bounty Hunter - A Cyberpunk Thriller - Neon Horizon Book Three.

Connection - A Cyberpunk Thriller - Neon Horizon Book Four.

Reunion - A Cyberpunk Thriller - Neon Horizon Book Five.

Eight Ways to Kill a Rat - A Cyberpunk Thriller - Neon Horizon Book Six.

Neon Horizon - Books 1 - 3 Box Set - A Cyberpunk Thriller.

∼

THE ALPHA PLAGUE:

The Alpha Plague: A Post-Apocalyptic Action Thriller

The Alpha Plague 2

The Alpha Plague 3

The Alpha Plague 4

The Alpha Plague 5

The Alpha Plague 6

The Alpha Plague 7

The Alpha Plague 8

The Complete Alpha Plague Box Set - Books 1 - 8

∼

BEYOND THESE WALLS:

Protectors - Book one of Beyond These Walls

National Service - Book two of Beyond These Walls

Retribution - Book three of Beyond These Walls

Collapse - Book four of Beyond These Walls

After Edin - Book five of Beyond These Walls

Three Days - Book six of Beyond These Walls

The Asylum - Book seven of Beyond These Walls

Between Fury and Fear - Book eight of Beyond These Walls

Before the Dawn - Book nine of Beyond These Walls
The Wall - Book ten of Beyond These Walls
Divided - Book eleven of Beyond These Walls
Escape - Book twelve of Beyond These Walls
It Only Takes One - Book thirteen of Beyond These Walls
Trapped - Book fourteen of Beyond These Walls
This World of Corpses - Book fifteen of Beyond These Walls
Blackout - Book sixteen of Beyond These Walls
Beyond These Walls - Books 1 - 6 Box Set
Beyond These Walls - Books 7 - 9 Box Set
Beyond These Walls - Books 10 - 12 Box Set
Beyond These Walls - Books 13 - 15 Box Set

∽

OFF-KILTER TALES:
The Girl in the Woods - A Ghost's Story - Off-Kilter Tales Book One
Rat Run - A Post-Apocalyptic Tale - Off-Kilter Tales Book Two

∽

Masked - A Psychological Horror

∽

CRASH:
Crash - A Dark Post-Apocalyptic Tale
Crash II: Highrise Hell
Crash III: There's No Place Like Home

Crash IV: Run Free

Crash V: The Final Showdown

∽

NEW REALITY:

New Reality: Truth

New Reality 2: Justice

New Reality 3: Fear

∽

Audiobooks:

CLICK HERE TO VIEW MY FULL AUDIOBOOK LIBRARY.

Printed in Great Britain
by Amazon